KARKLOOF BLUE

KARKLOOF
BLUE

A Maggie Cloete mystery

CHARLOTTE OTTER

English edition © Modjaji Books 2016
Text © Charlotte Otter 2016

First published in German by Argument Verlag in 2015

Modjaji Books Pty Ltd
info@modjajibooks.co.za
www.modjajibooks.co.za

ISBN 978-1-928215-05-9

Cover design: Martin Grundmann
Book design and layout: Liz Gowans

Printed and bound by Mega Digital, Cape Town
Set in Garamond, Geometric 415 and Geometric 706

For Andrew James, a genuine forest keeper

Prologue

The yellow winter grass left no footprints. The earth was hardened to cement, the grass so tough that not even the visitors who strolled across it every day from Ishmael's Howick Falls Tearoom and Cafe (Serving the Public With Pride Since 1982) to the amphitheatre to view the waterfall could buckle or bend it.

So neither flattened grass nor a trail of prints alerted Mr Ishmael's sleepy morning eye. He parked his car – an acid-green Toyota Camry that was the joy of his life and the bane of his wife's – in front of the cafe, as he always did. He opened the door and heaved one arthritic knee after the other onto the tarmac and stood up with a puff that was visible in the chilly air.

Mr Ishmael breathed in deep lungfuls. He could smell charcoal fires from the township just west of Howick town centre and the scent of freshly-baked bread from the Spar down the road. He had picked up twenty-four bread rolls. Soon he would cook some chicken pieces and make his famous chicken and coriander mayonnaise rolls. The ladies who worked in the insurance company next door loved these. They came every day to pick up three for their lunch.

Mr Ishmael slammed the car door shut and his thoughts turned to his morning treat. First he would put the kettle on to boil. Then he would put a teaspoon of instant coffee into the mug that Amil had given him on Father's Day when the boy was still a silky seven-year-old who loved and respected his Daddy. While the kettle boiled, he would get his illicit tin of condensed milk (Mrs Ishmael worried about his arteries) out of the fridge and drizzle some onto a spoon, which he would suck clean. Then he would pour hot water over the coffee granules and add a good tablespoonful of the sweetened milk into his coffee.

Then he would sit at the best table in the cafe and stare out of the window towards the waterfall. Ten years ago, he would have been able to see it from there, but now the bushes and the foliage had grown so dense that the only place to view it was from the amphitheatre beyond the traffic circle.

Ten years ago, Mr Ishmael would have up lit up a cigarette to enjoy with his coffee, but Mrs Ishmael had banned them after he had had a lung scare.

'Do you want to live to see your grandchildren?' she scolded. 'Then stop smoking those ridiculous death sticks.'

The death sticks had helped his mind relax. Without them, Mr Ishmael's mind was full of worries. He worried about improvements that needed to be made to the cafe, he worried about his sons – two gadflies who were showing no signs of producing the grandchildren his wife had promised him nor any signs of taking over the cafe so that he could retire early, a personal dream, and he worried about the foliage.

Mr Ishmael had more than once informed the municipality that the foliage ruined the view from Ishmael's Howick Falls Tearoom and Cafe. The municipality had replied to Mr Ishmael's letters that tourists should not be viewing the waterfall from the cafe. Tourists should be viewing the waterfall from the amphitheatre, a sturdy structure that the municipality had built and now maintained for the very purpose of viewing the waterfall. However, Mr Ishmael knew that tourists, having viewed the waterfall from the municipality's amphitheatre and taken the requisite number of photographs with their cell phones, would like to visit the cafe, eat one of his famous chicken and coriander rolls and enjoy the view from a sitting position. And all the foliage and bushes the municipality had allowed to grow unimpeded ruined that.

Mr Ishmael had more than once paid for the bushes and foliage to be cut back. These outlays had not improved the view for long and they had further delayed his chances of early retirement.

He was now impatient for his treat, his tastebuds ready for the sweet hit of condensed milk. Bread rolls in a paper packet under one arm, he jangled his key ring as he walked towards the cafe, the twin calls of caffeine and sugar luring him inside.

With that promise driving him urgently onwards, it was unusual for Mr Ishmael to glance up as he walked the short distance of tarmac and grass from car to cafe.

But he did.

His eye caught something white flapping on the bushes.

Grumbling that his double morning hit was being further delayed, Mr Ishmael trotted across the grass towards the flapping thing. It was probably a plastic bag caught there, and if there was one thing Mr Ishmael didn't like, it was litter. Litter spoiled the natural beauty of the falls, and if the natural beauty of the falls were spoiled then fewer tourists would come and spend their very welcome money at Ishmael's Tearoom and Cafe. Then he really would have to worry about his chances of retirement.

Mr Ishmael huffed to the foliage, where he found it was not a plastic bag. It was a white shirt, a formal work shirt, with a collar and cuffs, the kind of shirt that men put on every morning for the office, either with or without a tie. It was not caught on the branches, but carefully tied, although some black thorns had impaled the cotton weave. Below the shirt, resting on the ground, was a pile of clothes – pants and sports jacket – with a pair of men's shiny black brogues resting on top. Tucked into one shoe was a roll of socks and into the other, a red tie.

Mr Ishmael untied the shirt and folded it neatly. Then he bent down and, groaning slightly, picked up the shoes and clothes.

As he stood up, something brushed his hand. It was a butterfly, an ordinary enough sight. But it was winter and few butterflies could survive the icy winds that blew off the Drakensberg.

It took off towards the amphitheatre in that ragged way, as if it were not able to make up its mind which way it was going, and he followed it, still carrying the shirt and shoes. When it reached the amphitheatre, the butterfly flew towards the waterfall, rising and falling across the empty space where the land dropped away to nothingness.

His eye followed its trajectory down to the blackened rocks and there it was, a slash of white.

A body.

Chapter 1
Saturday, 8pm

Light from the windows strafed the dark grass outside the Old Scout Hall. It had been easy to find. Maggie still had an instinct for Pietermaritzburg. There were cosmetic changes to street names and facades, but it was still a small town full of intrigue and whispers and far too much dirty history.

She parked the Golf next to a clump of vehicles including a VW camper van emblazoned with surfing stickers at the back and decals of the Forest Keepers on its flanks. As she slammed the car door, she could see her breath rise in white puffs in front of her.

The hall was warm with bodies and fervour. People sat in chairs arranged in a semicircle as if for an AA meeting or some form of group therapy. A tall, middle-aged man stood at a flip chart, drawing what looked like a misshapen swimming pool. She leaned against the door jamb and listened to Alex Field speak. He had the light of an evangelist in his eyes.

'This is 12,000 hectares of forest.' Not a pool, then. 'Sentinel has turned most of it into a pine plantation. What very few people around here know is that inside this forest lies a secret and pristine piece of natural heritage.'

He drew another misshapen rhomboid inside the larger one. 'One of the few remaining pieces of natural forest outside state or private property in the whole of KwaZulu-Natal. Sentinel owns this natural forest, which goes by the name of Karkloof Extension 7. This tract is our heritage, packed with hundreds of plant and animal species.'

He put the lid on the marker, and placed it in the tray underneath the flip chart. 'Our intelligence shows that, within days, Sentinel plans to log this forest, to tear up the ancient trees and replace them with profitable pine. They want to add to the monocultures of pine, eucalyptus and cane that have taken over this province.'

There was a rumble in the room. 'Exactly!' He began to pace. 'We have to stop them. Sentinel have effectively persuaded the public that they are the good guys, greenwashing their profit-chasing with marketing campaigns about reducing their environmental impact. People actually believe them.'

He stopped to run his hand through his hair. He still had a lot of it, though it was turning white at the temples. 'This is very bad. What Sentinel plans to do is evil. But it is a gift for us. Finally, they are nailing their colours to the cross. We now know who they are – the ultimate capitalist profit-mongers who will do anything to save their share price. And now we can show everyone what they are, by protesting outside their offices.'

This group usually met to talk about dry environmental topics like water tables, erosion and overgrazing. Field had said that tonight's topic would make a potential story, which was why Maggie was here. The company Field called Sentinel – Sentinel Forestry Corporation – was well-known and well-respected. If they were about to do something nefarious, she needed to know.

She also hoped to see Christo.

There he was. Two chairs away from the speaker, face upturned towards him like a flower to the light of the sun. Alex Field was Christo's new hero. Maggie was allergic to gurus, but Field's concern for her brother after his release from hospital had warmed her. Field had given him a job and a place to live and had provided this community of environmental activists as a support network.

But Christo also needed family, which was why she was here.

'Any questions?' Field asked.

Someone in a grey knitted beanie put his hand up. 'Protesting is a form of action, but how can we really stop them logging?'

'Protests are our first step. But please be aware this could be a long fight. These corporate giants have the government in their back pockets. With their campaigns and clever marketing they have persuaded the ordinary person in the street that they are benevolent supporters of sustainability, and they have given so many sops to their unions that these are now overfed and plumped into a coma like battery chickens.'

He strode from one side of the room to the other while he talked, arms waving. He had the trim figure of man half his age.

Grey beanie nodded. 'So you are saying it is a war.'

Field stopped. 'It is a war! If anyone thinks we'll be parked outside Sentinel's offices for a couple of hours sipping latte macchiatos, then they needn't join us. If they don't meet our demands, we will have to take it to the next level and occupy the forest.'

'Occupy!' Grey beanie stood up, pumping a fist in the air. He looked around him, as if surprised to find himself on his feet, then promptly sat down again.

Maggie undid the zip of her coat. The hall was getting warmer as the emotional temperature rose.

She watched her brother's face. After Christo's release from the private hospital where he had spent nearly twenty years, his balance was still delicate. Dr Kruger, his psychiatrist, insisted he needed family nearby to help ease his exit from the institution. Maggie was his family. There was no one else. She'd decided to move from Joburg, at least for a short time, to help him find his feet.

She'd put through a call to her contacts in Pietermaritzburg. Her former boss, Zacharius Patel, had sounded exactly the same on the phone. She told him she needed to spend time with her brother and help him transition back into society. Zacharius, as always, had an answer. Now she had a short-term job on the local newspaper.

What she had not mentioned was that she also needed to get the hell out of Joburg. She had become persona non grata in certain circles. Very non grata. Very high circles.

She felt her phone vibrate and pulled it out of her pocket. It was a text from Leo.

Can I watch Skyfall?

No, she texted back. *You are too young.*

Maggie, I am nearly 12.

Not exactly. Still six months to go.

Dad says it's okay with him if it's okay with you.

She sighed. It was typical for Joachim to leave the hard parenting decisions up to her.

Tell Dad it is not OK with me.

Thanks for nothing.

My pleasure.

She buried the phone in her pocket again. Leo wouldn't be pissed off with her for long. His father Joachim was hardly an ideal childcare option, but he was her only option. He worked as an explosions expert in the film industry, had a gap between sets, and was prepared to move into Maggie's flat and look after their offspring while she spent time in her old home town. Joachim was not the type for regular meals, homework checks or timely bedtimes. She had to live with that. She needed him. Temporarily.

She sighed and pulled her attention back to the meeting. Field was still on his feet. 'By destroying the natural forest that is Karkloof Extension 7' – he thumped the swimming pool, causing the flip chart to wobble – 'Sentinel is robbing all of us, the whole country, of its natural heritage. This may seem like a tiny piece of forest, but it is yet another piece of the jigsaw that makes up corporate greed across the whole country, and the whole continent. We have to fight them, to preserve Extension 7 for our children, and for all the species that live in that forest and will have their habitat destroyed.'

Christo's head turned to scan the group and he caught her eye. He quickly turned away again. Dr K thought it was a good idea to have Maggie nearby. Christo did not.

'We need people with commitment,' Field continued. 'This will be hard. It will be scary. It will be dangerous. I only need people with me who can do without creature comforts. I need people who are tough, who don't need hot showers and three-course meals. I need fighters and warriors, people who are mentally and physically strong.'

He stopped pacing and turned to the group. 'Who's in?'

Every single person in the room, including Maggie's brother, put their hands up. Alex Field had found his warriors.

Chapter 2
Monday, 6am

Maggie poured the grounds into a filter and filled up the creaky machine. While she waited for the drips, she grabbed each foot and stretched her quads. Today's run had been a killer – all the way up Old Howick Road to Hilton and back again. Joburg had hills, but none with the vicious elevation of Town Hill.

Coffee in hand, she walked the lino corridor back to her desk. Front pages from the newspaper's history hung haphazardly on the walls, framed in black plastic. No longer buried in Victorian buildings in the heart of town, *The Gazette* now resided in a faceless, featureless office park on the outskirts of Pietermaritzburg, surrounded by other businesses that could no longer afford the downtown rent. Everything about the new premises was cheap.

Cost factors, the editor told her, during one of her interviews. Editorial and print brought together under one roof. 'Synergies' was the word Tina Naidoo used, making Maggie wince.

She switched on her computer and perused the wires for an outline of today's news: crime, corruption and power outages in South Africa; hell on the Gaza Strip; a plane crash in the US; the Tories busting out for austerity in the UK. At least the rest of the world was equally messed up.

The swing door that led into the newsroom screeched and Menzi strolled in, accompanied by a subterranean beat. He was the crime reporter, always early, always smiling, ears always covered by giant headphones.

'Morning, boss,' he waved as he walked past, short dreads bobbing.

She waved back and flicked through the Monday edition, making mental notes of stories that would need following up when she conferred with Patti at seven. Her start with the deputy editor last week had not been good. The less Patti saw of Maggie, the happier the deputy was.

'Cops say there's been a suicide at Howick Falls, boss,' Menzi called from his desk.

'Got a name?' Out of respect for the family, they wouldn't use it, but journalistic instincts die hard. Get a name, work the story from there.

'Dave Bloom, 43, Clarendon, wife and two kids.'

'OK, just a para, Menzi.' She would bury it somewhere on page five.

Now she heard Patti arrive. She waited until the deputy editor had inhaled her first coffee, then she plonked herself down in a chair next to her desk.

'News editor, reporting for duty.'

Patti glanced up, her face framed by wire glasses and a short grey crop. 'Hi.' The glories of this sunny winter morning were lost on Patti. Atmosphere as thick as Hilton mist swirled around her.

Maggie ignored the mist. 'I have a story list. Let's talk.' She reeled off her day's stories, while Patti stared at her screen.

'Anything for page one lead?' The deputy editor turned to Maggie and placed her glasses on her head. This was the first time she'd actually looked at her.

'Menzi's farm murder, maybe, if the evidence is good. I'll let you know after conference.'

Patti pursed her lips. She didn't like Maggie. Ed had explained why.

'Let's just say you were not her preferred candidate,' the pics editor told her over lunch on her first day. They were sitting outside on a bench in the sun, eating a couple of sad sandwiches from the lunch trolley.

'Who was?'

'Johnny Cupido really wanted the job. Patti supported him.'

'And they chose me because?'

'You're an outsider.'

'Which means?'

Ed put a hand on her shoulder. She could see Fortunate at the receptionist's desk, straining to hear what they were saying.

'It means you're easier to get rid of.'

'So I'm expendable. Fucking great.'

'It gets worse,' Ed said. 'There's money on it. An office pool.'

'On what?' Fortunate's ears were flapping now.

'On whether you'll last. Odds are on Patti winning and Johnny being news editor by December.'

'What makes them the favourites and not me?'

Ed grinned and slapped her on her back. 'Your reputation, Maggie. Everyone knows you're a trouble magnet.'

No one knew that better than Ed. They had worked together at *The Gazette* for years, before the shine of the big city lights had drawn her away. They had done a lot more than work together, but there was no electricity between them now; just a friendship, comfortable as an old shoe.

'What time do we meet the editor today?' she asked the deputy, whose frown was frosted into her forehead.

Patti put her glasses back on and frowned at the screen instead of at Maggie. 'Three pm.'

In all the other newsrooms she'd worked in, editor's conference was a regular meeting with a set time. A floating meeting was bloody awkward, but Patti had made it perfectly clear last week that no complaints would be tolerated. Tina Naidoo was a law unto herself, and Patti and Fortunate propped up the regime.

At nine, she made her way to the conference room for her daily meeting with the news team. Most of them were already there. Some looked at her expectantly, others were bent over their smartphones, tapping and swiping. She heard the swoosh of an email being sent. Johan Liebenberg took a loud sip of coffee and clanked his mug back down on the conference table. Did he have money riding on Maggie's early departure?

She gestured to Menzi, whose earphones were nestled around his neck and thudding gently. 'What's on for you today?'

'Ja, the farm murder is in the High Court at the moment. We're expecting evidence from the accused today unless something goes wrong.'

'Thanks, Menzi. That's our potential lead, for now. How about photos, Ed?'

'Sure, Maggie. Ahmed's already posted outside the courts to get a pic of him coming in. If he doesn't get anything now, we'll try again at the lunch-break.'

The days of light desks and contact sheets were gone. Ed's team now operated a bank of computers where they selected and filed the newspaper's photographs. It was a small department – a couple of geeks to run the computers and webmaster the digital edition – and three photographers.

The geeks were known for not talking to anyone but each other; the photographers were known for their laid-back attitude, their magnetic attraction to women and their access to the best dagga in KwaZulu-Natal.

'Anything else from the cops, Menzi?'

'I spoke to Ernest this morning. Only the suicide.'

'Suicide?' Liebenberg looked up.

'A guy called David Bloom jumped off the Howick Falls on Saturday night.'

Liebenberg gasped and put a hand over his mouth.

'You know him?' Maggie asked.

'I worked with him for a long time at Sentinel.'

Johan Liebenberg was *The Gazette*'s new environmental reporter, recently poached from the forestry industry. Naidoo had told her proudly during her interview how the paper needed to position itself on the cutting edge (quote) of environmental issues and that Johan was going to lead them there.

So far, Maggie had seen nothing cutting edge from Liebenberg, including today's offering – a press release from Sentinel about a new racing track they had created in one of their Zululand plantations.

'Downhill or motocross?' Maggie asked. Her scrambling days were over, but the town's plantations had been her playground.

'Downhill,' Liebenberg told her. 'Sentinel aren't behind motocross. They say it's too noisy, and not environmentally friendly.'

'Sure, they can say that.' According to Alex Field, Sentinel had gutted the KZN grasslands to plant thousands of acres of identical trees for the paper industry, yet they still managed to position themselves at the acme of environmental sustainability.

Fatima Rajab, health reporter and amateur football fanatic, had a story on a new fasting diet that was guaranteed to ensure the dieter high-speed weight loss. It was a hit amongst Pietermaritzburg schoolgirls, who were fainting by the dozen in class.

Once they had finished she clapped her hands. 'Right to work, everyone. Give me a heads-up by lunchtime on how your stories are progressing. Let's not let anything slip through the cracks.'

Everyone shuffled out. Menzi strode off to court and Maggie watched him go. She wanted to walk out with him – out into the fresh air, into the world where it was all happening – to find a nugget of news, develop it and feel that familiar prickle of a story down the back of her neck. Right now, however, she was keeping her head under the parapet. It was best that way.

Instead she could follow a story from her desk. She called her brother.

'World Shoes, Chris Cloete.' He worked in Field's shop, tooling peasant-style leather sandals and boots, the kinds that left-wing university students or gnomes might wear. Since his release from hospital, he had anglicised his name. That was fine; it was a long time since anyone had called her Magdalena.

'Hi, it's Maggie.'

'Hello.' His tone was icy.

For a long time, she'd chased him through the crazed landscape of his mind until she decided he was never coming back. Against the odds, he had, and was unable to forgive her for deserting him.

'I was at the meeting on Saturday night.'

'I noticed.'

'Christo, I think there's a story in there somewhere.'

'This is not about a story. It's about a genuine need to take action.'

It was like communicating with him over a two-meter wall topped with spikes, shards of glass and razor wire.

'Look, there is something I need to ask you.'

'Ask.'

'Dave Bloom. Local ecologist. Do you know the name?'

'Yes. He works for Sentinel.' That confirmed what Liebenberg had said in conference. 'Why do you want to know?'

'He was found dead at the bottom of Howick Falls on Sunday morning.'

'Oh shit.'

She glanced up and saw Liebenberg hovering. He was wearing

designer hiking pants, with nifty pockets to store Swiss Army knives and trail maps and snack packs of raisins and peanuts. The kind of pants that cost a fortune in camping shops.

She put up her hand to tell Liebenberg she would not be long. 'Better get going, Christo – I've got a newsroom to run.'

'And I've got shoes to fix.' Christo paused. 'Ask Spike about Dave Bloom.'

'Spike?'

Maggie's ex – now married, with three children – was a university lecturer in sustainability, and was often invited to speak to Field's group. He and Maggie had parted badly and there was no way on any planet, in any universe, for any story, that she was calling Spike.

Liebenberg perched his butt on her desk, without permission. In the old office constellation the news editor's desk had been right in the middle of a giant newsroom, placed where the ed could see everything. Now it was tucked away in an alcove, for privacy and status, she presumed, but it also gave people the chance to ambush her.

'I didn't want to say in the meeting,' Liebenberg began, 'but Bloom did have some issues.'

'Were you close?'

'Not friends exactly,' Liebenberg said, 'But good acquaintances. Dave Bloom is – was – manic depressive. Bipolar. It was well-known.'

'And this is relevant because?'

Liebenberg looked rueful, shook his head. 'Suicide can be a risk.' He paused. 'Will you get Menzi to talk to the family?'

'Not in the case of suicide, no. They are going through enough pain as it is.'

Liebenberg stood up, hooked his thumbs into his belt loops and squared his shoulders. 'Just remember that, if this story goes any further, the environment is my beat.'

Maggie stared at him. 'And if it turns out that Bloom was pushed and didn't jump, you remember that crime is Menzi's.'

Chapter 3
Tuesday, 5am

Maggie woke, startled. Where was she? She sat up and saw the dried flower arrangement on a chest of drawers under the window of her rented bedroom. She hated cut flowers. Dried ones were worse.

She got up, grabbed the flowers, vase and all, and threw them into a cupboard in the second bedroom, where they joined two Impressionist prints of misty European landscapes, three cushions dotted with rosebuds and some tea-light holders.

Cleansed of corporate cute, she pulled on her running gear, adding layers against the cold. It was time for some pain. Head-torch lighting her way, she pounded the suburban streets, past high walls protecting large houses. The houses had become grander since she left ten years ago, and the walls even higher.

The road forked. She could choose: uphill to the larger homesteads or down to town. Nostalgic for the city centre, she turned left and ran downhill, her blood pounding in her ears.

A silver Audi with Gauteng number plates drew alongside her, its windows smokey and impenetrable. Maggie ran faster but the car stuck to her side, matching her pace. The streets were deserted, not even a dog-walker in sight.

At the bottom of the hill, a traffic light turned red and the Audi stopped. A taxi pulled up and disgorged its passengers, mostly women heading to their jobs as domestic workers in the suburbs. She considered leaping in, but she had no cash. Instead, she accelerated down Peter Kerchoff Street, taking a swift left in order to bury herself in the streets beyond.

She glanced over her shoulder. No Audi. Ridiculous. She had spooked herself.

She turned right onto another main road and ran towards the city centre, her old stamping ground. She spotted a karate dojo and made a note to go in. She needed to keep up her training, especially if people who drove Gauteng Audis decided to get out of their cars and address their concerns to her in person.

She passed the City Hall. The clock donged sonorously, letting her know it was six o'clock. She stopped to glug some water on the pavement outside *The Gazette*'s old offices. She missed the heart of town, beating as it did with the life of the city. The office park where the newspaper now resided was soulless.

Minibus taxis streamed down the one-way street, hooters blaring, music pumping from a hundred different woofers. Soon the offices, shops and restaurants would be crowded with people doing their daily business. The streets would be full of informal traders selling a weird and wonderful array of items in order to make a living. As she needed to make hers.

Hair still wet, Maggie parked the Golf in *The Gazette*'s new parking lot and stopped in the office kitchen to get coffee. Once suitably caffeinated, she headed for her desk to bury herself in the wires and plan her day.

Her phone pinged. A text from Christo.

I called Spike, because I knew you wouldn't. Quote. Dave Bloom is the most sorted guy I know. A passionate environmentalist. Trying to change the forestry industry from the inside. It's just not possible that he killed himself. Unquote.

She reread Spike's words, written there as if he had texted her himself. Their time together had been short – not much over a year – and intense. Spike had wanted more, a commitment that Maggie had not been able to provide. They'd had one disastrous lunch with his parents, where his mother had tried desperately to forge a connection with her.

'Are you the Ladysmith Cloetes?'

'Nope.'

'Jan Cloete, the former High Court judge? He's retired to Zimbali now.'

'Er, no.'

'Wasn't there a Mrs Cloete who used to run a boutique in Musgrave? Lovely little place.'

'No idea.'

Maggie's family was was not nearly so fancy. Her father had

had a nominal job in the civil service, and her mother had made a career out of cooking stodgy meals for her family and eating all the leftovers. Even her father's hobby of tooling leather Bible covers had not been an earner. After Christo's ignoble departure from the South African Defence Force and subsequent sojourn in an apartheid jail, her parents had quit their church and departed for the South Coast in shame. There had been no Cloetes of her family left in town, except for herself and her brother. Who, at that time, was still in a mental asylum.

On the way home, Maggie told Spike that it would be the first and last Sunday lunch with his parents.

'You'll get used to them,' he'd said.

'Maybe, but they'll never get used to me.'

He'd had no reply to that and she ended it soon after. Spike needed harmony, all parts of his life flowing together in one happy symphony. She would always be the discordant note, the Afrikaans underclass piercing the bubble of his family's WASP privilege.

Maggie sipped her coffee. It was cold. Thinking of Spike was a mistake.

The swing doors to the newsroom squeaked open. A well-perfumed man bounded into Maggie's alcove, arms wide open.

'Darling!'

Maggie got up and hugged him. 'Aslan, how the hell are you?' The arts editor had been on leave when she'd started last week.

'Well, I would say magnificent, except for this.' He slapped yesterday's edition of the paper down on the desk. It was carefully folded into a neat rectangle, featuring the arts page.

Aslan Chetty had taken over the arts desk when its previous incumbent had debunked to a PR company in Cape Town. It had been his life's ambition to be headhunted and move to a real metropolis, but he had foiled his own ambitions by developing a reputation for discovering and launching new artists in KZN. Now he worked two days a week for *The Gazette* and freelanced as an art consultant.

Maggie examined the rectangle. 'What am I looking at?'

'My fresh hell.'

'I don't see it.'

'The subs have ruined my article. Look.' He stabbed the paper. 'Three errant apostrophes. Not to mention the headline.'

Maggie had seen the headline yesterday – Art Attack. She thought it was quite good, but Aslan clearly did not agree.

'Goddammit, Maggie, I have a reputation to protect. I won't have it sullied by childish puns and substandard editing by three-year-olds who can't do basic grammar. It's just not good enough.'

He flung himself into the chair opposite hers and started chewing his nails.

'Is that a new habit?'

'Yes.' He carried on chewing. 'Started today. Brought on by the goons who edit my work.'

'I'll talk to the subs.' They were supposed to check every word and prevent things like this from happening.

'Fat good that will do. They care not a jot for quality.' Aslan stopped chewing and folded his arms. 'Anyway, what are you doing back in this dump? You managed to escape and now you're back. No one ever comes back.'

'Well, Christo's out of hospital and he needs me around.'

'He is? That's amazing, Maggie.'

She nodded. Some spark had guided him back to the real world. Just not to her.

'So what do you think of the new place?' Aslan gestured to the cubicles around them.

'Grim,' Maggie said. 'I miss town.'

'Telling me,' he agreed. 'Remember those days, wandering out into the city, grabbing a curry, watching the buskers and the jugglers?'

The first time Maggie had met Spike he was juggling in the back streets of Pietermaritzburg. Aslan cocked an eyebrow at her. 'Remember the juggler?'

'The juggler is now married with three children.'

'Jane says happiness in marriage is entirely a matter of chance.'

She remembered her friend's tendency to quote Austen. It was part of his project to get Maggie to read something beyond motorcycling and running magazines.

'Aslan, I'm here to work, and keep an eye on my brother. I have zero interest in jugglers, past, present or future. This is just temporary. I'll leave when Zacharius comes back from his sabbatical next year.'

'If he comes back.'

'What do you mean?'

'The guy's tired, Maggie. He's been doing this job for twenty-five years. I reckon he's having a test-run for retirement.'

He grinned and stood up. 'Listen, I've got a couple of stories to file. See you later.'

At conference she asked Menzi to contact Natalie Bloom.

'I know it's a tough call,' she told him. 'But a couple of sources suggest that he was not a candidate for suicide. Maybe she has something to add.'

'The guy was manic depressive.' Liebenberg said, rocking his chair back on two legs, and folding his arms across his chest. 'Suicidal tendencies are one of the symptoms.'

'Thanks for the insight, Johan. What's on your agenda for today?'

'Sentinel's taking a minibus full of press out to the new track. I'd like to go along, check it out.'

'What's new? Sounds like yesterday's story.'

'I might get some good photos.'

'We don't have a photographer to spare.' Ed was scheduled to photograph some new city councillors, and Ahmed, his number two, would be tailing the farm murderer at the High Court. Musa was sick, and Sakhile had the day off to attend a funeral.

'I can take them. I have a great little SLR.' Of course Liebenberg would have a designer camera to match his designer hiking pants.

'Nope, you can stay here. We can't only file forestry stories. Find out what's going on at the Land Claims Court. Ask if they have resolved any cases lately.' The court was notoriously slow, held up by bureaucracy and file-pushers.

'I don't have any contacts there.' Liebenberg stopped rocking his chair.

'Then make some.' Maggie stood up. 'It's called journalism.'

People filed out. Liebenberg stayed in his chair. As Maggie passed him, he said, 'Can I talk to you?'

Against her better judgment, she agreed and closed the conference room door.

'How long have you been a journalist?'

'Nearly twenty years.'

'I admire your experience. I was really good at my old job. Just before I left, they offered me a huge promotion, major salary, fast track to the board.'

'And you didn't take it?'

'My mother is elderly. Very frail. I knew if I took the role, I wouldn't have the time I need to dedicate to her.'

'What about compassionate leave? Aren't corporates supposed to be really good about that sort of thing?'

He placed a hand on her arm, all conspiratorial. 'To be honest, after years slaving away for that place, I really needed a lifestyle change.'

'And you thought you would have a better lifestyle working on a paper? Take a look around. You'll see stress, overwork, people with addiction problems.' Not to mention people being tailed by silver Audis with Gauteng number plates. 'Look, I don't have time for chit-chat. I need to brief the editor and get this paper rolling.'

'I am just asking for some leeway. I'm still learning.'

'Ok. You can have leeway, but not for the Sentinel thing. That's just a pointless jolly. If you don't want to go to the Land Claims Court, then I suggest you spend the day in the archives. Take a look at the files, see which environmental stories hit the headlines in the last six months, find out who the players are, make appointments, go and see them. You need a contact book. It's time to make one.'

'Thanks, Maggie. Will do.'

She nodded and let herself out. After her meeting with Naidoo and Patti, she headed for her desk. As she sat down her cell phone rang. An unknown number.

'Cloete.'

'This is Natalie Bloom. Dave Bloom's wife. Spike Lyall gave me your details.'

The hairs on Maggie's arms stood up. Bloom's wife. Plus Spike fixing things in the background of her life. 'Hello.'

'Can we talk?'

'Sure. Now?'

'I want to show you something. Are you free?'

Maggie looked at her watch. It was ten past eleven and close enough to lunch to merit a jaunt from the office. However, it was only her second week on the job. She really should stay present and visible.

'Look, Mrs Bloom, I can't leave the office now. I can get hold of our crime reporter and ask him to stop off and see you on the way back from court.'

'No,' the woman said. 'It's you I want to see. Spike said you were the best.'

Best at what?

'It's you or no one, Ms Cloete.'

Maggie agreed to meet her and stopped off at Fortunate's desk on the way out of the office. 'Where do I get a car?'

'Is it *Gazette* business?' the receptionist asked, fingernails stabbing her keyboard.

'Ja.'

'We don't maintain a fleet any more. Staff use their own cars and file a requisition for petrol.' Fortunate stopped typing, dug around in a tray of papers and pulled out a dense, two-page form.

'I fill this out each time I use my car?'

'Yes, please. Note your before and after kilometres here and here.' Fortunate tapped the form with a long red fingernail. 'And your before and after petrol usage there and there. You get reimbursed with your paycheck.'

'And all this other stuff?' Maggie waved her hand at the form.

'The system requires it.' Fortunate flashed Maggie a giant smile. Her lipstick matched her nails.

She put the Golf's key in the ignition. Nasty offices, more paperwork and crap sandwiches. How things had changed at *The Gazette*.

The car coughed into life and she wound her way to Roberts Road, looking for the Bloom's house. It was easy to find – a long, white wall on the right, as Natalie had said, guarded by a giant tree. The house was an ordinary suburban single storey. Life looked so normal when you judged it on outside appearances.

Maggie rang the buzzer.

'Come in,' a woman's voice said. Maggie pushed open the security gate and trotted up the shallow steps to an outside courtyard dotted with pots of herbs.

The door opened and Natalie Bloom stood in the doorway. Death's brutal tokens were written on her face – dark shadows under her eyes, an unsmiling mouth, skin that looked porous and vulnerable.

'Hello.' Her voice was quieter in person than on the phone.

'Hi,' Maggie said. 'I am really sorry for your loss.' The words always sounded empty. She had used them countless times in her work as a crime reporter.

'Come in,' the woman said, leading Maggie through a small galley kitchen and into a dining room, where eight chairs were ranged around a circular table. 'Please sit.'

Maggie complied. Natalie Bloom sat too, looking down at her hands clasped on the table top. She dug the fingernail of one thumb into the cuticle of another, and seemed unable to lift her gaze.

'We buried Dave yesterday.'

The woman dragged her gaze towards Maggie's face. 'In the Jewish tradition, suicide is an abomination. Suicides don't get a funeral service and they cannot be buried in a Jewish cemetery. However, our shul is Reform and the rabbi turned a blind eye. I had to beg him to give Dave a honourable burial, within the bounds of our faith.'

Maggie nodded. 'That's good.'

'You don't get it, do you?' Natalie had stopped digging in her cuticles.

'Not sure I do.'

'There is no way that my husband committed suicide.'

'He had good reasons to live?'

'Absolutely!' Natalie Bloom's small fist banged the table, making the fruit-bowl rattle.

She stood. 'Come and I'll show you.'

Maggie followed her down a corridor, where she opened the door to a room.

'Firstly, this.' The room was empty of people, but it contained two of everything. Two beds, two desks, two chairs, two built-in cupboards.

'Our twins. They're seven and the apple of Dave's eye.' As she spoke, her face lightened, and then the shadows crossed it again.

Maggie noticed the present tense.

'Where are they now?'

'Well, they should be at school, but they have some time off due to circumstances. Right now they're with my mother.'

She pulled the door closed and led Maggie further down the corridor, where she threw open another door.

'And then this.'

She gestured for Maggie to step into the room, which she did. It was dark, the curtains firmly drawn in the small office.

Natalie switched on the light.

The room was plastered with butterfly pictures – paintings, photographs and blown-up photostats of newspaper and magazine articles. Maggie peered at the pictures on the walls.

'It's all the same butterfly.'

'Well done,' the woman said, with a wry look. She stood in the doorway, as if entering the room was too hard for her.

'Which one?'

'*Orachrysops ariadne*. The Karkloof Blue.'

'Is it very rare?'

'It's very vulnerable. There are only four colonies left in this province and all of them are endangered.'

'Endangered by what?'

'Goats, cattle, herbicides, all of which destroy the habitat. And by my husband's company. They want to pull up all the indigenous trees and bush in the Karkloof and plant pine.'

Maggie thought of Alex Field's rhomboid. 'Do you mean Karkloof Extension 7?'

'I do indeed.'

'And what was he doing to stop them?'

'Everything he could – meetings with senior managers, internal campaigns to educate people on the dangers of removing the habitat, any kind of activism that he could think of. In summer, he took small groups out in the Karkloof to show them the butterfly in its various colonies.'

'Was he alone?' Maggie watched pain shimmer across Natalie's face. Standing on the precipice on that cold, dark Saturday night must have been the loneliest moment of Dave Bloom's life. She could have kicked herself for the question. 'I mean, did he have an activist group at work?'

'No, I think not. That was his greatest frustration, that no matter how he hard he worked and how much he talked to people, he couldn't seem to convince them.'

Maggie leaned in closer and looked at one of the photos of the Karkloof Blue. Its wings were a delicate fawn colour, with blue radiating out from its body in a fan shape, and tipped with white. Very pretty, but in the end, it was just a butterfly. It was hard to imagine someone devoting their whole life to an insect.

She turned to Natalie, who was still in the doorway.

'Could he have given up?'

'What do you mean?'

'Is it possible that your husband saw there was no point in pursuing his cause, that no matter what he did, how much he protested, they wouldn't be stopped?'

The corners of Natalie's mouth turned up slightly. 'That is not Dave's style. He is a very determined person. He would not just give up.'

Maggie thought of Liebenberg's words, the suggestion of emotional instability.

'The struggle, the fight to save the Karkloof Blue, could it have been getting him down? Was he depressed?'

'He was human. He had up and downs, just like we all do.'

'Was he psychologically stable?'

'What kind of a question is that?'

Maggie sat at Dave Bloom's desk. If Natalie Bloom was going to pursue this line, then she would have to get used to difficult questions. The desk chair had a soft seat and a firm, tall back. Here Bloom had sat, night after night, researching the Karkloof Blue, planning ways to challenge the timber industry, to fight for the life of a small vulnerable insect.

And now he was dead.

She turned to Natalie. 'So if you don't believe it was suicide, what do you believe?'

'There's only one option,' Natalie said. 'He was pushed.'

'Okay,' Maggie said, slowly. 'And have you told the police this?'

'They've dismissed it. Suicide. Case closed.' She put her face in her hands and took a deep breath. 'I really need help, Maggie.'

'Would you think about getting a lawyer?'

'Lawyers are expensive. And I'm just a teacher.'

She reached out to Maggie with one hand. 'You have to believe me – he would never have left us like this.'

Maggie took a deep breath. 'I do believe you.'

'Then please help me. Spike Lyall says you're an investigative journalist. He's says you're the best. Please help me prove that my husband didn't voluntarily jump off that waterfall.'

Spike Lyall said she was the best. Part of her was faintly flattered. Part of her wanted to slap him for going around saying nice things about people and making them feel good about themselves while being married to someone else.

'Natalie, you need to know I am not an investigative journalist any more. I am the news editor, which means I sit behind a desk and tell other reporters what to do. However, I will do my best to help you.'

'Thank you,' the woman breathed, leaning her shoulder against the doorway, as if tired of the effort it took to prop herself up.

Maggie walked to her car, stomach grumbling. She stopped at a tearoom and bought a guava juice and a cheese roll to eat at her desk. Back in the car, her cell phone buzzed. It was a text from Alex Field.

Urgent developments. Please stop by.

Self-important, typical of Alex. She should ignore him and head to the office, but whatever was next on his agenda to rule the world involved her brother, so she obeyed.

As she came to a halt at a traffic light, a small beggar approached her car. He looked about twelve, dressed in a thin ragged jersey and a pair of shorts. He had cut holes in his takkies to account for his growing feet and his toes protruded out. He tapped on her window. She rolled it down.

He cupped his hands. 'Money for food?'

She grabbed the packet of food and passed it to him.

'Thanks, madam,' he said. In her rearview mirror, she saw him hobble to the side of the road and wolf down the bread roll.

Maggie parked the Golf and headed for World Shoes. As she turned into the lane where the shop was situated, a shadow blocked the sun behind her. She spun around. Nothing. Spooked again. She made a mental note to contact Jabu to ask how things were going.

A bell rang as Maggie walked into Field's shop. It smelled of leather and oil. The usual neat racks of shoes were overwhelmed by piles of equipment: a half-folded tent, several camping stoves, rolls of sleeping bags. Christo was stuffing a sleeping bag into a sack.

He glanced up. 'What are you doing here?'

'Alex asked me to come.'

'Ja, well. We heard Sentinel's going into the forest sooner than planned. End of this week or early next. They are going to start pulling it down and we need to stop them.'

'How?'

'We're going to camp there, form a human shield.'

Alex Field had already summoned his warriors.

'And twenty of you parked in the trees is going to stop them?'

He grimaced. 'We have no choice. They are destroying our bio-diversity to grow a monoculture, and the rest of the population just claps their hands and says lovely Sentinel, look what they are doing for the environment.'

He dropped the bag into a pile and started rolling a second one.

'Chris's right.' The bead curtain that separated the front and back of the shop shimmered as Field stepped through. 'We have to stop Sentinel by force. It's the only way.'

'You need a real campaign behind you. Strikes me your voice isn't being heard.'

'We have people outside Sentinel's offices. We've been there since yesterday and we've sent in a list of demands. No reaction from management. No support from the public. Makes no difference. No one cares that we're there.'

'One day isn't exactly enough to win hearts and minds.'

Christo shook his head and kept rolling and stuffing. Maggie turned to Field.

'Alex, let me help. I'll send a journalist to go and interview the Sentinel people, take some photos of the protestors and see if we can whip up some kind of response.'

Alex rubbed his beard. 'It's too late. You can write what you like and investigate what you like. We're calling the protestors back and heading to the forest. The war's on.'

The last thing Christo needed was another war.

Chapter 4
Tuesday, 1pm

Maggie googled Sentinel's corporate headquarters, which were in the same office park as *The Gazette*. There was no sign of Liebenberg at his desk or in the archives, and he wasn't responding to calls, so she went to the Sentinel offices herself. Someone had to address the honchos hiding inside their glass castle.

'Maggie Cloete, from *The Gazette*,' she told the guy on reception, flashing her press card. 'I'd like to see Xolani Mpondo. I have some questions about the protestors from yesterday, and Sentinel's plans for Extension 7 in the Karkloof forest.'

'Please take a seat,' the guy told her, indicating an array of leather sofas ranged around a low square table. 'I will check with Mr Mpondo's office if he is available.'

Maggie sat. The leather chair under her squeaked. She sighed and looked around. The corporate world was antiseptic, with its buffed leather, well-polished glass and shiny floors. Unlike the world out there – the real world, the grubby one – where people like her brother were fighting to save a little patch of natural forest that no one seemed to care about. She knew which world she preferred.

Sighing again, she picked up a brochure and flicked through it. Last year's annual report. Columns of figures. Rows of profit, like tiny little soldiers.

She paged further. There were a few photos, mostly of acres of identical pine forests. This was the so-called sustainability on which companies like Sentinel built their reputations: planting trees yet not mentioning that the trees were aliens that destroyed both the rich soil and the animal life that natural forests preserved. Not mentioning the vast hectares of grassland or, in this case, forest, and the hundreds of species ravaged so that Sentinel could plant their pines.

Monoculture. That was what Alex called it.

She examined the photos further. There was a good mix of black and white faces. The government's equity programmes were seeing to that. But even these mixed groups were a monoculture – suited and booted corporate types with a single joint aim: to make as much money as they possibly could, and dupe the public and the government that they were being sustainable at the same time. The faces were as clean and buffed as this reception area.

Amongst those faces was Johan Liebenberg's. Standing at the back of a group of men, he was clean-shaven and dressed in the corporate uniform of suit and tie.

Maggie slapped the brochure back on the low-slung coffee table. Liebenberg had worked for Christo's enemy, earned a fat corporate package, and now was pushing pencils at *The Gazette* for peanuts. What had he said yesterday? He'd been offered a board-level position but had turned it down to achieve more work-life balance. To spend more time with his ailing mother. What crap. Once a corporate animal, always a corporate animal.

'Maggie Cloete?' A tall young woman stood before her, dressed in the female version of Johan Liebenberg's uniform but with a mass of intricate braids falling down her back. 'Is it really you?'

Maggie stood. 'Mbali. You've grown.'

They hugged and the young woman laughed. 'More than grown. I've grown up.'

'When did I last see you? You were fourteen, fifteen?'

'Yes, I think it was Grade Ten.'

Fourteen years ago, Mbali Sibanyoni had been a little girl in danger. Now she was a woman in a sleek corporate suit. For a few years after her rescue, Maggie had visited Mbali, kept in touch with her family, but after a while she had let her Pietermaritzburg contacts slide.

'What brings you here?' Maggie gestured to the sleek glass surroundings.

'Well I studied journalism and PR. Sentinel hired me after university. I've been here three years.'

'Run, now, while you still can. Before they take your soul.'

'You are so funny,' Mbali laughed. Then her face straightened. 'Actually, I really like my job. They pay me well – and as you know, I have three siblings to look after.'

Maggie did know. Mbali had two brothers and a younger sister. 'How are they all?'

'Well, thanks. Grace is in matric and the two boys are at UKZN.' She clapped her hands. 'Now I know this isn't a social visit. You wanted to see Mr Mpondo, but he is in a board meeting. I am part of the PR team and can answer your questions. Would you follow me?'

Mbali led Maggie to a spacious meeting-room with a polished wood table and leather chairs.

'Please take a seat.' She indicated a chair and then turned to an array of drinks. 'Can I offer you something?'

Maggie shook her head. She had lost her appetite.

The young woman sat down and flipped open a laptop. 'How can I help you?'

'The protestors that were outside yesterday issued a list of demands – including that Sentinel immediately pull out of the Karkloof Forest.'

Mbali wrinkled her smooth brow. 'Sentinel owns the Karkloof. How can we pull out?'

Maggie noted the 'we'. Mbali identified with the company. 'According to environmentalists, the section of the Karkloof where you plan to cultivate your next pine plantation is one of the last remaining habitats of the Karkloof Blue. If you raze it, the butterfly will die out. Not only that, it is one of the few remaining intact pockets of natural forest in the province.'

'Oh, the Blue,' Mbali smiled. 'But we have amazing plans for it.'

Maggie raised her eyebrows.

'So, we will capture the remaining butterflies and keep them safely in a purpose-built butterfly dome right here on our campus. It is being built and is nearly ready. Our scientists will look after them, and when we have increased the population to a significant number we will release them back into the wild.'

'What's the point of that if their habitat is gone?' Maggie asked.

'We are working right now to find other suitable habitats. You know there are other colonies. Our environmentalists have studied those and are working hard right now to find a matching alternative for the K7 colony. We believe we have identified at least three potential locations.'

She sat back in her chair and smiled. 'Really, Maggie, you need to rest assured that Sentinel is doing everything in its power to ensure the butterfly's survival. We have consulted eminent biologists and are convinced that relocation will be the best possible outcome.'

'But why relocate at all? Seems crazy to me to go to that expense when you can leave them right where they are.'

Mbali folded her arms. 'The forest is prime real estate. It is conveniently located close to our Pietermaritzburg factories. It's the next step in our growth plan.'

'And what about the protestors and their demands? Do you have any specific response to them?'

Mbali opened a blue folder and pulled out a piece of paper. 'Here's a statement.'

Maggie read it. It was a terse two-liner, saying that Sentinel would continue with its growth plan, the butterflies would be safely relocated and that the protestors were reminded to keep off Sentinel property. The company had a planting permit from the Department of Water and Forestry and nothing was going to stop them from going about their legal business.

It was a time bomb. She could hear the ticking.

'You realise that there are colleagues inside Sentinel who do not believe that the company has a legal right to raze this forest? Colleagues whom the company might organise to get rid of?' Maggie waved the media statement in one hand.

Mbali shook her head. 'I am not sure what you mean.'

'How about Dave Bloom?'

Mbali's air of confidence slipped slightly. 'Dave's death has affected us all, very deeply. We are all in a terrible state of shock.'

Maggie stood. 'So your message to the public is that Sentinel is on track with cutting down the Karkloof forest?'

'Our growth plan is on track, yes.'

'I don't think the protestors are going to be particularly happy to hear that.'

Mbali stood too, arms firmly folded across her chest. 'Then I am sorry to say they will find themselves on the wrong side of the law. Sentinel has the right to log its own forests. It's as simple as that.'

'Your boss will regret this, Mbali.'

The young woman walked her back to reception. 'Sorry not to be able to give you different news. I doubt you can make much of a story out of this.'

'That's my problem, not yours,' Maggie said. She thought of someone else who was her problem. 'Listen, before you go, is there anything I should know about Johan Liebenberg?'

'The guy who left?'

'Ja. He now works for *The Gazette*.'

Mbali leaned in. 'They say he was lazy. Made a big noise about how hard he worked, but never got anything done.'

'He claims he was a Board candidate here. That he was offered some huge promotion.'

Mbali widened her eyes and shook her head. 'More likely he was asked to leave.'

Back at the office, Johan was at his desk, feet up and flipping through *Getaway* magazine. Maggie wished he would go away.

She slapped his boots. 'Feet off the desk, cowboy. This is a newsroom, not a bar. I've got some real work for you.'

He sat up straight while she filled him in on the Forest Keepers' plan to occupy the forest, and Sentinel's statement of intent. 'We need a quote from someone in academia, who can talk about why logging the forest is going to be bad for the Karkloof Blue. Can you get on it?'

Half an hour later, he was hovering at her desk. 'Apparently, the local expert is Prof Mike Rankin. The Biology department says he's living in the forest right now, and doesn't have a cell phone.'

Maggie glanced up from her screen. 'Try one of his students. There must be a masters or doctoral student around who has something to say.'

Johan found someone to quote, a PhD student named Hope Phiri, and they wrote the story together under the byline Staff Reporters. Maggie handed it over to the night news editor with strict instructions to keep it on the front page.

Back at the flat, she changed into her warmest gear – long johns, a thermal undershirt, thick socks. Over these went her winter uniform of black jeans and a black denim shirt, followed by a fleece and her thickest leather jacket from her motorcycling days. If she was going to spend the night in the forest along with her brother and his cadre, then she could at least be warm.

In winter, darkness fell early. With only the headlights of cars and trucks to light the highway, she drove by instinct. She followed Hope Phiri's careful directions – turn-off at Midmar Dam, right across the highway, winding road to Howick, left at the crossroads, follow the acres of plantation down a long rural road.

At night, the trees were dark stakes in the ground. Clouds washed out the moon. It was cold and lonely out here. On a night much like this a few weeks before, she had waited outside a petrol station in Kyalami for her contact. He had never turned up, but his broken body was found days later on a Katlehong rubbish dump.

She pulled herself back to the moment. She was looking for a big Sentinel sign on the right. There it was, in green and black. Hope had said that the gate would be locked at night. She climbed out of the car and gave the gate a shake, prepared to climb over if necessary. It creaked open, chains slithering to the ground. The Forest Keepers had broken the lock.

Maggie drove through the gate, stopped on the other side and rearranged the chain to look as if it was still locked.

She followed the dirt road up a hill, trees marching on either side of her. Up ahead she saw a motley collection of bakkies and four-wheel drives – the tanks of the new environmentalists. Hope had said it was at least a ten-minute walk into the plantation to find the original, ancient one. She parked next to Alex Field's surfer van, with its huge Forest Keepers decal painted on the side, and followed the path into the forest.

She could hear voices and see the flickering light of a fire ahead. The Forest Keepers were not making a huge effort to be silent or circumspect. In fact, they seemed to be having a party. Gusts of laughter reached her and someone was playing a guitar.

She approached the fire, safely contained in a ring of stones, and caught sight of Christo, a beer in hand, laughing at someone's story. Her heart caught in her throat. He looked so happy. She hadn't seen him look like this since he was a rugby-playing schoolboy. His stint in the National Defence Force, carrying a gun for the apartheid government during its jumped-up wars against its neighbours, had dulled that look. His years in a Pietermaritzburg mental institution had killed it forever.

But there it was again, a light in his eyes. It scared her almost more than the dullness had. How little it would take to extinguish it. One glance at his sister was apparently enough. The light died.

'Welcome Maggie!' Alex Field greeted her exuberantly, and made space for her on the log he was sitting on.

'People, this is Christo's sister, Maggie, from *The Gazette*. We have the mighty news organ on our side.'

There was a chorus of hellos from around the fire. Maggie recognised a couple of faces. A skinny guy in a beanie next to her was smoking a cigarette as if his life depended on it. She remembered him from the meeting on Saturday night.

'Maggie Cloete, right?' he said, a double wisp of smoke snaking out of his nostrils.

'Ja.'

'Brad McKenzie,' he put out his hand for her to shake. 'You used to go out with Spike Lyall. I know him well.'

'Let me guess,' said Maggie. Everyone knew Spike. She might be the press, but no one was as well-connected as her ex. His network spread throughout the province like a spider web.

'School?'

Spike had attended a posh local boys' school, where half the province's captains of industry sent their sons. The other half sent theirs to the rival school thirty kilometres up the road. The two schools played bloody, violent games of rugby against each other in the winter and cruel, vicious games of cricket in the summer. In the holidays, they all hung out at the same beach or trout-fishing resorts. It was the tiny world of the wealthy, where, having had the briefest of introductions from Spike, Maggie had felt acutely awkward.

The beanie guy shook his head.

'Okay, university then.'

He shook his head again. There would be another connection. Maggie racked her brains.

'Family?'

This time he nodded. 'Almost. My family's beach cottage is next to theirs.'

She put a finger in her mouth and made a gagging noise.

'What?' He looked surprised.

'You people. You own everything.' It was true. Apartheid had come and gone, but an elite still held onto vast tracts of land. The Land Rights Commission was doing its best to return land to the previously disadvantaged, but like most government bodies it was hampered by bureaucracy. Submissions lingered for years, untended and growing dust, while people like Brad McKenzie's family raised their innocent eyebrows and grew ever richer.

'As far as I know there are no tribal claims to Ballito,' he said and sucked deeply and rancorously on his cigarette.

Maggie turned away. There was no point in trying to disabuse the privileged of the advantages their privilege had given them. They were blinded by a special blanketing cloud and a steadfast belief in their own glittering talents.

Christo had his back to her. She nudged him. 'So what's the plan?'

He turned to her, face blank. 'We camp here tonight and then in the morning, we will climb the trees. We stay here until Sentinel gives up. It's a going to be a war.'

Someone passed her a beer and she sipped it. The temperature had dropped and she was happy to be warmed from the inside and numbed against Christo's war.

She watched her brother accept one beer after another. Dr K had warned that he should keep away from stimulants. He was still fragile and there was no knowing what might tip him over the edge. The last time he'd drunk alcohol, she'd woken with his hands around her neck and her blood throbbing in her veins.

Beanie boy nudged her and she turned towards him. He passed her the glowing nub of a joint.

'No thanks,' Maggie said.

'Pass it on.'

Maggie leaned across Christo to Alex, but Christo expertly intercepted her and took a deep drag before passing the joint on.

She could already see the downward spiral back to Kitchener Clinic, the private institution that he had so recently left. 'Please, don't,' she muttered, despite herself. He turned his back to her again.

Maggie would have to try another tack with her brother. She let a few minutes pass, so that he could forget the insult of her last words. The gathering grew rowdier.

Then she tapped his shoulder. The coldness in his eyes knifed her.

'Can you show me where your tent is?'

'Why?'

'Well, if it's okay, I plan to sleep here tonight.'

'Didn't you bring your own tent?'

'I'm not much of a camper.' The old Christo would have known that.

Alex was watching their interchange. 'Chris, we have a four-man tent. Of course Maggie can share it.'

Her brother got up with a great show of reluctance, beer in hand, and led her to the tent.

She started taking her boots off. 'I think I'm going to sleep now. How about you?'

'Nah, I'll head back.'

He turned to go, but she caught his arm. 'Christo, please go carefully. You know what the doctors said.'

He detached her hand as if it were a maggot. 'I am a grown-up. I know what I'm doing.'

'You are a grown-up, but you are still vulnerable.'

'Fuck you and your judgments, Maggie. I've managed my recovery perfectly well without you. What makes you think you can swan in now and have opinions? You lost that right when you left here and left me in that place.'

'Christo, your doctors assured me there was no chance of a recovery. They were convinced you'd never leave.'

'Well they were wrong and so were you. You abandoned me, just like our useless excuses for parents. And the only thing that pisses me off more is you coming back here with your saviour complex, thinking you can rescue me. I don't fucking need you.'

The reproach in his eyes was hard to bear. He turned and walked back to the fire.

She burrowed fully clothed into a sleeping-bag and tried to

sleep. It was futile. The truth of Christo's words rankled. She had let her career pull her away from here to Joburg, later to Berlin and then back to Joburg. She had paid for his care in Kitchener Clinic and had visited, but there was no denying that she had left. He had every right to resent her.

The noise from the fire grew from loud talking to shouting and hooting. It was a full-blown party and Christo was right in the middle of it, butching it out just to show her how successful his recovery was.

The noise from the party died down. At one point in the night, she woke with the awareness that other bodies had joined her in the tent. She relaxed back into sleep.

Suddenly there was shouting again. Lights flashed and there were screams from the other tents. She heard a dog bark.

An arm flung their tent flap open and a light flashed in her face. She scrunched her eyes against the blinding whiteness and lifted an arm across her face.

'Police,' said a voice. 'You are under arrest.'

'For what?'

'Trespassing. Now get the hell out of this tent.'

Maggie crawled out with Christo and Alex just behind her. She could feel Christo loom tall behind her, aware of the bulk that had made him a rugby player in his schooldays.

Maggie floundered around in front of the tent looking for her boots.

'You can't do this,' Christo told the cop.

'Yes we can,' the policeman replied.

'I'm not going anywhere!' Christo bulldozed the cop aside and ran for the trees. The Forest Keepers had earmarked their respective trees already. She guessed he was heading for his.

'Stop him!' the cop yelled and gave chase. Christo ran, surprisingly fast. Another cop jumped into his path and tried to grab him but he shoved him aside. The cop hit the ground with a bump and pulled himself back onto his feet. Now there were three policemen after her brother. In the melee, Maggie tried to follow them, one boot on and one in her hand, but someone held her arms.

'Don't get involved.' It was Alex.

'What are you doing?' She struggled against his grip.

'You can't help Christo. He is on his own now.'

'Fuck you!' She writhed, but his hands were huge around her biceps. She could feel the musculature of his chest behind her like a wall. Anger coursed through her. She tried to get her elbow up into his neck, so that she could swing around into a roundhouse but he held her too tightly. In frustration, she kicked back and downwards. There was a satisfying crunch of shoe against bare foot and he yelped in pain. There was a reason she still wore steel-capped Docs.

She ran tumbling through the darkness after her brother, her second Doc still in her hand. The cops' torchlights grazed the trees, a confusing mix of blinding light and shadow. She followed the noise of their boots crashing through the undergrowth and their shouts.

'Can you see him?'

'No man, he's got lost in the forest.'

'Then we need to go, man. Get the rest of them locked up.'

Panic gripped her heart. They were going to leave Christo in the forest, all alone in the dark.

A cop wrapped his fist around her arm. 'Come on, you.'

'But my brother ...'

'... wants to die of exposure, apparently.'

She could just make out the figures of the Forest Keepers hunched over with their arms behind them as the cops marched them back along the forest path and into waiting police vans.

A cop pushed her into the back of a van and she found a space next to one of the women. She put on her other boot as the van rattled into motion. Perhaps it was better that Christo not join the other Forest Keepers in prison. He had been in jail before. A night in the forest would be infinitely more bearable for him.

Chapter 5
Wednesday, 2am

The Pietermaritzburg lock-up smelled of damp and fear as it had during Maggie's first stint there years before. Then, there'd been the camaraderie of political prisoners united against the state, singing protest songs late into the night. Now, she was here as a petty criminal. And in need of sleep.

There were only two beds in the holding cell, and these had already been taken when Maggie and Bettina from the Forest Keepers were pushed inside. She tried to sleep upright, but there was cramp in her leg, a pulse of pain that knotted in her muscles. She rubbed it and then her neck, which was pressed against the cold cell wall.

'You awake?' Bettina whispered.

'Unfortunately.'

'What's going to happen to us?' Bettina had a German accent, thinly disguised by some South African vowels.

'Well, they will either charge us and let us out, or not charge us and let us out. We just need to get through tonight.'

'The campaign didn't exactly have a chance to get going,' Bettina said. 'One night in the forest and we were already arrested.'

Maggie didn't want to think about the forest. 'Tell me about you. What are you doing here?'

Bettina was a sustainability student from Leipzig doing a placement at UKZN for a few months. She was sleeping with Patrick, one of the Forest Keepers, and was now engaged in complicated arrangements with her faculty to try to extend her time in the country.

Maggie rubbed the back of her neck. The cell walls were chilly. Even the warmth of other people sleeping around them wasn't enough to defrost the atmosphere.

'What if the campaign got more coverage? Would they let you

extend if they saw what you were involved in?'

'Maybe,' Bettina said.

'It needs to be more visible. Right now, you look like a bunch of radical tree-huggers. You need to get ordinary people on your side. Sentinel appeals to them with all their greenwashing. You guys need to do so too.'

'How?' Bettina closed her eyes. She was getting sleepy.

'Well, social media for one. Someone needs to be on Twitter with an eye-catching hashtag.'

'Save our forest?'

'Something like that.'

'I'll suggest it,' Bettina yawned and closed her eyes.

In the dark, her thoughts turned to Leo. She missed his skinny arms around her neck and his chirpy voice, reciting a stream of consciousness that centered on Harry Potter, the South African rugby squad and Minecraft.

Later, she heard feet stomping down a corridor and the clashing of keys.

'You two, get up.'

'Why?' Bettina asked.

'You're being released. Charges have been dropped.'

The Forest Keepers milled on the pavement outside the police station, their breath puffing before them in the cold morning air. She stretched and felt a twinge in her shoulder. Spending all night sitting on a hard, cold floor had not done her body any good.

Alex Field addressed the group. 'People, our cars and things are impounded until 2pm. I suggest we all get home and get some sleep. We reconvene later. We need to ramp up the protest at the Sentinel offices.'

'What about Christo?' Maggie said. 'You're all going to have a nap while he is stuck in a tree in the middle of nowhere.'

Field turned to her, arms held out in an appeal. 'Maggie, we understand that you feel worried, but Chris is a big boy. He will be fine. We cased out the trees yesterday and put supplies in all the likely ones. There are at least fifteen backpacks scattered around that forest with food, water and survival blankets. He knows where every single one is.'

'Yes, but for how long?'

'As long as it takes, really.'

'You are making him a martyr.' She heard her voice get louder as blood thumped in her ears.

'A very well-fed, well-cared for martyr, yes.' Field glanced round at the crowd, and there were murmurs of amusement.

'I don't think he's safe. We should drive out there and collect him. Right now.'

He pulled both corners of his mouth down. 'Makes for a good story, doesn't it? Man in tree versus evil corporation. I think the public might find his plight appealing.'

'I don't believe you. You are going to sacrifice my brother, just like that?'

People started to move away in clumps. Field walked up to her. 'Pull yourself together, Maggie. This is Chris's big moment, the one he's been training and planning for. He knows exactly what he's doing.'

'Don't tell me to pull myself together,' she hissed. 'You know very well that a few short months ago, Christo was still in a mental institution. You know very well that his balance is extremely fragile. You yourself said that the forest occupiers would need to be mentally tough.'

He put a hand on her shoulder. 'Chris is tough. And you know very well that this cause means the world to him. He lives for it. Wouldn't you rather he was out there, fighting for something he believed in?'

She sighed. 'I suppose so. But I want a fixed plan on how and when we get him out of there.'

'I promise you, Maggie, you and I will keep in constant touch. I will let you know about every decision we make.'

She needed to get back to the flat and have a furious shower. But first she had an important errand. She walked the few blocks to Alpha Garage. Pete Dickson was in the office, as she knew he would be.

'Howzit, Maggie?' Pete gave her a klap on the back. He had always treated her as one of the boys.

'Sit, sit,' he pointed to the chair opposite his. The seat was fake leather and it leaked foam.

He pointed to a tall pump-action thermos. 'Coffee?'

Maggie groaned at the smell of fresh coffee as Pete poured it, thick and black, into a styrofoam cup. He handed it to her and she gave it an appreciative sniff.

'So what brings you back to town?'

'I'm working here again.'

'Great.' Pete had been one of her running friends. He had zero interest in her job. 'Listen, I joined a new club, the PMB Pelicans. Great group, you must come along.'

'Doesn't sound too promising,' Maggie laughed.

'I know, I know. We are considered seniors now too.' Pete sipped his coffee and looked at her speculatively. 'Have you seen Spike?'

'Why does everyone ask me about Spike?'

'You used to be close.'

'Yes, we were close. For one year, nearly fifteen years ago.' She tried the coffee. It was delicious. 'But for the record, no, I have not seen him and I don't plan to. All reports suggest that he is very happily married.'

'That he is.'

'How about you, Pete?'

'I'm also happily married. To wife number three.'

'Congratulations.' Just as Pete wasn't interested in Maggie's work, she wasn't interested in the women who moved through the turnstile of his front door.

'So listen, I'm sick of my bloody Golf. I want to trade it in.' She didn't need to mention that her car was presently in police lock-up.

'You want another car?'

'Well, potentially.' Maggie knew that Pete knew where this was going.

'I have a very nice motorbike. You could have it for free. You've been paying its license for the past twelve years.'

'Show me.'

Pete led the way into a back office which led to the workshop. It was spotless, heady with the smell of motor oil. He unlocked the back doors of the workshop and threw them open. Maggie followed him outside, where he had a series of small lock-ups. He fiddled with a set of keys. Their jangling and her breath were the only sounds she heard on the quiet winter morning.

'Got it,' Pete turned the key in the lock and threw the door open.

Maggie stepped into the garage. She watched as Pete whisked away the blue tarpaulin.

'There she is.'

And there she was. A Yamaha XT 350. Tweaked for off-road, but still excellent on tarmac. Shiny bodywork, pristine tires. The Chicken.

'She looks in good nick.'

'She is, Maggie. We do an annual service, plus I take her out every couple of months just to make sure the engine's in order.'

'And?'

'It's in order.'

'Where's the key?'

Pete dug in his pocket and passed it to her. The care he took also meant not leaving the key in the garage along with the bike as a gift to passing thieves. Maggie rocked the bike off its stand and pushed it outside. She swung a leg over the seat and put the key in the ignition. It started first go, despite the cold.

She grinned at Pete over the roar. 'Sounds good.'

'As good as ever, Maggie.'

She lifted her foot off the ground and let the bike's pull take her on a couple of circuits of Pete's yard. It was heaven, so much better than the crappy Golf.

She circled back to Pete.

'I'll take her.'

She borrowed a helmet from Pete and drove straight to the office. There was no time to shower or change. They were going to have to cope with her smelling of eau de police cell.

Someone else had got the first pot of coffee going. She poured herself a cup, then headed for her desk with a copy of today's edition under her arm. She read through the paper. Political reporter Johnny Cupido's lead on a war of words between the ANC and the opposition was a good one. She had supplemented it with additional reporting from the wires. The night ed had put the forest story on the front page, as promised.

Her desk phone buzzed.

'Can you go and see Tina?' Fortunate asked.

'Sure,' Maggie got up and grimaced as her shoulder twinged again. Why couldn't Naidoo call her herself? They had their own conference, along with Patti, in a couple of hours anyway.

She walked down the corridor to the editor's office, knocked and went in.

'Morning Maggie.' Tina Naidoo gestured to the chair opposite hers and she flopped into it, one hand reflexively rubbing her shoulder. She hoped she didn't smell too much. Tina Naidoo was as buffed and polished as Maggie was sweaty and tired.

'No prizes for guessing which executive was on the phone this morning complaining about our front-page story.' Naidoo pushed her reading glasses onto her head. Her fingernails were the colour of dried blood.

'Xolani Mpondo?'

'Correct.'

'What did he have to say?'

'He is stunned that we might consider a protest from a tiny group of radicals a story, and he feels we gave too much weight to the academic opinion of a PhD student and not enough to Sentinel's vision and mission.'

'Sentinel's vision and mission is to make as much money as humanly possible for Xolani Mpondo. Plus I asked for his comment and he was not available. His PR person stepped in.'

'Sentinel's one of the biggest employers in the province and does grow trees. It's not as if it is building shopping malls or pouring concrete onto the ground, Maggie.'

'He's sending in tractors to raze a patch of ancient forest. It's one of the last pockets left and one of the last habitats of a butterfly. The protestors, and Hope Phiri, want people to know what he's sanctioning. That's all.'

'I'm not against the article, Maggie. I just want you to know that Mpondo is. And in almost unrelated news, his company does supply our paper.'

'Are you saying he threatened you?'

'It wasn't exactly a threat. He just felt, in the light of our close business association, that he had a right to register his complaint.'

Naidoo pulled her reading glasses back onto her nose and peered at Maggie over them.

'You are looking a bit rough. Are you okay?'

'Bad night,' Maggie muttered. There were things editors didn't need to know. Her night in a jail cell was one of them.

'Hmmm,' Naidoo's gaze returned to her screen. 'Mpondo also mentioned that Sentinel had arrested a bunch of protestors on their property last night.'

Maggie held her breath. Was this it? Was her job over already?

'He said they released them without charge, but the company decided not to wait any longer before logging the forest.' She looked at her watch. 'They should be there by now.'

She exhaled. 'I think they are going to have a problem with that.'

'What do you mean?'

'I hear one of the protestors got away. He's climbed into one of the trees and is holed up there with a week's worth of supplies.'

'Interesting.' Naidoo glanced at the story. 'Who wrote this article anyway? I don't see Johan's byline.'

'Teamwork.'

'Maggie, we hired you to be news editor, not another reporter. We have enough of those.'

Not exactly. It was nothing more than a skeleton staff.

'Tina, listen, I am not impressed with Johan. He can't recognise a news story when it jumps up and hits him on the nose, and he manages to absent himself from the newsroom when we're all on deadline.'

'Sounds like you need to get your newsroom under control.' Naidoo was already typing. News editor dismissed.

Maggie went into conference in a bad mood. Not even Ed's crinkly-eyed smile was enough to lift her. Menzi was expecting judgment in the farm murder story, Fatima was researching an increase in TB cases, Aslan had a movie review and a book review in the making and there were football matches to be covered.

'Ed, I need one of your guys out in Karkloof today. Sentinel are going to start logging the forest and they have tractors and trucks rolling in.'

'Sure, Maggie.'

'And Johan, please follow up with Sentinel. Apparently Xolani

Mpondo is feeling left out of today's story and is now dying to give his full and unvarnished opinion. I am sure you will have no trouble getting an audience with him.'

Johan smirked as she stalked out of the conference. Back at her desk, she texted Alex Field to let him know that Sentinel's logging was kicking off. Then, Natalie Bloom's entreaty in mind, she dialled the police liaison, Ernest Radebe.

He answered the phone after one ring. 'Radebe.'

'Hi Captain Radebe, it's Maggie Cloete. We haven't met yet, but I've taken over from Zacharius Patel as news editor at *The Gazette*.'

'Morning Maggie, how are you?'

'Good.' Apart from the fact that she needed a shower, some food and eight hours' sleep.

'Listen, the investigating officer on the Dave Bloom case, who is it?'

Radebe sucked his teeth. 'Let me see.' He rattled some paperwork. 'Njima. Takkies Njima.'

'Takkies?' Maggie couldn't keep the surprise out of her voice.

'Yes, apparently he was on the Olympic sprint squad. Hence the name.'

'Any chance of getting Takkies' cell phone number?'

'Well it's not standard procedure ...'

'I've got information for him on the Howick Falls suicide.'

He caved. 'Okay, just this once.'

Maggie took down the officer's cell phone number, thanked Ernest profusely and cancelled the call. She would phone Takkies Njima. She had promised to help Natalie Bloom yesterday, and maybe he would have some insight into Dave Bloom's death.

The number went to voicemail and she left the cop a message. Then she got on the with the business of the day. At lunchtime, instead of one of Fortunate's sorry sandwiches, she decided to take the Chicken out for a spin. Time to remind herself what the Yamaha was made of, and forget all the crap of the newsroom.

The bike hugged the highway's curves as she headed for Howick. She had forgotten the rush of freedom, the thin line between life and death as she opened the throttle. It was only the messages between her ganglia and the nerves in her fingers that kept her alive. She felt the blood course through her and her energy come pouring back. This was a lot better than dealing with recalcitrant reporters and grumpy editors. She even forgot the tweaking pain in her shoulder.

She parked the Chicken near the Howick Falls. A number of traders had set up stalls selling curios. A couple of them yelled sales patter in her direction. She ignored them and walked over to the viewpoint. With the lack of rain, the falls were thin, dribbling into a green pool at the bottom. She had been here once before in summer after a rainfall and remembered the roaring water, the mist rising up in white puffs.

Maggie saw figures near the top of the waterfall. What were they doing there? She looked closer and saw that it was a group of women, making the most of the big pools at the top of the falls to get their washing done. Behind them were a few lean-tos. It was a squatter camp. People with nowhere else to go had set up their lives there.

Would any of them know anything about Dave Bloom's death?

She walked back towards the Chicken, stomach rumbling. It really was time to find something to eat. The building behind her declared itself to be Ishmael's Howick Falls Tearoom and Cafe. She wandered in and sat at a table with red and white plastic tablecloths. They were slightly sticky, but she was hungry.

'What would you like to order?' A older man wearing a spotless white apron hovered at her right shoulder.

She consulted the menu. It had been a while since she'd had a square meal. 'I'll have black coffee, and your lamb curry.'

'Will that be all?' He reached for the menu in her hand.

'Hang on.' She checked the drinks. 'I'll also have a lime milkshake. Thanks.'

'Thanks, ma'am.' That was new. She always used to be miss or sisi. When had those days ended?

He brought the coffee and the milkshake at the same time. Maggie gulped down the shake, its creamy deliciousness slaking her hunger and her thirst. The lime flavour was in no way way related to real limes; instead it had a chemical tang that was weirdly satisfying.

The man slid a plate in front of her piled high with curry and rice. She wolfed it down, and then pushed the plate to one side. Staring out of the window, appetite sated, she sipped the coffee. It was great – dark, thick and tasty.

'Very nice.' She gave a thumbs-up to the guy.

He came over to get her plate. 'Glad you liked it.'

'Bit quiet, isn't it?' She pointed to the restaurant and the viewing-point. Both empty.

'Weekdays aren't great,' he said. 'We usually get busier at the weekend.'

'You all alone here?'

'I have a couple of staff in the kitchen. I do the front of house. Everything else too, in fact.'

'You wouldn't know anything about the guy who went over last weekend?'

He put the plate back down on the table. 'You mean the suicide.'

'Yes. Well. If that's what it was.'

'I found him.' The guy looked distressed. 'He was not the first, of course, but it was just so, just so ...' He was lost for words.

Maggie pointed to the chair opposite her. 'Sit, please.'

The man sat. He was older, perhaps in his sixties, cleanly shaved. He wiped his hands on his apron.

'Do you want to tell me what happened?'

He nodded, grateful to talk. 'I came in early. Well I always come in early. I was heading for the cafe when I saw something white on the bushes down there. I found a man's shirt, pants, jacket and a pair of shoes. Socks and a tie rolled up and tucked into the shoes.'

The man glanced at his hands. 'I picked them up and walked towards the amphitheatre. Then I saw him down there. Half in the water, half on the rocks. He was naked. Very white, some blood too. It was horrible. Horrible.' The man shook his head.

'I'm sure.' Maggie sipped her coffee. It was cold. 'Can I have a top-up?'

'Sure, sure.' He leapt up and returned with a coffee pot in his hand and refilled her cup.

'Does this sort of thing happen often?'

'Now and again. If someone is serious about ending their lives, then this is a good place to do it.'

'Anything different about this one?'

He looked over his shoulder, and lowered his voice. 'Well, he was naked. What suicide strips naked in the middle of winter before leaping off a waterfall?'

An elderly couple wandered into the restaurant. 'Excuse me.' He hurried off to see to their needs. Maggie sipped her coffee and stared out of the window. An ache went through her. Who or what had forced Dave Bloom to take his life?

She waved down the proprietor and paid for her food.

'Listen, I'm from *The Gazette*. We might end up writing about this, we might not. Can I take your name and number in case we have more questions?'

'Sure. It's Ishmael.'

'Thanks.' Maggie took down his number and left. She headed to the Chicken in the car park. She swung her leg over the seat and stood there for a moment. What about the squatter camp? People were living there right on the lip of the waterfall. Maybe one of them had seen something.

Then she looked at her watch. It was time to get back to the office. She sighed. This desk job thing did not suit her.

Her cell phone buzzed.

'Ms Cloete?' It was an unfamiliar voice.

'Yes?'

'Njima here. You called.'

Chapter 6
Wednesday, 2pm

He was waiting in reception, Fortunate staring at him as if he was a family pack of KFC, all hot and steamy and straight out of the fryer. She was just managing to not lick her lips.

'Maggie you have a visitor.'

'Solomon Njima.' He held out a hand for Maggie to shake and nearly crushed hers. His sleeves were rolled up and she could see forearms threaded through with muscle. Tall and broad, he wore small wire-framed glasses.

'I'm sure Ernest Radebe called you something else,' she said, leading him to a downstairs meeting room.

'Just a nickname. I used to be a sprinter.'

'Can I get you a drink?'

'No thanks. I just had lunch. I'm okay.'

They sat and Maggie told him of her visit to Natalie Bloom, of the woman's conviction that her husband was not suicidal.

'She has to say that,' Njima said. He sat leaning forward, forearms resting on the table, hands clasped. Maggie tried not to let them distract her.

'Why?'

'Firstly, for insurance purposes. Most insurers don't pay out in the case of suicide.'

'OK. So if he jumped, she gets no money?'

'Correct.'

'That's a good reason to protest loudly.'

'It is.'

'But it seemed like more than that. She's convinced that he was too dedicated to his children and to the Karkloof Blue to just give up. He had a cause.'

'We've closed the case, Ms Cloete. It was suicide and, hard though it is for the family to accept, it's cut and dried. No evidence, nothing to investigate. Dave Bloom took his own life.'

'In suspicious circumstances.'

'What do you mean?'

Maggie told him she had just seen Mr Ishmael.

'We interviewed Ishmael.'

'So what do you think about the clothes?'

'I acknowledge that it is odd that he left them there, but someone who is about to kill themselves by leaping off a waterfall is not in their right mind anyway. There is no telling what they might do.'

Maggie shrugged. 'So, if you are so sure it was suicide, why are you here?'

A grin played across his face and he readjusted his glasses. 'I just wanted to meet the famous crime reporter, Maggie Cloete. Your reputation proceeds you, you know.'

Now he was flirting with her. 'I'm not a reporter any more. I'm on the editorial team.'

'Is that boring for you? Do you break out into a little light investigation now and then?'

'Yes, it is a bit.' Maggie smiled. 'And I do. Like now.'

'Is that why I'm here?'

'Look,' she lowered her voice. 'Some protestors were arrested in the forest last night.'

'I heard the charges were dropped.'

'They were, but one of them got left behind.'

'In the forest?'

'Yes. Apparently the plan was for all of them to climb trees and tie themselves in today. One escaped the police and is now alone in the forest. I just need to understand his position, you know, from a legal point of view.'

'Well, he is trespassing.'

'So, if the police manage to get him down from the tree, what are we looking at?'

'A fine or a short jail sentence.'

'OK.'

'But there is a twist.'

'What's that?'

'If he can show a lawful reason for being there, then he can't be accused of trespassing.'

'Is protesting a lawful reason?'

'I don't think so.' He smiled ruefully. 'This has been delightful, Ms Cloete, but I do need to get back to work.'

'Of course.'

He stood up. 'It's been a pleasure.'

'Likewise.' Maggie walked him back to reception, aware as she did so of his height behind her. The man had a physical presence that was difficult to ignore.

At reception, they shook hands again and Solomon Njima walked out, both Maggie and Fortunate watching him go.

'Sjoe. He is something else.' The receptionist waved a piece of paper in front of her face like a fan.

Maggie smiled and went back to her desk. What was she going to tell Natalie Bloom? Her husband's case was a dead end, closed to further investigation.

Back at her desk, she checked the wires, read through Aslan's submitted copy and secured updates from Johnny Cupido and Fatima Rajah on the status of their stories. Sport was in the bag. It was just environment that was missing. She glanced in the direction of Johan's desk. The reporter was nowhere to be seen. She presumed he was out interviewing his former boss, as she had told him to do.

A text bleeped. *Thanks for the heads up. Got our cars. Now at K7, protesting.* Alex had woken from his nap.

Please check on Christo.

Maggie, the forest is under armed guard. We can't get near him.

Try and get a message to him.

We'll do our best. PS follow @ForestKeepers, hashtag #SaveOurTrees.

Maggie logged on to her Twitter account. Her last tweet was four months old. She had never really got her head around the platform. A couple of her Joburg colleagues were addicts, tweeting their breakfast, lunch and supper, as well as everything in between, but it had not been relevant for her brand of journalism, which tended towards long, slow, detailed investigations.

She checked @ForestKeepers, and joined their two hundred-odd followers. She typed in the hashtag to see if there was any action. There was a series of tweets from the gates of Extension 7.

Watching as the Sentinel loggers roll into KE7 to destroy the ancient forest #SaveOurTrees

Liebenberg chose that moment to walk into the newsroom.

'Johan, come and see this!' she yelled. He leaned over and stared at her screen.

'Someone from the Forest Keepers has a Twitter feed going. Please monitor that.'

'Sure, Maggie.'

'Did you get anything from Mpondo?'

'I have a statement, yes.'

@ForestKeepers chief Alex Field blocks Sentinel trucks at the gate to KE7 #SaveOurTrees

There was a grainy photo of Field, apparently in negotiation with a couple of truck drivers and two of the armed guards. He was waving his arms in the air. She had seen that look before.

@ForestKeepers chief Alex Field and other protestors lie down in front of Sentinel trucks at the gate to KE7 #SaveOurTrees #HumanShield

She dialled Ed. 'The Forest Keepers are taking matters into their own hands, lying down in front of the trucks. Hope Ahmed is on this.'

'He is, Maggie, no worries. He'll email us some pics in the next twenty minutes. I'll ping them to you.'

Johan was still hovering. 'Please follow the hashtags and see if others are tweeting this,' she told him. 'Also, keep an eye on the Forest Keepers followers and see if the numbers change.'

She wondered at the insane foolhardiness of Alex Field. He was prepared to risk anything, even the lives of his followers, to prevent Sentinel logging the forest. She couldn't understand that kind of commitment to a cause.

The pics came through from Ed minutes later. It was one of those stupidly sunny winter days, and the pines were shot in dark relief against the blue sky. A long line of Sentinel vehicles trailed into the distance down the main road. The driver of the front truck was gesticulating and trying to pull a supine figure off the dirt track in front of the Extension 7 gate. She could see the bodies of four other protestors.

'Forest Keepers now have over 500 followers!' Johan yelled from his desk. '#SaveOurTrees is trending in South Africa.'

Pics are great, she replied to Ed. *Any other news from Ahmed?*

He says he can hear sirens. Cops are on their way.

Police arrive to stop @ForestKeepers trying to save KE7 from Sentinel loggers #SaveOurTrees #HumanShield

Then her screen went blank. All the lights went off in the newsroom. There was a general groan. Unscheduled load-shedding was not what she needed right now, especially when she was on deadline.

She logged back in again. *The Gazette* had a back-up generator. Another photo had flashed online of cops trying to pull Alex Field and his troops to their feet. A second photo showed them being dragged by their arms out of the loggers' way.

Five @ForestKeepers arrested by police #SaveOurTrees

She had her front-page lead.

Chapter 7
Thursday, 11am

With Alex and a number of other Forest Keepers arrested, and Christo playing the hero in the forest, the Save Our Trees campaign had sparked widespread interest. A group of protestors had gathered outside Sentinel's glass offices.

Alex Field had got his wish. The campaign had got attention. But it had not stopped Sentinel.

After the daily conference, Patti told Maggie that Naidoo was at an all day editor's conference at the university. With the editor safely out of the way, she decided to track down the elusive professor.

Fortunate looked ostentatiously at her watch as Maggie walked out of the office. She would no doubt be reporting on the news editor's comings and goings next time she talked to Tina Naidoo. Or maybe the receptionist had a stake in the office pool.

Maggie didn't give a stuff. *The Gazette* wasn't a police state. At least not yet.

She accelerated out of town and felt the Chicken roar beneath her. As she crested the hill at Hilton, the province spread out in front of her, yellow winter grass slashed by dark ribbons of pine. Workers in fluorescent jackets were cutting grass on the side of the road. The government keep their service delivery – when it happened – as overt as possible. Just like the small scattering of RDP houses on the left. Tourist buses en route to Durban would be sure to see these. Townships with no running water were hidden from view.

She turned left off the highway. The Chicken nosed past a cemetery, the many new headstones still dark grey, not yet weathered pale by the elements. On the other side of Howick, rows of identical houses spread across the landscape. Old-age housing on an industrial scale. The elderly were shipped out here to the countryside to rot.

The road dipped down a hill and up the other side and the Karkloof rose in front of her, forerunner to the mighty Drakensberg that flanked the west side of KwaZulu-Natal. Farms extended on both sides of the road, herds of velvet cows grazing in large fields.

Now where would she find Rankin? Hope Phiri had said he was living in a part of the Karkloof Forest that was on Anderson property. She passed signposts to various farms and eventually found the Anderson signage.

She and the Chicken followed a bumpy dirt road. She saw a couple of men walking in her direction and stopped the bike.

'Excuse me.' She pulled off her helmet so they could hear her. 'I am looking for the professor. He lives somewhere on the farm. In a caravan.'

One gave her directions. When she thanked him, he said, 'Be careful.'

'Why?'

'He is a bit crazy, that man. They say he talks to the trees.'

The two men laughed and Maggie pulled on her helmet. She could deal with crazy. Crazy was her territory and had been for years. It wasn't nice, normal, non-murdering people who made the news. Plus there were shades of crazy. Living off-grid in a caravan in a forest, the professor was probably just gently dotty, a little off-kilter. Like many of the people inhabiting Christo's world, people whose passion for their subject impeded their ability to accept practical reality. Like Christo himself.

She found the big tree, turned right and saw the parking area. She hopped off the bike and parked it. Carrying her helmet in one hand, she walked into the forest. It would come in handy if the professor did turn out to be truly crazy.

The path twisted and turned through thickets of ferns. Trees rose to her sides and above her, densely packed together. This was no plantation, this was ancient, lush, natural forest, trees growing where seeds dropped. Luckily for this patch of forest, it was on private property.

She found the clearing where the caravan stood to the left, the land around it falling quite steeply towards a bank. She could hear running water; perhaps a stream. There was a washing line, with clothes hanging out to dry. The clearing was dappled with shade and the air was chilly.

Maggie walked towards the caravan. Once a mobile home, it was now propped up on bricks, its entire underside overgrown with weeds. She walked up the three short steps – wooden and creaking – and knocked on the door. There was silence from inside. She knocked again.

'Hello!' Still no answer.

Maggie listened, hoping for a response.

She walked towards the stream, following a path down a steep bank. She could see the path continued on the other side of the stream. Should she cross the stream and follow it, and get herself lost in the process?

'What are you doing here?' said a voice in her ear.

Behind her was the prof. He had shimmered into being, seemingly out of nowhere. He was dressed head to toe in khakis, the style Liebenberg adopted, except that the prof's gear was covered with genuine flecks of mud and dirt, unlike Johan's.

'I'm Maggie Cloete,' she put out her free hand but he declined to shake it, keeping both hands resolutely stuck in his pockets.

'I'm from *The Gazette*. We've been covering the Sentinel affair. They've started logging their patch of the forest. Alex Field got himself arrested trying to stop them, and another of the Forest Keepers has tied himself to one of the trees in protest. If I could learn anything that would stop Sentinel ...'

Mike Rankin grunted. 'Nothing will stop them. It's their land. They can do what they like.'

'But what about the Karkloof Blue? I believe that's your speciality.'

'The butterfly will lose another habitat. That is true.'

'Doesn't that enrage you?'

'I have given up on rage. It's pointless and depletes energy. And now I want you to leave. I have work to do.' He turned, about to shimmer back into the forest.

There were no newspapers out here in the forest. Certainly no Internet access.

'Dave Bloom died.'

'What?' He turned back to her, face pale.

'He fell, or was pushed, off Howick Falls. No one is sure.'

'Good God.' Rankin stared at her. 'I cannot believe it. What do the police say?'

'They say suicide.'

'Don't believe them!'

'That's what people keep telling me, except for people at Sentinel, who tell me he was bipolar and prone to depression.'

'Bullshit.'

Maggie was silent. In the distance, she could hear a whining sound, as if a thousand mosquitoes were gathering.

'Is that noise what I think it is?'

He nodded. 'Sentinel, hard at work with their chainsaws.'

'Can you take me there? The guy tied to a tree is my brother. I would really like to find him.'

'I don't have time to conduct tours. I have work to do.'

'Please,' Maggie begged. 'You can tell me more about the forest. Introduce me. I am such a city dweller that I can hardly tell one tree from the next.'

That seemed to change his mind. 'You get an hour of my time, and then you need to be on your way.'

He turned and led the way into the forest. She followed him along a track. Now that they were further from the stream, the forest grew denser. The track was indistinct. Without Rankin, she would be lost in here.

He stopped. 'If you look around you now, you'll see that the forest is made up not only of trees, but of climbers and shrubs.'

She looked. It was true. The space between the trees was jammed with other plants, verdant and alive. She could practically hear them growing.

'You'll find over a hundred different species of trees here. They are all in different stages of life, from this old *Celtis Africana* here,' he patted a grey trunk that reached high into the forest canopy as if it were a favourite pet, 'to medium-sized trees and saplings. Each forest is a tree nursery for new baby trees.'

'How do the new trees grow?'

'Well, they sow seeds themselves. Or they get help from the forest birds.'

'Are there other animals that live in the forest?'

'Apart from the hundreds of different birds? Yes. We have various kinds of antelope, genet cats, fruit bats, insects, tree frogs, lizards, snakes, land crabs and bush pigs. It's teeming with life.'

'What happens when their habitat goes?'

'Some run, find new spaces to live, others die.'

'Can't they live in a plantation?'

'The trees are a rich food source. When you replace a hundred types of tree with just one kind, the food sources die away. The Celtis, for example, feeds birds and monkeys with its fruit and seeds. If it went, along with all its other tree compatriots, the animals would have to go elsewhere.'

'Does the forest support people? Apart from you, I mean?'

'Well, the local people do forage here. So yes, the forest supports people apart from me too.'

'Anything else?'

'Anything else, what?'

'I'm trying to understand what the Forest Keepers say – that it's an ecological disaster when a forest goes. Is there anything else that might support that?'

'Well there is floral substrata. These are the tiny plants that grow amongst the trees. They, along with the leaf and animal litter, play the role of sponges, arresting and absorbing run-off in times of high rainfall.'

'Stopping floods and soil erosion, you mean?'

'Exactly.'

'And what else?'

'A natural forest acts as a water purifier, helping to conserve and store water.'

'While a plantation ...?'

'Is a water consumer. We're talking excessive amounts.'

'And this forest we're in – is it in danger?'

'No, it's safe while its still in the Andersons' hands. They understand its value.' He ran his hands through his hair. 'We just have to hope that they never need to sell.'

'Because Sentinel will be the highest bidder?'

'Sure they will.'

'Can you explain to me why no one but a small group of radical environmentalists gives a damn about what Sentinel does? Why does no one care?'

'Sentinel is good at PR.'

'But it's more than that. It's as if they put everyone to sleep. No one seems to notice or care that they are systematically getting rid of all the natural forest and replacing it with tree factories.'

Rankin nodded. 'People are anaesthetised. It's true.'

He led the way deeper into the forest. He was light and fast on his feet, like a buck, slipping between trees and in and out of shadows. The rhythm of her blood rose to match her footfalls as she trod carefully behind him.

They came to a barbed wire fence.

'This is where the Anderson's part of the forest ends, and Sentinel's begins.'

He put one boot onto the bottom two rungs of the barbed wire, pushing them together and to the ground, and gripped the top two with one fist. 'Here you go.'

Maggie climbed through and then did the same for him.

'And now we are trespassing.'

She didn't mention that she had done the same a couple of days ago and been arrested for her sins. 'Looks the same as on your side of the fence.'

'It is. Now do you have any idea where you think your brother will be?'

She tried to remember where the Forest Keepers had positioned their camp and what direction Christo had run.

'Just follow the sound of the chain-saws. He will be somewhere nearby.'

Rankin led on without cracking a twig or bending a branch. This was bush lore, becoming part of the natural world instead of intruding upon it. He was following a path, but not one that she could discern. It was the path of the animal inhabitants of this forest, who glided through the undergrowth, their heads down, cropping on plants, or heads up, alert to danger.

While they walked, she glanced upward to the canopy, hoping to see the khaki-clad figure of her brother. The noise grew to a crescendo.

Rankin stopped. 'There they are.'

Through the trees, Maggie could see green and black Sentinel vehicles and people moving around. The whine of the chainsaws made her head throb.

He crouched down. 'We can't go any further.'

She crouched next to him and watched the activity, a hive of workers swarming over the forest. The logging seemed to be happening in three layers: an advance guard that slashed the undergrowth with pangas, a second group that attacked the trees with chainsaws and used a large crane to swing fallen tree trunks onto the flat beds of trucks, and a third group that dug up the tree stumps and any other vegetation left behind.

Behind them was a small space they had already stripped naked. It looked torn and bruised.

'Sometimes they'll burn instead of strip. Grasslands they'll nuke with military-grade herbicides,' Rankin whispered to her.

'Why don't they burn now?'

'Too dry. Fire would be too hazardous, especially given the proximity to the Anderson farm.'

'And to the precious plantations.'

Rankin watched the loggers, an inscrutable look on his face, while Maggie scanned the canopy in hope.

She heard crashing from nearby and a figure slid down from a tree.

'Christo,' she breathed.

He put his finger to his lips and beckoned.

She shook Rankin's arm. 'Look, there he is.'

Maggie and the professor followed Christo into the depths of the forest. When he stopped, she did too. He was in the same clothes he'd been wearing on the night of the forest occupation, had three days' worth of beard and smelled of dried sweat.

'What the hell are you doing here?' So he hadn't changed his attitude either.

'Just checking on you.'

'Too little too late, dear sis.' There was no affection in his tone. He turned to Rankin and put his hand out. 'Chris Cloete.'

'Mike Rankin.'

Maggie's brother peered at the prof. 'You're Mike Rankin? Wow, you're kind of famous.'

'Only to a few,' Rankin said, still not smiling. 'Glad we found you.'

'You won't believe the wildlife I've seen, man. Owls, bats. I think I even caught a glimpse of a leopard.'

'Seen a porcupine yet?'

'No, but there was some loud rustling around my tree last night.'

'There you are, then. You've heard one. How are you surviving?'

'I'm fine. There are backpacks dotted in various trees. I have food and drink. I'm good.'

'What happens when they reach your tree?' Rankin looked curious.

'That's when the stand-off happens.' Christo allowed himself a small smile. 'I am quite looking forward to it.'

'Listen,' said Rankin. 'They've stopped.'

Maggie cocked her head. The mosquito whine of the chain-saws had died down. Instead there was shouting.

'Something's going on.' Rankin led them back towards to the foresters. 'Keep your heads down.'

They ducked down and followed the prof. He found a vantage point in a stand of trees closely grown together, thickly enmeshed with undergrowth.

Maggie peered through, much of her vision obscured by branches. 'What's happening?'

'They seem to have found something.'

A group of workers were clustered close to a shallow hole where they had pulled up a tree stump. A foreman stood at the lip of the hole, hands on his hips. More people crowded around, then some fell back, shaking their heads. They retreated to their vehicles, lit cigarettes and leaned up against the wheels of the trucks to wait for the instruction to start work again.

The foreman got down on one knee to look more closely. He picked something up, examined it, then dropped it fast. He leapt up. Maggie's head prickled.

'Call the cops!' he shouted. 'There are bones in there. Lots of them and they are not from any animals.'

They had found a grave.

Chapter 8

They pile into a minibus, some talking in overdrive out of sheer excitement, others awed into silence by the magnitude of their adventure. They are the chosen ones, the driver has told them. The boldness of their actions means they have been hand-selected, picked out by wiser, older men grizzled by life on the run to join their cause. They try not to think of mothers, sisters, girlfriends. Love is a domestic shackle. Now they will be free. One day they will return and the women will be proud.

The driver tells them to sleep, as the drive is long. He is tall and strong, and they see themselves in him, a freedom fighter with a just cause. Some sleep, resting their heads on their backpacks. Others stare out of the windows into the darkness, watching the familiar shapes of the township turn into the less familiar hills of the province.

One young man feels less the anticipation of adventure, and more the burning anger of what happened to his father. Men just like his father, men who looked like him and talked like him, took his life away. Now he is nothing but anger. He wants training. He wants to learn to take apart an AK in under three minutes. He wants to learn Russian and become a decorated soldier. He wants to kill the men who killed his father. He wants his mother and his brothers and his sisters to have something to live for again.

They are woken by potholes in a road. The driver stops the mini-bus, tells them they will sleep here tonight. They rub their eyes, still boys, and troop into the crumbling house. There is another man there, a white man. They stop, look at each other, but the driver says he is a cadre. They are given food. Neither the driver nor the white man eat. The boys find somewhere to lie down. Seven young men lie down to sleep. It takes several days for them to die.

Chapter 9
Thursday, 2pm

Christo climbed back up his tree while Maggie hightailed it back to civilisation. She pulled over on the side of the road back to Howick to call Radebe. There'd been no cell phone reception in the forest.

'Cloete here. I have eyewitness accounts that loggers have found evidence of a mass grave in the part of the Karkloof Extension 7. Any comment?'

'Police are heading out there, but it is too early for us to confirm what the loggers have found. How the hell did you get eyewitnesses?'

'That's for me to know, Captain.'

He exhaled. 'We are not used to these strong-arm Joburg tactics here. Can't you leave us poor provincial cops in peace?'

She decided to ignore that. 'I need to know how many bodies there are, how long they have been there and what the cops are planning to do about them.'

'I'll try to get an answer for you.'

'I need it by four-thirty at the latest please.' She put her helmet back on and gunned the Chicken's engine, startling a few pedestrians who yelped and dived into the grass on the side of the road. This was a major scoop, and she needed to get the story before the national press pack started chasing it.

Back in the office, she strode straight to Liebenberg's desk. There was no sign of him.

'Where's Liebenberg?'

Fatima's desk was nearby. The health reporter looked up. 'He said he had a follow-up interview with Xolani Mpondo about the logging at K7.'

At least Johan was focused on his actual job even if he was interviewing the chief executive on the wrong topic. He should be asking him why the loggers had found the remains of bodies in the Karkloof forest.

His phone went through to voicemail, so she phoned Mbali Sibanyoni.

'Mbali, I hear the loggers are at work in the forest.' She got straight to the point.

'Yes.' Mbali's voice was cool. 'That is true. They started logging Karkloof Extension 7 yesterday.'

'I have an eyewitness account that says logging stopped today. Apparently they found a grave containing human remains. What is Sentinel's response to that?'

'I cannot comment. Only Mr Mpondo is authorised to comment on that.'

'Can I talk to him?'

'I believe he is presently in a meeting with one of your reporters.'

Liebenberg, who did not know about the latest developments in the story. 'Can I come around to your offices and join the meeting?'

'I don't think so – in ten minutes, Mr Mpondo will be getting into the company jet to fly to Johannesburg.'

'Mbali, this is a PR disaster!' Maggie exploded. 'I have an eyewitness account and the cops are about to give me their side of the story. I am going to print on this, with or without word from Sentinel. You really mean to tell me you have nothing more to say?'

'I have no comment,' Mbali told her. 'Sentinel has no comment. Xolani Mpondo has no comment.'

Then she put the phone down.

Maggie sent Liebenberg a text – *Ask Mpondo about the mass grave loggers have just found in K7* – and then called Alex Field, now bailed on trespassing charges, for his comment. The activist sounded exhausted and dismayed, but he summoned the energy to skewer Sentinel with words.

Then she tried the cops again.

'Ernest, I am going to print with this story. What can you give me?'

'We will release a full statement tomorrow, but I can confirm that human remains have been found in part of the indigenous forest belonging to Sentinel. All logging has been stopped while police investigate.'

She relaxed for the first time since leaving the forest. Now she had a story.

'Any idea how long the bones have been there?'

'Forensics will be able to tell us soon, but we're estimating well over ten years.'

She thought of the media outlets that had harassed her earlier in the day. 'Anyone else contact you about this?'

'No, you're the only one.'

If it stayed that way, she would have a major scoop. 'Thanks, Ernest.'

'No problem, Maggie. There will be a press conference tomorrow. We'll let you know more details then.'

She wrote the story, printed it out and took it with her to afternoon conference with Naidoo and Patti. There was still no sign of Liebenberg. On the way to the meeting, she stopped at Fortunate's desk.

'If Johan arrives while I am still in conference, please send him in.'

'Sure thing,' Fortunate flashed her a smile.

Maggie handed Naidoo the story without a word and sat down. Patti glanced up briefly from her laptop. There was silence in the room as the editor read.

'This is an interesting one.' Naidoo passed it to Patti. 'But we can't run it without word from Xolani Mpondo.'

'His PR person says they have no comment.'

'Which could also mean she is too lazy or scared or intimidated to track him down and ask him. Let me do it. I'll call Xolani. If we can get a statement from him, we'll run the story.'

Maggie checked her watch. 'Apparently, he's on a plane to Joburg right now. And I really don't see why we need Sentinel's permission to publish a story in our own newspaper.' She folded her arms.

'It's not about seeking permission, Maggie. It's about right of reply.'

'Which we have already offered them.'

'Maggie, if we run this tomorrow without Mpondo's express

knowledge, then I will have both him and Timothy Richardson on my back.'

Richardson was CEO of Gazette Holdings, a family business that would do anything to remain independent and not be snapped up by one of the bigger news outlets baying to add *The Gazette* to their stable. As long as circulation and advertising revenue stayed above a certain level, the Richardsons could keep their dream. Keeping their main paper supplier sweet was part of that delicate balancing act.

Maggie couldn't stand corporate politics wading into the newsroom and strangling press independence. She breathed, slow and deep. What the hell was she doing on this two-bit provincial newspaper that couldn't recognise a major story when it jumped up and bit it on the butt?

She tried to keep her tone reasonable. 'Tina, this is a huge story. No one else has got it and they are only going to hear about it when they wake up tomorrow morning and read our headlines. We've scooped the whole country. We need to run the story.'

Naidoo turned to her deputy. 'Patti?'

'It is a good story,' Patti acknowledged. 'And a major scoop.'

'Timothy will freak if we don't get Mpondo's side, though.'

There was a knock on the door and it creaked open. Liebenberg appeared, looking extremely self-satisfied. 'I have Mpondo's comment on the mass grave if that's what you're talking about.'

He had seen her texts and been a decent journalist for the first time and put the question to Xolani Mpondo.

Naidoo clapped her hands. 'Great job, Johan! Come in.'

He obeyed orders. 'Mpondo says all logging will stop until police complete their investigation into the human remains found in the forest.'

'Excellent. Now get the story finished. We have an hour to deadline.'

Maggie stood up to go.

'And one more thing, Maggie. Make sure Johan gets a byline on this. Without him, there would have been no story.'

Maggie's blood boiled. Johan looked smug and a half-smile played around Patti's lips.

Chapter 10
Friday, 9am

Mass Grave Found in Karkloof Forest
Johan Liebenberg and Maggie Cloete, Staff Reporters

Logging in the Karkloof Extension 7 – one of the few pockets of natural forest left in KwaZulu-Natal and home to the Karkloof Blue, an endangered butterfly – was brought to an abrupt halt on Thursday when workers clearing bush between the fallen trees stumbled upon a mass grave.

Eyewitnesses report that logging activities started on Wednesday but stopped suddenly late afternoon Thursday, followed by the arrival of the police. 'They were digging out an old tree stump when they stumbled on the bodies. I saw the foreman bend down to examine the hole and then jump up again very quickly,' said the witness, who did not want to be named.

Police liaison officer Captain Ernest Radebe confirmed that logging had been stopped because workers had found a number of bodies in a mass grave. Police were unable to establish how many bodies there were, but said they showed signs of severe decay. 'Forensics will give us a clear timeline, but we believe that these remains have been there for ten years, possibly longer,' said Captain Radebe.

Karkloof Extension 7 belongs to Sentinel, a national paper company with its headquarters in Pietermaritzburg. Chief executive Xolani Mpondo said the company was distressed about the discovery in the forest.

'We will do everything in our power to assist the police in their investigation.'

Sentinel has been in dispute with the environmental group Forest Keepers, which has been protesting against the logging of the forest. Forest Keepers spokesperson Alex Field and a number of other members of the organisation were arrested on Sentinel property on Thursday.

They were released on trespassing charges late Thursday.

'We believe that Sentinel's logging in the Karkloof is an illegal effort to rob our country of its natural heritage. We should be protecting our last remaining forests, and the flora and fauna they contain, not ruthlessly cutting them down for profit. While I am sad that there are bodies in the forest, I am happy that Sentinel has been forced to stop and take a hard look at what they do,' said Field.

He confirmed that one member of the Forest Keepers had managed to infiltrate the forest and was still there.

In a press release from earlier this week, Sentinel confirmed that logging in Karkloof Extension 7 would continue as part of the company's growth plan. 'We will safely relocate the butterflies. Protestors are reminded to keep off Sentinel property and not stop the company going about its legal business.'

Until police complete their investigation, all logging activities have been stopped, Officer Radebe confirmed last night.

Thanks to Maggie, *The Gazette* had scooped the rest of the country. All the news desks would be chasing Ernest Radebe for comment. His moment of fame had arrived.

Coffee in hand, she read the wires. One report made her heart stop. *Joburg Sun Journo Mugged at Knifepoint.* She read the story, and dialed Jabu's number. They had agreed to not talk over the phone, but this was an emergency.

'Hello,' her former colleague sounded groggy.

'Jabu, it's Maggie. Are you okay? I just saw the story.'

'Howzit Maggie. I'm okay. Just a bit roughed up. But they took my laptop.'

For their investigation, Jabu and Maggie had installed elaborate encryption on their computers. If Jabu's muggers were ordinary muggers, they wouldn't find anything. But if they were hackers of any merit, all the details of their work so far would be laid bare.

Girls lured to Joburg with the promise of jobs found themselves enmeshed in prostitution and then, went they wanted out, were given the chance to leave the country as drug mules. Sex, drugs and money. The usual trifecta, this time made more complex because it appeared that the son of a government minister was the lynchpin. No one knew if his venerable father was involved.

Maggie's contact was going to provide proof a couple of months ago, until he was found dead in a rubbish dump.

It was painstaking, dangerous work. Both Maggie and Jabu received death threats. When Dr K had called her about Christo's surprise recovery, her editor on the Joburg Sun agreed that a hiatus would be healthy. Jabu was not so lucky. He had to stay in the city, write stories and remain visible – and now he had paid the price.

She told him of her suspicions that she had also been tailed.

'I wouldn't put anything past them,' Jabu said. 'You'd better watch out.'

'Are you pursuing any of it?'

'No, like you, I'm laying low on this one.' Which was all very well for them, but terrified teenagers were still being shipped out of the country to brothels in the EU with drugs hidden on their bodies. There was no freedom for them at the end of their journeys, just an endless stream of faceless men.

Maggie had met one of the girls on the streets of Berlin. Standing behind her in an Aldi, she'd heard the accent, recognised it in her blood. She'd followed the kid outside and watched as she lit a cigarette with trembling hands. Her thin anorak was no protection against the biting northern cold.

'Are you okay, sisi?' Maggie had asked. Just that one familiar word had caused the trembling to turn to tears. Maggie heard the whole story in a coffee-shop, while Nombulelo drank one *Milchkaffee* after another.

'What do you want?'

'I just want to go home to my mother.'

Maggie was working as a stringer for Reuters and a couple of other news agencies. She was getting great experience but only just scraping by, and what she earned she sent home to pay for Christo's private hospital. She found the money for Nombulelo's ticket and sent the teenager home to Durban.

She spent a few more years in the *Hauptstadt*, perfecting her bad German and developing an in-depth knowledge of Berlin beer gardens, nightclubs and men. She met Joachim and fell pregnant with Leo. Then the *Joburg Sun*, a daily with the advantage of being read in the townships and in the polished northern suburbs, had called her back to head up their investigative unit. She headed home, with Leo and Joachim in her slipstream.

The first thing she did in her new job was poach Jabu Sibiya, crime reporter extraordinaire, from *The Gazette*.

Over the years, Nombulelo had haunted her. On a visit to Pietermaritzburg, with Leo in tow, she'd looked the woman up and interviewed her in a local hair salon where she was working as a junior hairdresser, to find out how the recruitment process had worked. With new knowledge and the blessing of their editor, Maggie and Jabu began to unlock the complex twists and turns of the network.

She wished Jabu well, and focused her attention on the day's work. Menzi told her that the mass-grave press conference had been pushed out to Monday.

'Okay, but we can't let the story die. Menzi, dig around your police contacts and find out who the investigating officer is. See if you can pump him or her for a new angle. Johan, why don't you make an appointment with Hope Phiri and get more on the Karkloof Blue?'

Then she called Natalie Bloom. 'It's not looking good. Cops aren't budging. They are still calling it suicide.'

'I feel like no one is listening to me,' Dave Bloom's widow whispered. 'Why is no one hearing what I say?'

Maggie thought of Mr Ishmael's description of Dave's naked body and his neatly folded clothes. Whether Bloom's jump was voluntary or not, the despair he felt would have been acute.

'Listen, so I can understand better, could you tell me what happened the night he disappeared?'

'Yes,' her voice was quiet. 'We went out for dinner on Saturday with some friends. When we got back Dave drove the babysitter home. He never came back.'

'Did he behave differently during the evening?'

'No, he was the same Dave - laughing and joking. Fun, as always. Except—'

'Except what?'

'The weird thing with the clothes. He put on really smart clothes, as if he were meeting someone he respected, or wanted to impress. Not the kind of clothes you'd wear if you were desperate enough to kill yourself.'

'And after dropping the babysitter, he never came back.'

'No.' It was a tiny word, expressed as the smallest exhalation, but it held a world of pain.

Natalie Bloom didn't sound like a woman chasing an insurance payout. She sounded like a woman whose life had been torn apart.

'Editors' conference, please!' Patti yelled across to Maggie. Welcome to the floating meeting. She picked up her notebook and headed to Naidoo's office.

'Timothy Richardson was on the phone this morning,' Naidoo told the two women once they sat down. 'We have major negotiations with Mpondo on Monday. Timothy has expressly asked that we run no forest stories until then.'

'That's bullshit!' Maggie exploded. 'This is a huge, high profile story and I've asked both Menzi and Johan to follow up different angles.'

'Save it for the Tuesday edition,' the editor said calmly. 'We can't afford to antagonise Sentinel.'

'Tina, the country's press is crawling all over this story. Do you mean to say that we, the ones that broke it, are now expected to sit back and shut up. I call censorship.'

'And I call pragmatism,' Naidoo said, turning to Patti. 'I'm leaving early today. Can you deputise?'

'Can do.'

Patti and Maggie left the editor's office. Maggie fumed all the way back to her desk, and then kicked her helmet, because it was there.

What a shitty two-bit paper *The Gazette* had become. Zacharius Patel would be shocked. His commitment to news reporting and telling truth to power was beyond reproach. He would not have stood for corporate interference.

Her cell phone buzzed. It was a text from Menzi. *Cop in charge of the mass graves investigation is Solomon Njima. Won't budge on details.*

Maybe she could make him budge. He answered his phone quickly. 'Njima.'

'It's Maggie Cloete.'

'I was expecting your call.'

'Our crime reporter says you don't want to talk to him.'

'He's right. I have an investigation into a mass grave and I don't need press interference.'

'How's that investigation going?'

'I really can't tell you.'

'OK, off the record then. How many bodies do you have?'

'We can't tell yet.'

'Do you know how they died?'

'We can't tell that either.' He went silent. 'Look, Ms Cloete, I appreciate that you're trying to do your job, but I am also trying to do mine.'

He killed the call. So that was a no-go zone. She looked for Liebenberg. Not at his desk. She could only hope he was in a tête-à-tête with Hope Phiri, learning everything there was to learn about the Karkloof Blue.

She stared around the newsroom. People had their heads down, working. She heard the swish of a message being sent; someone coughed. The drip-drip of office life was like water torture. To make time go faster, she went to get a coffee from the kitchen. As she sat back down in front of her computer, her desk phone rang.

'Someone for you,' Fortunate told her.

'Is that Maggie Cloete?' The woman sounded hesitant. 'I ... I am phoning about the story you wrote. About the bodies in the forest.'

'Yes.'

'Well, I think one of them might have been my brother.'

'What's your name?' Maggie pulled her notebook closer and grabbed a pen.

'Thandi.'

'Surname?'

'I don't want to give it. So much has happened to my family. I would prefer to remain a bit anonymous. But I do want to talk to you.'

'That's fine, Thandi.' Her desire to get the hell out spiralled upwards. 'Listen, can we meet? It would be easier for us to talk in person.'

'Yes.' They made a plan, and Maggie gratefully swung her helmet onto to her arm and headed out of the office, mindful of Fortunate's eyes piercing her back as she left. She waited for Thandi as planned on a bench between the City Hall and the library, her helmet next to her. Despite the thin winter sun, it was chilly. She wished she had brought a cup of coffee.

'Miss Cloete?' A woman stood near her, clutching a handbag. 'I am Thandi.'

Maggie invited her to sit. Thandi perched on the edge of the bench, handbag in her lap. She wore a thin grey fleece.

'So you mentioned on the phone that you think your brother's body could be one of those found in the forest?'

'Yes,' she said. 'It's a long story, though.'

'That's okay,' Maggie replied. *The Gazette* could wait.

'I grew up in a loving family. My father was a priest and my mother was a teacher. We lived in Sweetwaters. We were three boys and two girls. My parents were kind; they were leaders in the community. But then came the time of the violence. The IFP and the ANC were against each other. My father was ANC, but he always offered help to anyone in the community. One night, the IFP firebombed our house. We ran out of the house into the forest to hide there, but my father was trapped in the house.'

'I am sorry,' Maggie said. These stories were familiar to her. In her first stint at *The Gazette*, she covered the violence that sprung up in the province and had ridden with Ed into the townships to cover protest marches or attend the funerals of those who died.

'As we ran out of the house, they shot at us. The bullet hit my younger brother in the leg. We managed to carry him into the bush with us. The next day, we returned to see our house. It was burnt down, with my father inside. My mother decided it was not safe for our family in Sweetwaters any more, so we went to live with her sister in Edendale. My brother went to hospital; the doctors took off his leg. He went around on crutches, but it was hard for him, so my mother said I had to stay at home at my aunty's place to look after him.

'My sister and my other brother went to school. My injured brother and I stopped school. My mother tried to teach us at night, but she was so tired from working all day and looking after all of us, that sometimes she would not. We all missed my father, so much. He was such a kind and good man. He wanted nothing more than a good education for his children. He wanted us to better ourselves.'

Thandi's eyes glistened. She dug in her bag and pulled out a handkerchief and wiped her eyes.

'My oldest brother, Vuyani, was angry about what happened to my father and to our family. He joined the ANC Youth. He went to meetings, and when he came home he was even more angry. Sometimes the police came to our house and beat him up. The next time they detained him for three weeks. He came back, so thin, you know, with marks all over his body. The last time I saw him was in 1988. I was eleven years old.'

'How old was he?'

'Nineteen.'

'What happened after that?'

'He did not come back.'

'What did your family do?'

'My mother went to the police station to ask for him. The police told her told her he was a troublemaker and that he had run away to Swaziland to join MK.'

The armed wing of the ANC had taken up residence just outside the borders of South Africa, near enough to make raids but beyond the jurisdiction of the apartheid state.

'Was that true?'

'Oh no,' Thandi shook her head. 'He was a good boy. My mother knew he would never leave the family. We knew the police had him. Then a kitskonstabel who lived near my aunty told my mother he had seen Vuyani in the cells in Plessislaer. He had been tortured. Again my mother went to the police, and again they told her he had gone to Swaziland.'

Thandi sighed. 'We never saw him again.'

'Did you testify?'

'Yes, we spoke at the TRC.'

'And?'

'We told our story, but we were not able to find out more about what happened to Vuyani.'

'Did you get reparations?' The Truth and Reconciliation Commission had paid some funds to families who had lost loved ones.

'We received a once-off sum. My mother used it to pay for operations to my brother's leg. They gave him a false leg.'

The clock in the City Hall chimed two. A couple of doves fluttered into the air.

'I must get home now,' said Thandi. 'My kids are waiting.'

'What do you do?'

'I work for Mrs Henderson in Mayor's Walk.'

'As a domestic worker?'

'Yes,' she sighed. 'It is not the job I want and not the job my parents wanted for me, but after my father died, I did not return to school. There are no other jobs for women who only have a Standard Five.'

Maggie felt a wave of pain. She pushed it down. Years of practice. 'Your brother, Vuyani. Why do you think he might be one of the bodies in the mass grave?'

'It will sound crazy.'

'Try me.'

''Do you remember the attack on the power station in Umlazi? Mid 80s maybe? We heard, a couple of years ago, that a cell of ANC youth had pulled that off. They disappeared shortly afterwards. None of them have ever returned.'

'The Umlazi 7.'

'Yes.'

Thandi stood up. 'I must go.'

Maggie looked up at her. 'Thandi, I will protect you, but to do my research, I do need to know your brother's surname.'

The woman dug her hands into the pockets of her fleece and looked around her. She exhaled. 'Mshenge.'

Maggie stood too and put out her hand. 'Thank you so much. I will do what I can to find out more.'

They exchanged cell phone numbers and then Thandi walked away, a tall dignified figure.

Maggie sent Solomon Njima a text. *Vuyani Mshenge. Try that name.*

Chapter 11
Saturday, 8am

She woke to a terse text from her editor. *Urgent. Meet me in the office this morning. 9am.*

Maggie seared herself with hot water in the shower. It was nothing compared to what Naidoo's reception was going to be.

She was right, except the editor was not hot; she was ice-cold. Her fingernails were painted gravestone grey and she enunciated every word slowly as if she were talking to an intransigent toddler.

'What in God's name were you thinking?'

'I thought Johan's piece was excellent. It's the first real piece of journalism I've seen from him. A thought-piece, timely and well-written.'

Johan had done an in-depth interview with Hope Phiri, in which she talked about the four remaining colonies of the Karkloof Blue The most endangered of these was the one in the Sentinel forest. Hope explained how the Karkloof Blue caterpillar had a symbiotic relationship with the sugar ant, crawling into its nest to feed and be cared for by the tiny ants while they drank a sugar solution from a gland on its back. Maggie had put it on the op-ed page – prime newspaper real estate, guaranteed to get readers' attention.

And that of rabid forestry executives.

'Yes, it's good journalism. But you deliberately published something about the forest without ratifying it with either Patti or me.'

'Technically, it's about the butterfly.'

'Oh Jesus.' Naidoo stalked to her office window and looked out on her view of the car park. 'You know exactly what I mean.'

She turned back to Maggie and Patti. The deputy editor, rendered silent by Naidoo's rage, plucked at an invisible speck of dust on her shirt. 'I say, no forest stories, you say ok, and after Patti leaves you swop out Fatima's TB op-ed with Johan's piece on the butterfly.'

Maggie couldn't argue. That was exactly what she had done.

'And now Mpondo's ballistic, as is Timothy.'

Maggie shrugged. 'It's a good piece of writing and it does not even reference the mass grave. I take full responsibility. Publishing it was my call.'

Naidoo leaned in over the back of her chair. 'And it's going to be my call when Xolani Mpondo arrives for a meeting first thing Monday along with Timothy Richardson and the rest of the board. We've been fighting him on paper prices for the last three months, and now he's going to leverage today's op-ed to squeeze a price hike. Timothy is enraged. As am I.'

Naidoo paced the room. 'And you know what's worst of all? You really don't care. That's what gets me.'

'I care about news. And if *The Gazette* continues to publish strong news stories, and break stories instead of following others' leads, then you'll balance out your circulation and advertising problems. It's a good story.'

Naidoo stopped pacing. 'From where you sit, it is good story. From where I sit, it's a fucking shambles.'

'There's a press conference on Monday. I'll go and make sure we cover the dead bodies angle and completely drop the evil forestry angle.'

'You will do no such thing!' Naidoo exploded. 'You leave this one well alone.'

'Oh for God's sake, we broke the story.' Maggie stood up. She was taller than Naidoo, who was in her weekend attire of jeans and takkies. 'We need to cover it. We can't just drop it.'

'That's exactly what you'll do,' Naidoo spat. 'You will stay right here in the office, monitoring other people's copy, until further notice.'

'Okay, I'll send Menzi.'

'You'll send no one. *The Gazette* is dropping that story, right here, right now.'

'But ...'

'No buts. Go!' She pointed one long grey fingernail at the door.

Maggie and Patti staggered out into the corridor.

'I can't believe she is deliberately scuppering the news in order to appease some executive,' Maggie said.

'And I still can't believe what you did.' Patti's perma-frown deepened on her forehead.

'Listen, Patti, I am not sorry about publishing the story,' she said, 'but I am sorry about putting your head on the block.'

Patti stopped, drew herself up to her full height of five feet nothing. 'It's clear you're not remotely sorry. Zacharius Patel always used to say you were trouble, and now I see why. The sooner you're off this paper, the better it will be for everyone.'

She turned and left. Maggie felt a simultaneous wave of relief – at least Patti's feelings were now out in the open – and of rage.

She flung herself onto the Chicken and headed out of town with no destination in mind. What was she doing here, wasting her time in this dead-end town, chasing great news stories that nobody appreciated. Her brother was up a tree, her boss was freaking out over mediocre butterfly stories and the real evil – people who pushed other people off waterfalls or sent teenage girls into institutionalised prostitution – was being ignored.

Without thinking, she took the highway turning to Howick and drove towards the waterfall. Before crossing the river bridge towards town, she turned right and headed down a small road that led past a disused factory. A dog ran out of the bushes, snarled at her and tried to bite her leg. She accelerated and left it yapping in her wake. Yapping dogs, barking editors; they were all the same.

The road turned into a track and Maggie slowed down. She saw the shacks and parked the Chicken. The houses were spread out, not squashed together like some urban squatter camps she'd seen. Some of them had fires outside, and she could see women bent over cooking pots.

A couple of children were playing football nearby. Their football was made of plastic bags tied together and their pitch was a patch of dry earth. A boy ran past her after the ball. He looked about the same age as Leo, stretched and skinny, the roundness of childhood now just a memory.

'Sawubona,' Maggie called out to him.

'Sawubona,' he answered.

'Are your parents here?' Maggie's Zulu petered out. After years of living in Joburg, seldom using it, what knowledge she had of the language had gone. It was embarrassing.

'That's my mother,' he pointed to a wizened woman outside a nearby shack. She had a baby tied to her back with a mottled brown and white blanket.

Maggie nodded her thanks and approached the woman.

'Hello. How are you?'

The woman was bent over, stirring the pot. She straightened, rubbing her back. The baby stirred and then resettled into a new sleep position.

'I am fine. How are you?'

'Well, thanks.'

The woman stared at Maggie, suspicious. Her face was young, but her body was thin and wasted by disease. She carried herself like a much older person, slowly, and as if in pain.

'I am trying to find out about the man who fell off the waterfall last Saturday.'

'I know nothing.' The woman shifted the blanket under her armpits and pulled the knot tighter. Despite the cool morning, sweat beaded on her forehead.

'I need to know if he fell off or maybe if someone pushed him.'

'I know nothing.'

'It's important to his family, you see.'

'You can talk to Xoliswa. He is our community leader. I don't know anything.'

'Where is Xoliswa?'

'I will call my son. He will show you.' She yelled at the boy, who came running.

They exchanged a few words and then he beckoned to Maggie. She followed him.

He led her along a track, the grass flattened by many feet. The track weaved between the shacks and Maggie could feel eyes on her back. She was a stranger here.

'That is him.' The boy pointed to a tree, close to the river. Here were the deep pools that the river made before it tumbled over the edge. Underneath the tree, a group of men squatted, rolling dice.

'Which one?'

'The small one.'

The boy went forward, and stood just outside the circle of

men. They looked up at him and then towards Maggie. The boy beckoned her again.

She approached the men. They did not stand up or stop their game as she got closer. Xoliswa rapped something curt in Zulu.

'He says you may speak,' the boy told her.

'Hello, my name is Maggie Cloete. I am from *The Gazette* newspaper. I am trying to find out about the man who fell off the waterfall last Saturday. I am wondering if anyone who lives here might have seen something.'

'The police have already been here,' Xoliswa still didn't look up at her. 'We told them we saw nothing.'

'Maybe someone here saw if he was alone or with another person.'

'We saw nothing and we know nothing.' He grumbled something in Zulu and another man answered in a similar grumble.

'His family are very sad. They want to know what happened on his last night.'

'I have told you.' Xoliswa stood up and took a step towards her, one hand pointing at her. 'We know nothing. We told the police we know nothing. You will find out nothing.'

She saw that his other arm hung loosely at his side, shorter than the one pointing at her, no hand. His shirt was knotted over the stump.

A man said something; another barked with laughter. Xoliswa glanced at them and then back at Maggie. 'We do not like them, these people who go over. They bring us bad luck. They bring the police and other busybodies and we do not like that.'

It was time for her to go.

'Please, if anyone remembers anything, I am at *The Gazette*. Maggie Cloete is my name.'

She turned and the boy was waiting to lead her back towards his home and the Chicken.

'What is your name?' she asked him as they walked.

'Sandile.'

'Well, Sandile, thank you for your trouble.' She dug in her jeans pocket for a coin and produced five rand. 'Here's something for you.'

His face lit up. 'Thank you, miss.' He ran ahead and showed the coin to his mother. She took it from him and slid it into a pocket, face blank as Maggie walked past. Maggie lifted a hand in farewell, but the woman ignored her.

Chapter 12
Monday, 8am

Maggie stood at her desk and stretched, keeping an eye out for Patti. She had been to a class at the dojo yesterday, followed by a long run up Town Hill. Her biceps and her glutes were aflame. As soon as Patti arrived, Maggie went right over to her desk. 'I'm sorry about Friday.'

The deputy editor looked up from her computer screen. 'Are you?'

'I am sorry that I messed up your Saturday. I am extremely sorry that *The Gazette* won't be attending the press conference today. I am not particularly sorry about publishing the butterfly story.'

'So the story comes first?'

'Sure it does,' Maggie said, nodding.

'For you, maybe, Cloete, but not for me. I am five years from retirement and I intend to ride those years peacefully and not get tossed around on a tidal wave of trouble.'

'So you think Tina made a mistake hiring me?'

'A large mistake, yes.'

Heads were turning in the newsroom as Patti's voice grew louder.

Maggie crouched down at her desk. 'Patti, I'm not intending to go anywhere. I suggest you get used to my style.'

Patti's eyes widened. 'No, you get used to mine,' she hissed.

'You mean avoid conflict at all costs? Is that what you recommend?'

'Yes.'

Maggie got up. 'Sorry that's not going to happen. I put news before personalities. Even if it means pissing off the editor.'

She went back to her screen, leaving Patti spitting and cursing at hers, and checked her email. There was an invitation from Radebe to the press conference that morning. Thanks to Naidoo, she would have no journalists in the room.

She searched on Twitter for the story, and found the hashtag #KZNgraves on the feed of a freelance journo called Shane Venter. His handle was @Ventersdorp. Twitter was perfect for reporting on a press conference, where the news came in soundbites. She would keep an eye on Mr Venter's feed.

Then she went into news conference with her team. Johan was there, looking pasty, as was a freshly laundered Menzi. Fatima had the day off because she had worked the Sunday shift. Aslan was out today too, busy being a kingmaker for the artists of KwaZulu-Natal.

As she walked in, a neatly dressed man in his thirties stood up.

'Hi, I'm Johnny Cupido.'

Her rival for the role of news editor. Patti's pick. Maggie stopped to shake his hand. 'Good to meet you.'

He smiled, extra-white teeth flashing. 'You too. Your reputation precedes you.'

'So Parliament is on break now?'

'It is, so I have returned to the centre of the world.'

Johnny split his time between Cape Town, where Parliament sat, and Pietermaritzburg. It sounded glamorous and many reporters yearned for six months a year in Cape Town, but it was hard to sustain any kind of family life. Johnny already had one marriage behind him. It was rumoured that his Cape Town girlfriend was an ANC MP.

'Couldn't stay away myself.'

He smiled and sat back down.

'So people, we have an embargo on the mass grave story.'

'What?' There was general jabber around the table.

'Yes. We've stepped on Sentinel's toes once too often and they're threatening the board with a paper price hike. Naidoo is spitting mad, so I recommend keeping well out of her path today.'

'I do already,' Menzi quipped and there was laughter.

'So, we're basically going to look like idiots today, as newspapers around the country carry the story we broke while we remain silent. I need a quality lead, badly. Who's got something for me?'

There was silence.

'Menzi, what's on the cards today?'

'I was hoping to cover the mass grave.'

'I hear you. Me too. But you need to find something else, and something pretty bloody compelling.'

Menzi kept his equanimity. He always did. 'Sure, Maggie. I'll head for the courts and see what's happening.'

Maggie looked at her watch. 'You'd better go now.' If Menzi didn't collar the prosecutors before they went into court, he could waste the day court-hopping and come out with nothing.

The crime reporter gathered his belongings into his leather satchel.

'Get me something lurid, please,' she told him.

'I'm on it.' He closed the door behind him.

'Johnny, anything on your side?'

The political reporter flashed her his shiny grin. She could see where his reputation as a ladies' man came from. 'Well, I'm going to have to call round my contacts and remind them I'm still alive.'

'I hope the KZN political scene is full of intrigue and scandal,' she said.

'Yes, me too.'

Liebenberg was clutching his notepad and looking eager.

'Johan?'

'I have the beginnings of a thought piece on fracking in the Karoo,' he told her proudly. Evidently the thrill of the op-ed had caught him.

'Excellent. Send it to me.'

'Well, it's not quite ready yet. I have a few more sources to interview.'

Maggie sighed. 'Johan, we are a daily newspaper, not a Sunday. We have little time for long investigations or ruminative thought pieces. What we turn over here is news – short, sharp, and preferably headline-generating.'

'Today's headline is Sentinel,' he said.

'Indeed, but we've been warned off. I'm asking you for something else.'

'I don't have anything else.'

'Well, work on it.' She stood up. 'Conference dismissed.'

Maggie watched Shane Venter's feed. No news yet. Cops coming and going. The press conference about to start. Crowds in the conference room. TV cameras. A one-hour delay.

She picked up the coffee that she had left on her desk before conference and took a sip. It was ice-cold and nasty. The only thing worse than bad coffee was cold bad coffee. She heard a hum from her cell phone. *Christo is back at work.* It was Alex Field. *Logging is off. He left the forest yesterday.*

Good that her brother was out of harm's way, a privilege that Thandi Mshenge did not have. Who had wanted Vuyani dead and how had he died? So many questions, and she had no idea how she would find the answers.

South Africa had a history of secrets, buried under the weight of second chances. In their rush to reconcile under the rainbow banner, the government had given those who'd confessed to apartheid-era crimes their own walk to freedom. During the Truth and Reconciliation Commission, many of their secret crimes had been unearthed, but there were hundreds of families still living without knowing what the apartheid state had done to their loved ones. Some had been killed inside the country by the police, others had been killed while serving the ANC outside its borders. And some had just disappeared, victims of ordinary crimes.

Peace had been achieved, but not justice. And if the cops continued on their current tack there'd be no justice for Dave Bloom either.

Maggie dialled a number. 'Hi Hope, it's Maggie Cloete.'

'Hi Maggie.'

'Congrats on the butterfly story. Were you happy with it?'

'Sure, I was. It's a nice article.'

'How about the mass grave, any ideas?'

'Whoa, Maggie, I'm a scientist. I can't talk to South Africa's dirty history.'

'Okay, just thinking aloud here. Is there a community that potentially might have a stake in the forest?'

Hope went silent. Maggie bit her lip.

'I seem to remember something,' she said. 'Something about a land claim, a couple of years back, but then it went away.'

Shane's feed lit up with a new tweet. *Police introduce investigating officer, Solomon Njima. Says investigation will take weeks, months.*

#KZNgrave

Maggie's heart dropped into her stomach at the name. She remembered his forearms and faintly flirtatious manner.

'Thanks, Hope,' she said. 'Appreciate your help.'

The scientist went back to her work, and Maggie went back to watching the Twitter feed. While she did so, she texted Menzi.

When you have a moment, please check the Land Claims records to see if there was a claim against Karkloof Ext 7.

Will do, boss.

Got any news for me?

A local politician accused of using party funds to run shebeens and brothels. Would that do?

Absolutely!

Maggie loathed emoticons, but she was sorely tempted to type a smiley. She loved working with Menzi.

Her desk phone rang. It was Fortunate.

'Maggie, please schedule 2pm into your diary. The board would like to see you.'

Maggie scheduled 2pm into her non-existent diary. Was this it? After two weeks as news editor were they chucking her off the job for extreme commitment to following the news?

She glanced at Twitter again.

Early forensics show bodies in forest for over 20 years, says investigating officer Njima. #KZNgrave.

Shane and the other hacks were getting themselves a great story.

Maggie had a roll off Fortunate's cart for lunch, and went back to filling the newspaper with news. While she was chewing, Johan flapped a piece of paper onto her desk.

'Here's a reactive statement from Sentinel. They will halt all logging in the forest until the police investigation is over.'

'Thanks, Johan. Pity we can't do anything with it.' She indicated the chair on the other side of her desk. 'Sit.'

He obeyed.

'How's the fracking piece?'

'Not so great.'

'Got anything else for me? Any news from your contacts at the Parks Board?'

'There's been a spate of rhino poaching in northern Natal.'

'There's your story, Johan! Rhino poaching is huge news. Get me ten paragraphs and I'll put your story on the front page.'

'I have to take my mother to the doctor this afternoon.'

'What time?'

'Three.'

Maggie looked at her watch. It was shortly before one. 'If you can get a statement from the Parks Board, and a bit of background, you could easily have a story by two-thirty.'

Johan slumped in his chair.

'Listen, nothing gets the middle-classes more riled up than rhino poaching. More than gang rape, more than AIDS babies, even more than mass graves.' She was tempted to clap her hands. Anything to light a fire under the guy. 'This could be a major story for you. Get to it!'

He pulled himself up and moved sluggishly to his desk, the picture of enthusiasm.

Just before two, Maggie walked to the conference room where the board were meeting. The door was closed and she was not sure whether to wait or barge in. On the dot of two, Naidoo opened the door.

'Come in.' She pointed to a spare seat and Maggie sat. She looked around the table. She and Naidoo were the only women.

'Thank you for joining us, Ms Cloete.' Timothy Richardson was head of the board, CEO of Gazette Foundings and head of the clan that owned *The Gazette*. He was grey, wore reading glasses over which he squinted at her, and was of indeterminate age – anything between fifty and seventy.

'Thank you for inviting me.'

'We have just said goodbye to Xolani Mpondo, who was extremely exercised about the butterfly op-ed.'

'And so he should be – not only is his forest a graveyard, but he can't turn it over for profit, because police have called a halt to all logging.'

'Yes, he is exercised about that too. However, it appeared to me that Mr Mpondo was mostly up in arms about the way we have been reporting on events in the Karkloof. Board members, would you agree?'

Heads with varying degrees of baldness nodded. Where did

these suited and bespectacled men spring from? Could one go to a casting agency and order them? *Get me ten men, late middle-aged, in cookie-cutter business suits, from mildly to completely bald, wearing glasses and severe expressions. Must exude gravitas.*

'And what do you think of how we've been reporting the Karkloof events, Ms Cloete?'

'We've done a great job. We had contacts on the ground who informed us about the police presence, and by putting pressure on the police liaison we were able to turn over a strong story which scooped all other national newspapers. Then we followed up with an in-depth on the butterfly. In my mind, it's been a great success.'

'From a news point of view, perhaps. From the point of view of our relationship with Sentinel, it's been a complete disaster.'

'Well a free and independent press will tell stories that others don't like. That's our job.'

Timothy Richardson allowed himself a small, tight smile. Others around the table reflected the same. *Must be adept at facial mimicry.*

'Sadly, we are not that free. We are tied in a business relationship with Sentinel.'

'Paper prices.'

'Indeed.'

'I thought the price of newsprint had gone down since the financial crisis.'

'It has, but we are renegotiating the terms of our contract with Sentinel at the moment. This gives them leverage.'

'Okay. So what are you telling me?'

Richardson leaned his pointy elbows on the conference table and placed his fingertips together. It was a gesture that caused Maggie instant irritation, employed as it always was by men of a certain standing and power. Had any woman anywhere in the history of the world ever steepled her fingers? She thought not.

'I am telling you two things. One, don't leave your editor out of editorial decisions. Tina is on board with our considerations and can speak to the goals of this newspaper.'

Naidoo nodded. She also had her elbows on the table, each wrapped by one of her hands. That wasn't steepling; that was self-protection.

'Yes, I am sorry for that mistake,' Maggie said. Naidoo

unwrapped her elbows and sat back in her chair. She looked more relaxed.

'And the other is, please keep *The Gazette* out of Sentinel's firing range.'

'So you're telling me not to cover the mass grave? This is one of the biggest stories of the year.'

'I'm telling you to keep Sentinel off the front page. Report the story if you must, but no more headlines. Bury it.'

'And if the bodies in the forest turn out to be little green men from Mars, do we still bury it?'

Richards steepled his fingers no longer. His hands were flat on the table. He clearly felt like slapping her.

'If the story merits the front page, Naidoo will consult with me. We will also offer Sentinel adequate time to respond.'

She always offered a chance to respond. That was part of the job.

'Okay. Consultation. I hear you. Now I'll get back to work.' She stood up. Richards looked even more irritated. He was obviously used to telling people when he no longer needed them.

Maggie left the conference room. On the way back to the newsroom, she dialled Solomon Njima. No one had told her not to follow up on the mass grave story. Just to bury it.

Chapter 13

A gloved researcher and his assistant examine the seven bodies, make notes. The men grow impatient; they wish to get rid of them, but burial must wait for science.

Eventually, they are given permission. It is harder to move seven dead teenagers than it is to move seven live ones. In the end, they pile them on top of one another in the boot of the minibus. They are dead after all.

They drive the potholed road from the crumbling farmhouse back to the main road. From there, they head for the forest. There is a man who waits for them. He is holding the gate open as they drive in. He climbs in after shutting the gate. They have chosen him because he knows this land well. It is the land of his forefathers and mothers. He knows the secret hiding-places where bodies will never be found. His people do not like the battle that the teenagers have chosen. His people have chosen a middle route, a dangerous straddling of two worlds that pays now, but will not always pay.

He doesn't know this yet. But he knows the ways of the forest. Three of his men wait amongst the trees. They make several trips between the mini-bus and their chosen place deep in the forest, hoisting the bodies by their arms and feet.

They reach a small clearing. The driver fetches cans of petrol from the minibus. They douse the seven bodies, making sure each is thoroughly soaked. Then they set them alight.

None of them has ever burned a body before. None of them expected it would take this long. They take it in shifts, some watching the flames while others sleep in the bus. Twelve hours after they first set the boys alight, the bodies are charred beyond recognition. The sun is already high in the sky when the final flame goes out.

Now they must bury them. Six men with shovels should be able to dig a grave, but the ground is hard and threaded through with tree roots. It is almost impossible to dig deeper than twenty centimetres. They should have brought a chainsaw to saw through the roots, but no one thought of it.

Eventually, at noon, sweating, their nostrils sickened by the smell of charred flesh in the sun, they have dug a rectangle big enough for seven bodies. Using spades they push the bodies into the shallow grave. As they push, an arm falls off one of the corpses. A man vomits in the bush. Years later, he will hang himself, unable to live with the torture he perpetrated on scores of people.

Then they cover the bodies with soil. They pull branches off trees and undergrowth to cover the grave.

Money changes hands.

The two men return to their office in Durban, while the four go back to their lands, their wives and their goats.

All are confident that the grave will never be found.

Chapter 14
Monday, 5pm

Menzi came in to write his story about the local politician who had been spending provincial road repair funds to set up a string of shebeens across KwaZulu-Natal. Maggie signed off his pitch-perfect copy. It was a relief to have him on the team. She was still labouring on fixing Johan's rhino poaching story. The guy had his lead paragraph buried halfway down the story. But at least he had turned over two stories in two days, which was more than he'd achieved all of last week.

'Maggie, just one thing before I go.'

'Yup,' she glanced up from Johan's interminable paragraphing.

'I looked up that land claim on Karkloof Extension 7.'

She nodded. 'Carry on, Menzi.'

'It was dropped a couple of years ago. The community suddenly decided they were no longer interested.'

'Just like that?'

'Yes.'

She puzzled over that. Land claims were usually serious affairs. Communities that decided to try to reclaim land through the courts were mostly aware that there were long legal battles ahead. They didn't go into them lightly, or give up.

'Most interesting, though,' Menzi shifted the strap of his backpack on his shoulder, 'was the name of the community spokesperson.'

'Uh-huh.' She spotted something in Johan's copy that needed urgent fixing.

'Someone you might remember from way back.'

'Who?' She looked up.

'Lucky Bean Msomi.'

The name sent a chill through Maggie. Lucky Bean Msomi was a local gangster. She had almost succeeded in getting him behind bars years ago. Through judicious payments to the right people, he had escaped bail, and later the charges against him were dropped. Lucky Bean Msomi always got what he wanted by whatever means, including stalking, extortion and kidnapping, as well as vicious beatings for people who stood in his way.

She pushed memories of Msomi away as she pulled together the day's paper. It was a decent edition. She led with Menzi's story, while Johan's much-edited text was second lead. Following consultation with Naidoo, she had been graciously allowed to report on the mass graves story with a fulsome quote from Mpondo. This she and Patti put on page five, next to a story about a local entrepreneur who had sold her line of homemade peanut brittle to Harrods. Talk about buried.

It had been a long day in the office. What she needed now was food and a drink. Especially after hearing that Lucky Bean Msomi was involved with the forest story, even tangentially. She called Aslan.

'I've already eaten, sweets,' he told her.

'Come and watch me eat? I'll buy you a spritzer.' Aslan's taste in alcohol did not run to hard tack. Maggie's most certainly did.

'Sold. Where do you want to meet?'

They chose Guido's, an old establishment in the centre of town, where she ordered a hearty steak and thick-cut chips. She waved away the idea of salad. Leaves were for rabbits.

She downed her vodka, and ordered another, while Aslan took polite sips of his spritzer.

'So, how have your first two weeks on the job been?' he asked.

Maggie told him about it, leaving out the arrest in the forest last week. She loved Aslan about as much as he loved talking. He could quite easily let it slip in front of Naidoo, no malice intended.

'So two weeks in, and you've already been called in front of the board and reprimanded? That's the Maggie we know and love. I'll drink to that.'

They clinked glasses. Maggie took her drink slower this time, enjoying the fire in her belly. She could feel it warming her from the inside, radiating outwards and helping her relax. It was a relief to enjoy a drink or two, knowing that she wouldn't be getting up in the morning with the full responsibilities of parenthood on her hands. For now, she had only herself to think about. A luxury.

'So ... bodies in the forest?' Aslan said, as her steak arrived. 'What do you make of that?'

She cut a piece of steak and chewed it. It was glorious.

'Njima says they could easily have been there for twenty years or more. Takes us right back to the bad old days.'

'You mean NIS?' The apartheid government had had a web of spies and secret police. Some of their deeds had come to light during the Truth and Reconciliation Commission, but not all. There were still families grieving the loss of people who had been detained without trial and had disappeared into the system, never to be seen again.

'Sure, why not?'

Aslan sipped his spritzer. 'It just never goes away.'

Maggie spiked a couple of chips into her mouth. Apartheid was two decades away. It was going to take much, much longer for it to work its way out of people's memories, and out of the system. Its poison had been too strong.

She was full. She pushed the plate towards Aslan. 'Want some?'

He took a chip and chewed it.

'Tell me about the art world.' She was ready to be transported elsewhere, far away from the mundane daily grind of stories in and stories out.

'It's fantastic. My latest customer is Spike's brother Rick. He's hired me as an art consultant. I am going to fill his pristine white walls with expensive African art and then take a huge cut.'

'Congratulations. Sounds like a good business model.'

'It is.'

Maggie listened as Aslan expounded on his business model, which was largely about making rich people feel insecure about their taste and then telling them what to buy in order to make them feel better about themselves. He broke them down and then built them up again. It was working well.

'Doesn't sound like you need *The Gazette* any more.'

'I don't,' he said, trying to look modest, but failing. 'But it gives me some cachet. If they see I'm also an arts reporter, then I'm even more credible.'

'And it gives Mrs Chetty pleasure.'

Aslan nodded. He was the apple of his mother's eye.

'Yes, and distracts her from the fact that unlike all her friends' sons, I'm not hunting for a wife and getting married.'

'Does she still cut out your articles?' Mrs Chetty kept scrapbooks of all Aslan's stories.

'No. She has arthritis in her hands. No cutting.'

'Please don't tell me she's stopped cooking.' Mrs Chetty made the world's best curries.

'No, she'll go to her grave with a wooden spoon in her hand. She makes my dad do all the chopping, then she does the important part – the assembly.'

Aslan's parents were a team united in their love of Aslan and each other. She found them fascinating, especially since there was a parent-shaped gap in her own life. Maggie hadn't seen her own parents since their departure down the South Coast to escape the shame of Christo's defection. Her father had tracked her down in Joburg a few years before to tell her her mother had died of diabetes.

Maggie had not gone to the funeral. When they deserted both their children, leaving Maggie in charge of the wild-eyed, psychotic mess that Christo had become, she had lost interest in both of them. She didn't know if her father was still alive. She had managed to persuade herself that she didn't care.

It was time to forget. 'Does Crystal's still exist?' she asked Aslan. Crystal's used to be their late-night hangout.

'No, it's now a furniture shop.'

'Oh hell. When did that happen?'

'Years ago. But don't despair – there's a new place.'

Maggie went in Aslan's car. He now drove a small BMW.

'You used to have a Golf.'

'This is my overpaid, over-sexed bachelor's car.'

'I love it.' Maggie settled down in the passenger seat. Black leather, of course. It held her snugly as Aslan drove towards the university.

'Streets are quiet tonight.'

'Tonight? It's always so. This city is dead at night.'

He pulled up to a bar in a strip of shops, its name lit up in neon.

'Aslan, I'm not going to a place called Barry's Bar.'

'It might be hard to believe, but Barry's is the hip centre of town. It's where it's all happening. Your only other option would be The Wagon Inn in Hilton and there the patronage is all grey-haired and over sixty-five.'

Maggie got out of the car and slammed the door. 'If I see one grey-haired person here I'm leaving.'

Aslan was right. Barry's Bar was packed, even on a Monday night. Aslan cornered a table up against the glass front window while Maggie fought her way to the bar for a vodka and sparkling water.

'I miss Crystal's,' she said, passing Aslan his drink. 'This place is half the size and there's no dance floor.'

'People don't want to dance any more,' Aslan told her. 'They just want to drink and get laid.'

Maggie watched people doing the former and trying to snaffle someone with whom to do the latter. The crowd and the music, were loud.

'Excuse me,' A woman squeezed through the crowd to their table. 'Are you Maggie Cloete?'

'Yes.' Maggie sipped her vodka. Only in town a week, and she was already being recognised in bars. This place was far too small. She missed the vast anonymity of Joburg.

The woman put out her hand. 'I'm Hope Phiri. We just talked.'

'Of course.'

'My cousin knows you. See, over there,' Hope pointed across the bar to a tall man standing in a group. He waved at Maggie, a big grin splitting his face.

She waved back and then turned to Hope.

'You're Dumisane's cousin?'

'Ja.'

Dumi Phiri was a city councillor and former lawyer. Given his broad grin, he had decided to forget his past spats with Maggie. She introduced Hope to Aslan, who offered to get the next round of drinks. She asked for a beer – she needed a drink that lasted, not one that disappeared in seconds. In the years she'd spent out of Pietermaritzburg she'd forgotten how small it was. Everyone was somebody's cousin or employee or ex-boyfriend. The anonymity of Berlin and even Joburg had been a relief.

'So what do you think of the latest in the forest story?' Maggie asked Hope.

'Well, at least the Blue is spared. For now.'

'That's true. And the bodies?'

'South Africa has many dirty secrets.' Hope gave a half-smile. 'I guess you're going to try and uncover the secret of these bodies.'

'I certainly am.' Maggie said. 'I followed up on that land claim you mentioned, but looks like they retracted. I'm wondering what that's about.'

'You should go and talk to them,' Hope said. 'Let me know if you need a bodyguard.'

'I might just take you up on that.' Maggie's Zulu was so rusty now, she would also need a translator.

A woman twined her arms around Hope's waist. 'Ready to go, my sweet?'

Hope's face lit up. She caressed her companion's arms.

'Let me introduce you. Maggie Cloete, this is my girlfriend, Chloe Steyn. Maggie's the reporter I told you about.'

'Hi.' Chloe moved from behind Hope, and shook Maggie's hand. 'Nice to meet you.'

'And you.'

Chloe draped one arm around Hope's shoulders. 'You covering the logging story?'

'I am. Or should I say, *The Gazette* is.'

'You know what I find weird about the whole thing?' Chloe said. 'Is that nobody, apart from a few protestors, seems exercised about an entire natural forest being cut down. Everyone gets up in arms about poaching or about crime, but when it comes to the forestry industry, we're all passive as hell.'

'You're right,' Hope agreed. 'Profit is legitimate.'

'Have you driven up the coast lately?' Chloe asked Maggie. She shook her head.

'Once you pass the sugar-cane, it's all gum trees. The whole way up the North Coast, one vast plantation after another. And because the only people who live there are poor and uneducated, and grateful for the minuscule amount of jobs the industry offers, nobody notices or cares.'

'Are you also an environmentalist?'

She shook her head and Hope laughed. 'Chloe is an English lecturer. She specialises in nineteenth century women's literature. But she hates the monoculture.'

'Any kind of monoculture, be it eucalyptus, or sugar cane or patriarchy. I hate them all.' Chloe mock-frowned and put up two small fists in boxer pose.

Aslan returned bearing drinks and Maggie introduced him to Chloe.

'No introduction necessary,' he smiled, kissing her on both cheeks. 'We were undergrads together, a long time ago.'

The two began talking books. Maggie heard the words 'Jane Austen' and tuned out. She turned to Hope. 'I saw the professor last week. He also didn't seem to be up in arms about the forest. He said he was beyond anger.' The noise inside Barry's was growing. She had to shout.

'Scientists generally aren't good at corporate politics,' Hope shouted back. 'Plus I really think everyone feels it's hopeless. Sentinel owns the property, they have the planting permit and those rights supersede all others. Certainly the rights of one tiny butterfly.'

There was some shoving in the bar and raised voices. The noise swelled, and people crushed them into their corner. Maggie propped one hand against Aslan's shoulder to stop herself getting knocked over.

Someone was being escorted out. A large man held a smaller man by one arm and the scruff of his jacket and marched him through the crowd to the door. Maggie recognised him by his dirty grey beanie.

Brad Someone, one of the Forest Keepers who had been arrested with her last week in the forest. Owner of a Ballito beach cottage. Roller of joints. And, judging by the bouncer's attitude, starter of fights.

'Get out,' the bouncer shoved Brad into the street. He staggered a bit, and then righted himself, looking back at the bar as if he were about to attempt re-entry.

'Get!' the bouncer pointed down the street. Brad began to stagger away. Reassured, the bouncer made his way back into the bar. Brad leaned against a parking meter, staring back at the bar over his shoulder.

Inside, the shifting tides of people had righted themselves. Maggie took her hand off Aslan's shoulder.

She turned back to talk to Hope, but the woman was transfixed by something behind Maggie.

'Oh Jesus,' Chloe said.

Brad stood at the window, face pressed against the glass.

'Chloe,' he mouthed. 'Chloe.' His beanie was askew, and his eyes were struggling to focus. But he had definitely recognised Chloe.

Maggie turned to her. 'What's going on?'

She grimaced. 'My ex.'

Brad spotted Hope and his face grew thunderous. 'Lesbians!' he howled, staggering backwards and then towards the glass again. Now his face was even closer. 'Lesbians!'

Chloe put her face in her hands. Hope hugged her closer.

'Oh my God, he is gross,' she whispered. Maggie turned back. Brad was licking the glass, smearing it with his tongue, his whole face pressed against it like a dreadful whiskery crustacean.

He pointed at Hope. 'You are a lesbian!' Then he attacked the glass with his tongue again.

'He's been stalking me on Twitter,' Hope said, looking shellshocked. 'At least I think it's him. Leaving me abusive messages about corrective rape.'

Chloe's face was buried in her hands.

'I can't take this,' Maggie said to the others. She pushed her way through the crowd to the door.

As she got outside, the cold night air bit her. Brad still had his face to the glass.

'Enough of that,' She pulled him by his shoulder, and he staggered backwards again. Now his focus, what there was of it, was on her.

'Lesbian!' he yelled and wound up his arm to take a swing at Maggie. He flailed and missed.

'You're making an idiot of yourself,' she hissed. 'If you're trying to impress Chloe, it's not working.'

She glanced inside. Their faces, joined by many others, were watching her.

Her jaw jolted and her teeth rattled. Brad's next swing had made contact. Despite being disgustingly drunk, he was pretty strong.

Anger coursed through Maggie. She dropped him with one short kick to the lower legs. Since he was drunk and uncoordinated, he landed on his nose.

'You kicked me!' he yelled, pulling himself up onto all fours. He clutched his nose with one hand and blood dripped through his fingers. 'I can't believe you kicked me.'

Maggie held the side of her head. She could feel the skin on her jawline start to swell. She was going to have a massive bruise in the morning. Not her first.

'What's going on here?' She heard a familiar voice and saw Solomon Njima standing there, an elegant woman at his side. He had a smile on his face; she did not.

'Are you brawling in the street, Ms Cloete?' he asked.

Maggie nursed the side of her head. 'He threw the first punch. Plus he was aggravating my friends.'

Hope and Chloe were at her side. 'Aslan's getting ice,' Hope told her.

'This is Captain Njima,' Maggie said. 'My friends, Hope and Chloe.'

'Maggie was just defending herself, Captain,' Hope told him. He still looked amused. His companion pulled out her phone and distanced herself from the proceedings by scrolling on the screen.

Aslan arrived with two bags of ice. Maggie placed one against her face and Aslan took the other to Brad, who held it to his nose and howled.

'He's making it up,' Maggie said. 'It can't be that sore.'

The policeman put a hand on Brad's shoulder. 'Are you going to be okay? I can call an ambulance.'

'No!' Brad was clearly still feeling combative. He sat on the pavement, feet in the street, each elbow resting on a knee and both hands up to his nose.

'We need someone to take this guy home,' Njima said. 'Before he causes any more trouble.'

A man had come out of Barry's. 'I know him. I'll take him home.'

'Thanks,' Njima said. He looked at Maggie, amusement at the

corners of his mouth. 'And you're alright?'

'We've got her, Officer,' Aslan said. 'We're used to mopping up after Maggie.'

She glared at him, but he pulled gently at her arm. 'Come on, let's get you home.'

'How is your investigation going?' she asked the cop.

'Still early stages. Not much to report right now,' he smiled.

'Can I call you to find out more?' His girlfriend lifted her head. She was not quite as oblivious to proceedings as she wanted to make out.

'Sure.'

Chloe and Hope each hugged Maggie, patting her on the back and thanking her. They left hand in hand. Brad's friend got him standing and he staggered off. As she walked with Aslan through the parking lot to his car, Maggie glanced over her shoulder.

Solomon Njima's girlfriend was still staring at her screen, stilettos spiking the pavement. The policeman watched Maggie walk away.

Chapter 15
Tuesday, 7am

She stared at the bruise in the bathroom mirror. If she were the kind of person who used foundation, she could dab some on to lessen the effect, but she was not. Then she remembered the photography studio. Occasionally, Ed had to take an in-studio portrait, usually for the business pages. Rows of suits. Very boring. However, the suits were vain and liked a touch-up before going under the lights.

She pulled on her leather jacket and glanced into the fridge. There was nothing there except for a well-browned banana. No telling how old that was. She really needed to do some grocery shopping. Or get a housekeeper. One of the two.

She stopped at a fast-food place for a breakfast burger. There was a woman outside, begging, with a baby tied to her back. Maggie went back into the restaurant and bought a second burger and a bottle of water, which she handed to her.

Then she headed for the photography studio. Ed was in early, as always.

'Jeez, Maggie, what happened to your face?' he exclaimed when he saw her.

'Someone disagreed with me at Barry's Bar last night,' she said, picking a piece of bacon out of her teeth. 'He threw the first punch. Listen, do you still have your make-up stash?'

'I do.'

'Can you remember how to use it?'

'Of course. Take a seat, madam.'

Maggie sat still while Ed dabbed foundation around her jaw. The touch of his fingers was familiar. They had had an on-again, off-again relationship for many years. Before she left Pietermaritzburg to seek her fortune in the big wide world, it had become more on-again. She was hurting from the break-up with Spike, and Ed's girlfriend Sally-Anne, the former arts editor, had just left the city for Cape Town. They comforted each other.

Now Ed was married, and his second child had started primary school.

'So are you going to work here for ever?'

'Probably,' he said. 'Now this might hurt.' He was right.

'Why, Ed? You are such a good photographer. Any paper would have you.' It was true. He had won a couple of national awards for his photos of the Inkatha/ANC civil war in the run-up to the first democratic election.

'The family are settled. So am I. We like it here.'

'Hmmm.' Maggie couldn't imagine the tediousness of knowing you were going to live in one place for the rest of your life.

'But there is one thing I'd like to do.'

'What's that?'

'Try my hand at writing.'

'Seriously?'

His steady eyes met hers. 'Seriously.'

'You mean in private or journalism?'

'I'd like to write for the paper.'

'Have you told Naidoo this?'

'Many times. But I don't think she believes me.'

'Well, let's give it a go. If I have a story in need of a writer, I know who to call.'

'Thanks, man.' Ed turned away. She could tell he was pleased. She also knew that after years of tag-teaming with journalists, Ed understood the basic tenets of a news story. He'd know what questions to ask, when to ask them and how to shape a story.

'Take a look.' He passed her a hand mirror.

Maggie took the mirror and examined her face. Where earlier there had been black pouching around her jawline, there was now a pasty pink with undertones of yellow.

'I look like a circus clown.'

'Which is better than a bar brawler.'

She slapped Ed's upper arm. 'Listen, I owe you. Can I come back tomorrow? This thing is going to take a while to clear up.'

'Sure. I'm always in early.'

Maggie left the studio, promising to find a story that Ed could work on. She walked wordlessly past Patti on the way past her desk and sat down to read the wires. The journalists drifted in one by one and no one mentioned her face. It was going to be a good day.

After conference with Naidoo, the editor asked Maggie to stay behind. 'Listen, Sentinel have invited us to lunch,' she said. 'I think it's some kind of olive branch, so we should make the effort. Are you available?'

'Sure, when?'

'Today.'

Instinctively, Maggie patted her jaw. It felt tight and swollen.

Naidoo squinted at Maggie's face. She fumbled around on her desk, located her glasses and put them on. 'What the hell happened?'

'You really don't want to know.'

'No, I do.'

'Some guy in a bar last was throwing his weight around. I asked him to play nicely, He didn't like that so he punched me.'

'Jeez, Maggie that's bad.' Naidoo's face was all concern. 'Did you report it to the police?'

Maggie thought of Solomon Njima's tall figure, his cool, amused glance. 'The police were there. Everything was sorted out.'

'Good. So meet me in the lobby at 12:30. We can walk over to the Sentinel offices together.'

Maggie's morning went fast. She found a first assignment for Ed, a story on how locals were rejuvenating the town's traffic circles, which the provincial administration had allowed to become overgrown and weed-filled. It would make a nice photo-essay, with quotes from the different individuals. Ed was thrilled.

At lunch, she headed for the lobby. Naidoo clicked down the hallway in her stilettos, hands swinging at her sides. Her nails were forest green.

'Let's go,' she said, as if she had been waiting for Maggie and not the other way around. They walked out of the building, doors swooshing open and then closed behind them.

'How is it, being back in town?' the editor asked.

'Same but different.'

'I should hope it's different, after more than a decade.'

'Ja, I miss the downtown office. That had more buzz.' And access to better food.

'True. This place is a bit soulless. But it makes financial sense.'

'I am sure it does,' Maggie said. She said no more and they walked in silence. Naidoo was the queen of the conversational road-block.

They arrived at Sentinel's sleek offices. Behind and to the left, Maggie saw a giant, inflated tent. It was white and still surrounded by workers' scaffolding. A butterfly dome?

Inside, the Sentinel receptionist greeted them and asked them to sit down. 'Mr Mpondo will be out to receive you personally in a minute.'

They sat. Naidoo got out her mobile and checked her messages, scrolling with her green-tipped fingers. Apart from meetings with the board and writing her daily editorial, what did she do? Who were her many messages from?

'Oh, I've been invited to an editors' conference in Cape Town next month,' she answered Maggie's unspoken question. 'Patti will be holding the fort.'

'Okay.' Maggie took out her cell. Two could play the ignoring game.

'Welcome ladies!' Xolani Mpondo stood before them, arms and smile wide in greeting.

'Xolani!' Naidoo leapt up, and she and the chief executive shared a hug. Very friendly for two people whose organisations were involved in a price war.

'This is Maggie Cloete,' she said, when the hug had finished.

'Ms Cloete,' he said, putting out his hand to shake and then pumping her hand up and down. 'So good to meet you.'

He tucked Naidoo's arm into the crook of his elbow. 'Now if you come this way, I have a couple of people waiting to meet both of you.'

He led the way down a shiny corridor, all buffed floors and framed aerial views of forests.

'After you,' he said, throwing open a door. Naidoo and Maggie entered and Mpondo followed them in. There was a small group awaiting them, including Mbali Sibanyoni. Maggie grinned at her and she returned a half-smile. Were things not all that well in

Paradise Sentinel?

'Let me introduce you,' Mpondo said. 'Team, meet the neighbours!'

The team laughed obediently. 'This is Tina Naidoo, who is editor of *The Gazette*, and her news editor, Maggie Cloete.'

He indicated the group. 'Tina, Maggie, please meet Paul van Spruy, forestry manager, Midlands division.'

They both shook hands with Paul, who was tall and spindly, not unlike a mature eucalyptus. He was wearing his corporate suit awkwardly, as if uncomfortable in indoor gear.

'This is Mbali Sibonyoni from corporate PR. I believe you know each other.' He winked at Maggie. Mbali looked elegant in her corporate uniform, even if her smile was at half-mast.

'And please meet Themba Tlakane, our chief financial officer.' Maggie and Naidoo shook hands with Themba.

Mpondo introduced them to a woman from research and a man from the paper mill. Maggie immediately forgot their names. Her stomach was grumbling and the food laid out on the buffet looked tantalising. There was a pasta dish with her name on it.

'Thank you for coming, Tina and Maggie. We wanted to reach out to you as neighbours. I want you to realise we are not monsters, just ordinary people going about our ordinary business of growing trees and making wood products. Nothing sinister, nothing unusual. Just a business that makes jobs and helps people. Please talk to each other, exchange, and enjoy the food.'

Maggie didn't hesitate. Her breakfast burger was a mere memory. She grabbed a plate and heaped it high. She found a knife and fork and somewhere to sit. The guy from the paper mill joined her.

Maggie speared a piece of pasta. 'I'm sorry, I don't remember your name.'

'Max Govender.' He was in his fifties, and comfortable-looking. Surfing the last few years until retirement.

'That's right. And you run one of the paper mills.'

'Yes, North Coast.'

'Is there a Maritzburg one?'

'Ja, there is.'

'Who heads that?'

'The guy died, actually. They are busy looking for a replacement.'

Maggie chewed. Sentinel had a tendency to lose its employees to early death. 'What of?'

'Some kind of galloping cancer. He went to hospital one week, and died the next.'

Max Govender cut a piece of roast beef into neat slices. 'That looks good,' Maggie said. 'I might have to go and get some of that.'

'It is good,' he told her. 'I'm always happy when I have to come to HQ for lunch.'

'Did you know Dave Bloom? Environmentalist, based here. Also died recently.'

She heard a peal of laughter and looked up. Naidoo was head to head with Xolani Mpondo. She patted his arm and then wiped her eyes. Maggie looked around the table. The rest of the employees, brought in to show how normal everything was, were eating quietly.

'I'd heard of him,' Max Govender said, 'but I never met him. I'm not even sure what he did.'

Neither was Maggie. She glanced up and saw Mbali's serious eyes upon her.

'Just going to try that roast beef,' she said, getting up.

Mbali joined her at the buffet. 'So good to see you Maggie.'

'You too, young lady. How are you doing?'

'Just great, thanks. Really enjoy my job.'

'Listen, I realised I have no idea what Dave Bloom actually did here.'

'Research,' Mbali said, putting her plate down. 'He was looking into different kinds of more energy-efficient solvents, ones that could extract cellulose from wood chip much faster. I can introduce you to his colleague over there.'

The research person's name was Susannah Hynde.

'Yes, Dave was my close colleague,' she said, when Maggie asked. 'Our department is still in a state of shock. To lose someone just like that, overnight.'

Maggie remembered Johan Liebenberg's words. 'Was he depressed?'

'He had nothing to be depressed about,' the woman said. 'His life was wonderful.'

Depression wasn't like that. Even people with perfect lives

became depressed.

'What about the Karkloof Blue? Was he upset about that?'

'Sure. We all are. No one likes to see a species lose its habitat. But Sentinel has an amazing plan for it. Did you see the butterfly dome outside?'

'I did.'

'Mr Mpondo is going to take you on a tour. You'll be impressed.' Susannah Hynde had drunk all of Xolani Mpondo's Kool-Aid. There was no way she was going to be Maggie's whistleblower.

'And what about the bodies in the forest? Do you have any idea where they came from?'

'None. Obviously it's upsetting for us.'

'Right.' Mpondo stood up and clapped his hands, like a parent herding his children. Maggie realised that she had done just the same yesterday at news conference. She resolved never to clap her hands and chivvy people again.

'Hope you enjoyed your lunch.' Naidoo nodded, though Maggie didn't remember seeing her actually eat. 'Now we'd like to invite you outside to see our newly built butterfly dome.'

There was an expectant buzz, and people threw on their jackets and coats. Xolani waited in the corridor and when everyone was with him, he led the way to the back of the building. He pushed open a big safety door and they were outside.

They crossed a car park. The dome loomed above them, pristinely white. There was still scaffolding bracing it.

'I assure you it's secure. I have been in many times,' Xolani told the group as they neared the dome.

'It's a hard-hat zone, I'm afraid,' he said, handing out yellow hats that were waiting on a table. 'Each got one? Great.'

Mpondo led the way in and everyone trooped in after him.

'It's my first visit here,' Susannah Hynde's eyes shone as she whispered to Maggie.

'What we have here is a raised walkway, so that people can walk through the dome without disturbing the butterflies. We have planted only indigenous trees and shrubs, ones that match the Karkloof Blue's present habitat. Please feel free to have a walk, experience the dome, and let's gather here in ten minutes.'

The Sentinel employees surged ahead. Mpondo and Naidoo

took a more leisurely pace. Maggie glanced up. The dome was really high, cathedral-like. It was beautiful and the newly-planted trees gave off a lovely scent. Soon it would be nothing more than a prison.

Maggie's cell phone buzzed. It was a number she didn't know. She took the call. 'Hold on one minute. I just need to step outside.'

Outside she put the phone to her ear. 'Who is this?'

'Maggie!' There were sobs, a sound of gulping. 'Maggie, it's Chloe. Remember, from last night?'

'Sure I remember. What's up, Chloe?'

'Maggie, it's Hope. She's disappeared.'

Chapter 16
Tuesday, 1.30pm

'What do you mean, disappeared?'

'She left for university this morning, but she never arrived. No one's seen her; her office is still locked. We had a plan to meet for an early lunch at the cafeteria, and she didn't turn up. She's not at home and she's not answering her cell. It just goes to voicemail.'

'Have you told the police?'

'I have, but they tell me it's too early for a disappearance. They open a docket after forty-eight hours. 'Maybe she's shopping,' the one guy told me. Hope doesn't shop, Maggie. She is a creature of habit and she's completely reliable. I'm freaking out.'

Maggie thought of last night's performance, the tongue and whiskers pressed against the glass.

'Have you asked Brad?'

'Brad, no. Why?'

'He didn't seem too enamoured with Hope last night.'

'Brad is an idiot. He wouldn't know how to kidnap someone.'

'Let me go and find out. In the meanwhile, you keep looking for her and keep in touch.'

Maggie went back into the dome, shook Xolani Mpondo's hand in thanks and told Naidoo something had come up. She ran back to the office and grabbed her helmet. Then she dialled Alex Field.

'Hey Alex. Brad MacKenzie, where does he work?

'I think he's between jobs at the moment.'

'Okay, then where does he live?'

Alex gave her the address of a house that MacKenzie shared with others. It was on the lip of a hill overlooking town, just a few hundred metres above the tower-block where she used to live years ago. From what she could see over the security walls, it was an old Victorian, with deep sash windows and a wrap-around verandah. Nice spot for someone who was unemployed.

She leaned on the buzzer. No answer. She leaned some more. Silence.

She dialled the number Field had sent her for MacKenzie. It rang. Eventually, a groggy voice answered.

"Lo?'

'Brad MacKenzie, this is Maggie Cloete. I am standing outside your house, pressing the buzzer. Would you please let me in?'

Maggie heard muttering. Then the phone went dead and the gate clanged open.

MacKenzie stood on the verandah, topless and in surf shorts. His nose was puffy and bulbous.

'I don't know why the fuck I'm letting you into my house,' he said, running his hand through his sleep-wild hair.

Maggie grabbed his arm and marched him back inside. 'I'll tell you why. The woman you were abusing last night has disappeared. I want you to tell me where she is.'

'Chloe?' his face crumpled.

'Not Chloe. Her girlfriend, Hope.'

He slumped into a plush leather armchair. 'I don't care about her. She stole Chloe from me.'

'Your girlfriend left you, and quite honestly, I can see why. You're an unemployed rich kid who lies around sleeping all day, gets pissed at night and abuses people having a peaceful night out. Not to mention taking pot-shots at people who are trying to stop you embarrassing yourself.'

MacKenzie winced. 'That's not a pretty picture.'

'You're right, it's not. Now where the fuck is Hope?'

'I have no idea. Seriously. I've been here since last night, sleeping it off. My housemates will tell you.'

'Where are they?'

'At work.'

'Hope Phiri disappeared this morning on her way to work. You have no alibi to speak of.'

MacKenzie paled. 'Shit. I really don't know where she is. I wish I did.'

Maggie pointed a finger at him. 'She told me last night you've been abusing her on Twitter. Show me.'

He tried to look innocent, but there was a flash of a smile. The little shit was proud of himself.

'Get your laptop. Show me.'

'No.'

'Listen, MacKenzie, the minute I walk out of here you can delete your Twitter feed and all the disgusting abusive messages you've been sending to Hope. But there is such a thing as a history, and police computer experts need about five minutes to unearth it. If you insist that you are innocent, the least you can do is show me the crap you've been sending to Hope.'

He got up, went to another room and came back with a laptop. He clicked a button and they waited in silence as it warmed up. He located his Twitter account and passed the laptop to Maggie.

MacKenzie's handle was @MacRat and threaded throughout his feed, and amongst his many tweets about getting #wasted, were tweets to @Hopeful:

Do you like pussy?

All lesbians need to change their minds is a big, hard cock.

You're not hot enough to rape.

Maggie shut the laptop. In the scale of Twitter abuse meted out to women, it was amateurish, but with two or three tweets to Hope a week, it had the markings of a dedicated campaign.

'You realise that with these, last night's events that were witnessed by half of town and the fact that you have no alibi for Hope's disappearance, you will be a prime suspect when the police open a case.'

He stared at her. She hoped her words were getting through the fog of alcohol and self-regard in which Brad MacKenzie floated.

'Okay,' he said sulkily. 'What do you want me to do?'

'Phone Chloe, apologise for your behaviour – all of it – and offer to help her find Hope. Then help her. Do something for someone else for a change.'

He got up. 'OK. But stop lecturing me. You sound like Chloe.'

Outside she called Chloe and told her about Brad.

'He disgusts me,' the woman said. 'I can't believe I ever went out with him.'

Maggie left her thoughts unsaid. 'Any news from your side?'

'No Maggie, nothing. It's like she left for work and disappeared.'

'How does she normally get to work?'

'She gets up early and walks to campus, which is just around the corner from our house. I sleep in, drive there a bit later and then we always drive home together.'

Regular habits. These were not good. Anyone wanting to snatch Hope would observe her for a couple of days and learn them. Plus being a walker made her vulnerable.

'How about her friends and family?'

'I've called everyone I know. No one has seen her or heard from her.'

'What about Dumisane?' Maybe Hope's cousin could pull some strings.

'He said he would call his contacts and get them to open a missing persons case immediately.'

'Good.' There was no point having an ANC heavyweight for a cousin if he couldn't make things happen. 'Chloe, I must get back to the office. My phone is on. Call me anytime.'

She found a message from Naidoo in the in-house mail. *Have sent Ed to take photos of the butterfly dome. PR exercise to befriend Sentinel.*

Naidoo could do what she liked. She was the editor. She and Xolani Mpondo might think that a dome to re-home butterflies was a great PR exercise for Sentinel. Maggie thought it would have the opposite effect, that people would start to see that the paper company were dead serious about getting rid of a precious patch of forest. If they cared, that is.

She worked hard all afternoon, her work underlaid with concern about Hope. As the hours passed and there was no sign of her, her chances of survival grew smaller.

Aslan emailed in a book review, Menzi was following up on the shebeen story, as well as chasing Ernest for more on the bodies in the forest. Johnny Cupido had a long and detailed story on a city council meeting. No one would read it, but as an organ of record, *The Gazette* was duty-bound to report it.

Johan was typing busily. She was not sure what was keeping him engaged.

She tried to shape her thoughts by drawing pictures. She drew a circle for Dave Bloom, a man obsessed with the Karkloof Blue and yet doing Sentinel's research into better solvents, a man known and appreciated for his commitment to the environment, a man who was dead in an apparent suicide despite all appearances of having been happy and balanced. There was another circle for the Forest Keepers, eager enough to preserve the natural forest and save the Blue's habitat that they were prepared to risk arrest. She drew another for the bodies in the forest, a reminder of the horrors of South Africa's recent history.

There was the land claim, recently retracted by the local community whose organiser was the known troublemaker and gangster, Lucky Bean Msomi. There was Mike Rankin, a professor so obsessed with his studies of the forest that he now lived there, in the middle of winter, without electricity or plumbing. There was Sentinel itself, on one hand, threatening to raise *The Gazette*'s paper prices and complaining about negative publicity and, on the other hand, treating its editor and news editor to jolly little lunches and tours of their butterfly dome.

And now Hope Phiri, a PhD student and expert on the Karkloof Blue – whom Maggie had quoted in the paper last week – had vanished in broad daylight.

It was a big mess. Maggie stared at the circles. She was sure that they should fit neatly together, if only she could find a way of joining them. Something was missing. What had Alex said on that first night? Sentinel had everyone in their pocket: the government, the public and the union.

The union. She typed Paper and Allied Workers' Union in to the search engine and it threw up a series of links. She clicked on and scanned them all. The union's leader was a man called Joshua Ntombe. He was usually pictured with his right fist raised, shouting into crowds like a demagogue. It reminded her of the first Forest Keepers meeting where she had met Alex. He had been shouting and fist-waving then too.

Ntombe had a rich history in *The Gazette*'s records. He was a long-term unionist, had climbed his way up through the union, had been a committed Cosatu member and activist, had had periods of detention without trial during the eighties. There were photos of him at Cosatu rallies and later at the constitutional negotiations. A survivor.

What would his interests be? Better working conditions and

better pay for the union members. Would the union care if Sentinel were mowing down a forest in order to grow alien trees? Maybe all they would care about was jobs.

She called the union office and a harassed-sounding woman answered the phone.

'My name is Maggie Cloete. I'm from *The Gazette* in Pietermaritzburg. I want to talk to Joshua Ntombe.'

'We're in a meeting.'

At least he was in the office. 'When will the meeting end?'

'Hard to say. Try again in thirty minutes.'

Maggie left her number in case the meeting finished early. Then she sipped on her ninth cup of coffee and stared at her circles.

She followed the links on Joshua Ntombe down the rabbit holes of the Internet. There were campaigns leading back thirty years – Health and Safety Campaign 2006, PAAWU Celebrates 25 Years in Office – each accompanied by grainy photos.

She clicked on pictures of Joshua Ntombe heading protest marches surrounded by union stewards. She stared at the faces. One of them was a young Xolani Mpondo. The career path of a shop steward didn't usually end in the corner office. How had Mpondo swung that?

Her phone rang. 'Joshua Ntombe. I believe the press is after me,' said a genial voice in her ear.

'Thanks for calling back. I'm from *The Gazette* in Pietermaritzburg.'

'Yes,' he rumbled. 'Good paper. We have always had fair coverage from you people. More than I can say from the Durban crowd.'

Durban had a scattering of daily newspapers, all owned by various conglomerates. *The Gazette* was the only independently owned paper left in the province. It held onto that status with pride, but if circulation didn't keep steady and if the Timothy Richardsons of this world didn't keep earning their money, it would be in jeopardy.

'I just wanted a quick chat. Off the record,' she began. 'We've got a lot going on in your world at the moment.'

'The bodies in the forest. I know. I read about those. So terrible. I thought of the families.'

'I am sure you remember Dave Bloom.'

'Sure I do! How's Bloomie doing these days?'

Maggie told him and he went silent. Then he breathed deeply. 'He's not a union member. I did not know.'

Maggie thought of Alex's demagoguery, of Christo's face when he talked about preserving the forest for the insects and animals. 'Dave Bloom was very upset about what Sentinel is doing to Karkloof Extension 7, and particularly the habitat of the Karkloof Blue.'

'So here's the thing,' Ntombe's voice was back to its full strength. 'In the union, we worry about fair wages and about the safety of our workers. We have mouths to feed at home, Ms Cloete. We can't get worked up about a butterfly.'

'I think the butterfly has become a symbol for the fact that Sentinel will walk over anything for profit.'

'Profit is good for the workers, Ms Cloete. What's not good for the workers is when our health and safety is compromised for profit, when we become tools in the machine.'

'Don't you think you are already tools in the machine?'

He laughed. 'You are very direct, Ms Cloete. But yes, sure we are. We know that. But without us, the union, management would have carte blanche to walk all over everything and everyone.'

As they already do, Maggie thought.

Ntombe cleared his throat. 'I need to go. Is there anything else I can do to help you?'

Maggie remembered the photo of a younger and leaner Ntombe leading a protest march next to Xolani Mpondo.

'Apparently the boss used to be a unionist.'

'Indeed.'

'Is that an unusual path to the C-suite?'

'It is,' Ntombe chortled. 'But he was a very clever boy. He knew how to game the system. I can only admire him.'

'Is anyone bitter that their former comrade is now top management?'

'Not me. It's useful when we are negotiating wages to know he once was a lowly factory worker. There was some bitterness when he did a first round of lay-offs in 2008. That was ugly. But he has saved face since then by pulling up the share price and giving out a wage hike last Christmas.'

'So where are those laid-off workers now?'

'I don't know,' Ntombe said. 'If they are lucky they've found other jobs. If they are not, then they're living hand to mouth in a squatter camp somewhere.' He coughed. 'It's been a pleasure, Ms Cloete. I am always here. Let me know if I can help.'

She did a final check with the subs. Ed's photo of the butterfly dome was on the front page. She stared around the emptying newsroom. Everyone was gone except for Johan Liebenberg. If he wanted to be journalist, then he could be a journalist.

She walked over to his desk. He was thumbing his smartphone.

'Come with me.'

'Okay,' he leapt to his feet.

'Bring your car keys.'

Chapter 17
Tuesday, 5.30pm

Despite rebranding himself as a community organiser, Lucky Bean Msomi had not changed the glaring signals of wealth outside his large Edendale house: a three-car garage, Doric columns at the front door and a shiny black BMW parked outside, all surrounded by a large fence topped with barbed wire. Night was falling and the place loomed gloomy in the half-light.

'This is it?' Johan Liebenberg's voice grew squeaky. He had not been happy about joining Maggie on her trip to visit the former gangster, but she had told him to do some investigative work for a change. Plus she needed a driver.

'This is it.'

Johan parked outside the gate, and Maggie got out of his car and slammed the door. She was about to buzz the intercom when she realised that Johan was not with her. She gestured to him but he didn't move.

She walked back to the car and he rolled down his window. 'I'm a bit nervous.'

Maggie laughed. At least the guy was honest. His bluster was peeling away.

'I'm nervous too, but there's safety in numbers. Come on.'

Liebenberg got out of the car with a great show of reluctance that included wiping imaginary dust off his pristine cargo pants.

Maggie marched back to the intercom and pressed the buzzer before she or Liebenberg could change their minds.

'Yes?' A disembodied voice crackled through the machine.

'This is Maggie Cloete from *The Gazette*. I would like to speak with Mr Msomi.'

There was silence. A long silence. A curtain in a front room whisked open and then shut again. Maggie and Liebenberg were being assessed for their potential for danger. The assessor evidently decided they posed none, and the gate creaked open.

Maggie led the way to the front door where a man mountain stepped out and stood between the four Doric columns. He was as tall as a basketball player and as wide as a prop forward.

Msomi still merited a bodyguard, it seemed. Maggie had been instrumental in getting two of his previous employees locked up. Kidnapping, threat, unlawful destruction of private property and accessory to fraud were just some of the charges they'd been convicted of.

This guy was new to Maggie.

'What do you want?'

'We just want a short chat with Mr Msomi.'

'Who are you?'

She had already told him on the intercom, but blood had a long way to travel in a body that size.

'Maggie Cloete, from *The Gazette*. This is my colleague Johan Liebenberg.'

'And what do you want to talk about?'

'Karkloof Extension 7. The part that belongs to Sentinel.'

'Wait.' He went back inside, but left the door slightly ajar. In the gloom, Maggie could see black marble tiles and a hallway table that consisted of two black ceramic panthers with a sheet of glass resting on their heads.

'Follow me.'

Maggie and Johan followed him. The panthers' teeth gleamed in the half light.

He led them to a small sitting room. This wasn't the palatial home's main sitting-room, but a side event, to indicate how unimportant they were to his boss.

'Please wait here. Mr Msomi will join you.'

Maggie sat on a black velvet sofa. Johan stood, putting his hands into his pockets and then taking them out again.

He flopped down next to her. 'I don't feel well.'

He was greenish, but Maggie wasn't sure if it was the low lighting in Msomi's palace or if he was genuinely ill.

'Ms Cloete.' A short, round man entered the room, immaculately dressed.

'Mr Msomi.' Maggie stood up. She had to lean over Johan's half-prone body to shake their host's hand. She prodded her colleague's foot. 'This is Johan Liebenberg.'

Johan got up and offered his hand. Msomi shook it, his eyes moving from Liebenberg to Maggie and back again.

'You both look so familiar to me,' he said. She and Msomi had never met face-to-face, but he was the kind of person who'd make sure to know who his enemies were.

'Please sit.' He indicated the sofa behind them and sat opposite in an upright armchair.

They obeyed.

'Now, what is your little visit about?' His words were friendly, and his teeth shone, but his grin was not entirely genial.

'We have been covering the Karkloof logging story for *The Gazette*.'

'Oh yes, where they found the bodies.' He nodded. 'Terrible thing. Terrible.'

Maggie agreed that it was terrible. Johan Liebenberg said nothing. He kept his eyes trained on Msomi's face.

'Yes. So we are trying to understand all the various vested interests in that piece of land,' she said. 'There's Sentinel, the forestry company; there are the Forest Keepers, who are protesting against the logging.'

'The environmental lobby.'

'Exactly. And, our research shows, the local community, which has instituted and withdrawn a land claim on Karkloof Extension 7.'

Msomi nodded, his head moving up and down slowly. 'And you're here because you know that I was involved with the land claim.'

He was making it easy for her. Why?

'Yes.'

'The community decided it wasn't worth the fight, Ms Cloete. They realised it would be years of litigation against a company that has all the resources and all the funds in the world. Sentinel would have been happy to take us on. I persuaded the chief and his advisers to stop before they lost everything.'

How had he persuaded them, Maggie wondered. Did his persuasion come wrapped in R200 notes?

'Was the community happy with the decision?'

'You will always get your malcontents.' He smiled again.

'Now, Mr Liebenberg,' he turned to Johan. 'Let's talk about you.'

Johan squirmed next to Maggie.

'You say you are from *The Gazette*, but I remember you in another context.'

'Yes, sir,' Johan stammered. 'I used to work for Sentinel. We met during one of the community meetings.'

'That was it!' Msomi clapped his hands together, as if Johan was a clever pupil who had just given the right answer. 'And now you've moved over to the enemy?'

'Yes, a slight career change.'

'Journalism doesn't exactly pay,' Msomi said, his smile still wide.

'It was a lifestyle change.' Maggie knew all about Johan's new lifestyle. With his work ethic, his job was turning out to be pretty cushy.

'One more question, Mr Msomi,' she said.

'Sure.'

'Who is the chief and do you think I could visit him? I'd like to understand his claim on the land a little more.'

'Good idea! Let me arrange it. You and I can travel there together, reminisce a little.'

Msomi did remember her. Both she and the Chicken had suffered at his thugs' hands. Now he was offering her a lift and a chance to talk about old times.

'Johan would like to come too,' she said quickly. Whatever Msomi had in mind for her, she needed a witness.

Johan shot her a look of horror. He clearly wanted a chasm as wide as the Orange River between himself and Lucky Bean Msomi and now she was offering him a jaunt in the man's car.

'I'll talk to the chief and set something up.'

'Thank you. Here's my business card.' She put it on the coffee table between them. 'And now we'll stop disturbing you.'

Msomi slid her card into his pocket. 'It's been a pleasure.'

He stood up. As he shook Maggie's hand, he pointed to her jawline. 'Got some bruising there.'

'Yes, I had a difference of opinion with a drunk guy.'

'Did you win the argument?' Msomi smiled.

'I certainly did.'

'Glad to hear it. Vincent! Please see the people out.'

The man mountain appeared in the doorway. 'Please follow me.'

Johan led the way, his eagerness to leave Msomi's lair evident. Maggie followed. She turned once to look behind her. Lucky Bean Msomi stood where they had left him. He had a small white rectangle in his hand and was studying it intently. Her business card.

In the car, Johan sat still, holding the steering-wheel.

'The guy scares you,' Maggie said.

'I'm not feeling well,' he said, starting the car. 'Where can I drop you?'

'Back at the office.' As Johan drove, she called Chloe.

'Nothing. I've heard nothing,' the academic told Maggie. 'I'm frantic.'

'Can I come and sit with you?'

'Yes, please.'

Maggie headed across town towards the university, to the grid of streets where students and academics lived in old Victorian houses – some in disrepair, others neatly tidied up and renovated. She pulled up to a gate and buzzed the intercom. Security was high here, just like everywhere else in town.

Chloe and Hope lived in a cottage in the garden of another house. Once the gate trundled open, Maggie pushed the Chicken down the driveway, not wanting to disturb the inhabitants of the main house.

She parked the bike next to the cottage. The front door opened and Chloe stood in the doorway, backlit from inside. She was wearing a blanket around her shoulders.

'I'm so cold,' she said. 'I've got the heaters on, but I'm freezing.' She looked at Maggie, her face tear-stained. 'And I am so scared, Maggie, so scared for her.'

Maggie hugged her, and directed her inside. 'Can I make you something?'

'Cup of tea would be great.' Chloe slumped onto a sofa. On the coffee table in front of her were numerous cups of half-drunk tea. Maggie gathered them up and took them to the open-plan kitchen, where she put them in the sink and washed them while the kettle boiled.

She passed Chloe her tea, and the woman held onto it with both hands.

'So the police won't file a missing persons case until she's been gone forty-eight hours. They said Hope's an adult and she could have personal reasons for going somewhere without telling me. I've phoned everyone, Maggie, every single person who knows Hope – work, family, friends – and no one has seen her or heard from her.'

Chloe put the tea on the coffee-table, untouched. 'I feel as if I'm in a nightmare. She's out there, somewhere, and I can't help her. The people who are supposed to help us, the police, refuse to do anything, and every minute feels like an hour.'

'Have there been any changes to Hope's behaviour, any deviations from the norm, in the last few weeks?'

'No,' Chloe looked Maggie in the eye. 'Hope is the most dependable, most straightforward person I know. There are no games, no weirdness with her.'

'Was she feeling uncomfortable, feeling any sense of threat?'

'Apart from Brad MacKenzie's ridiculous behaviour on Twitter, no.'

'Did she take that seriously?'

'It felt like an invasion, sure, but as soon as we worked out who it was, we didn't take it seriously.'

Chloe leaned forward. 'I'm quite new to this business of being a lesbian, but Hope has been out since she was fourteen. Can you imagine? As a Zulu woman, here in Pietermaritzburg? Not an easy life decision. I admire her so much for that, for not taking the easy path, for being who she is no matter what people say or think.'

'How have her parents been?'

'Her mother is fairly open-minded. Hope says her mom keeps hoping it's a phase she'll grow out of.'

'And her father?'

'Her dad died when she was little.'

'What's her relationship like with Dumisane? You guys were

out with him last night.'

Chloe shrugged. 'Dumi is a social animal. He's fun to be around. He invited us to meet him for a drink.'

'And today? Has he been supportive?'

'Very. He's been making phone calls to everyone Hope has ever met, and his entire contact book. He's trying to persuade some high-level cop to subpoena the cell phone company so they can track her phone.'

'And?'

'Nothing yet.'

She picked up her cell phone and showed Maggie a text. 'See? There it is.'

How are you? No news from my side yet.

Chloe responded, one finger typing.

When she put the phone down, she shivered. 'I'm so cold and scared, and I keep thinking, wherever she is, she'll be more cold and more scared.'

'Maybe you need some sleep,' Maggie said.

'I can't imagine sleeping! What if Hope calls, or arrives at the front door, or she needs me?'

'How about you sleep for a couple hours, and I keep phone and door guard for you?'

Chloe accepted Maggie's offer and trailed off to the bedroom in her blanket. Maggie sat in the quiet house, listening to its creaks and moans. She pulled out her cell phone and checked Brad's Twitter feed. The creep had gone silent. She scrolled through Hope's feed. She'd linked to *The Gazette* articles about the forest, including the one where Johan and Maggie had quoted her. Maggie clicked through to the paper.

Logging Karkloof Extension 7 will be extremely damaging for the habitat and the potential survival of the butterfly known as the Karkloof Blue, said local scientist Hope Phiri.

'Building a butterfly dome to rehouse the butterflies is nothing more than cosmetic,' Phiri said. 'It doesn't deal with the core problem that our few remaining natural forests and grasslands are being sacrificed to capital gain.'

They had published two articles quoting Hope in the last two weeks. If someone was looking to punish people for speaking out against Sentinel, then *The Gazette* had a done a great job of leading that person directly to Hope.

Hours later, a harsh sound grated across Maggie's consciousness, jarring her awake.

'Hope!' Chloe, ran to the front door, still trailing the blanket. She pressed the buzzer. 'Who's there?'

Maggie sat up and rubbed her face. How long had she been asleep?

Chloe opened the door and stared out. Maggie got up and stood next to her. The gate was open, but there was no one in the driveway.

'Maybe just a prank,' Maggie said, but Chloe was fixed in the doorway.

'I think I can see something,' she whispered. 'Please come with me.'

Leaving the front door open, light from inside spilling out, Chloe and Maggie walked down the driveway. Chloe was right. There was a figure there, not standing, but slumped on the ground.

Maggie curled her fingers into a fist, nails digging into her palm. The driveway extended for miles, stretched into a different time zone, as she and Chloe hurried towards the figure at the end of the driveway, still slumped over.

'Hope!' Chloe began to run. Maggie broke into a run behind her. Chloe reached the figure, who was lying sideways on the ground with her feet in the gutter. She touched her shoulder and Hope rolled over.

Her face was a pulp of blood and bruises, both eyes swollen and her lips cracked and purpling. Her clothes were ripped and bloody.

'Oh God, Hope,' Chloe knelt next to her and stroked her hair. 'No. Oh God, no.' Tears fell down her cheeks.

'Quick, get the blanket around her,' Maggie said.

They wrapped her as best they could. With some effort, they manoeuvred her into a sitting position. She breathed heavily, gasping a couple of times in pain.

'I want to get her inside,' Chloe said, looking at the empty street. 'Those monsters could still be around.'

'Hope, can you stand?' Maggie asked.

Hope nodded, just one small incline of her head. Maggie and Chloe pulled her to a standing position as gently as possible. With one woman on either side of her, Hope lifted her foot and stepped from the gutter onto the pavement.

She doubled over. 'My ribs.'

Chloe bent down. 'Listen Hope, darling, we just need to get you inside. Then we can call a doctor and get you seen to.'

'No doctor,' Hope said, her voice sounding strangled. She straightened up.

If the walk down the driveway had seemed long, the walk back up it again was even longer. Hope's every step was hunched over in pain, but they made it, inch by inch. Inside the cottage, relief breaking like a wave over her, she wept. Not storms of sobs or great heaving breaths, just tears pouring silently down her poor broken face. Chloe led her to the sofa, where she held her.

'So tired,' Hope said. 'Let me sleep.' She lay down on the sofa, still wrapped in the blanket. Chloe lifted her feet up and tucked a second blanket over them. She switched off the sitting-room light.

'We really need to get her to the police,' Maggie said. 'And she must see a doctor.'

Chloe walked to the front door. She put a hand to the knob. 'I want you to get out.'

'What?'

'This is your fault. If you had left Hope alone, not pressed her for quotes for your bloody stories, we wouldn't be here now.'

There was truth in her words, but Maggie had not orchestrated an attack on Hope.

'Chloe, please ...' she stepped forward, hand out in appeal.

'Just go!'

Maggie got her jacket and helmet and walked out. Chloe slammed the door behind her. She could hear the gate rolling open at the bottom of the driveway as she pushed the Chicken towards the road. Once through the gate, she put her helmet on and straddled the bike.

She drove back to the flat through the empty streets. There were regular pools of light from the streetlights, but otherwise the streets and the hills surrounding town were dark. Tomorrow, town would be filled with people, their hustle and bustle, the busyness of daylight and commerce, but tonight was silent. The only commerce carried out now was sly and underhand and cruel, the business of people who chose shadows and corners, who acted according to a law of their own making.

Chapter 18
Wednesday, 5am

She woke early with a sense of dread as she remembered Hope's face, purple with bruises, and her bloodied clothes. She checked her phone for messages. Nothing from Chloe. She had another shower and took a hopeful glance into her fridge. It had not miraculously refilled itself.

Instead of heading to the office, Maggie went to town to find somewhere for breakfast. She parked the Chicken near the City Hall. Town was busy, with people arriving in taxis to start work, but the layer of winter chill kept everyone bundled up and withdrawn into themselves.

Maggie walked to the Mooi Boy. Tucked away in the alleys, her favourite cafe had provided easy access and cheap food for the shop and office workers of Pietermaritzburg. The red plastic table-cloths of the Mooi Boy were no more. Instead, vases full of roses and chrysanthemums in garish colour combinations filled the windows. It was now a florist.

She plumped for a Wimpy, which was low in atmosphere but high in calorific offerings. She had a black coffee and an omelette. While she ate, she checked her texts. Nothing from Chloe. A breezy good morning from Leo. And a missed call from Christo. Her brother had actually called her. Maybe there was a chink in the wall.

She walked to World Shoes. The shop wasn't open yet, but she knocked on the window. Christo unlocked the door for her.

'What are you doing here?' His tone was still chilly, but at least he was asking.

'You called.'

'I did. Just wanted to let you I was back. Enjoyed sleeping in a bed last night.' He looked at her more closely. 'What happened to your face?'

'It was one of your Planet Keeper friends.' She told him of the altercation with Brad, Hope's abduction and beating and possible rape, and of her suspicion that it was something to do with Sentinel.

'So you defend a gay couple in a bar, and the next day one of them is snatched off the street.'

'Pretty much.'

'And why her?'

'We quoted her a couple of times. She was speaking out against Sentinel. Do you think Brad MacKenzie could have done it?'

'The guy might be an idiot, Maggie, but he couldn't organise himself out of a paper bag. He's either drunk, stoned or hungover.'

'That could be an act,' she said. 'Maybe it's useful if everyone thinks you're a stoner.'

Christo rubbed his unshaven chin. 'She spoke up, just like Dave Bloom. And look what happened to him.'

'If that's the case, then why haven't they targeted you, or Alex? Or anyone else in the Forest Keepers?'

'We are too obvious. Safety in numbers. Instead, if you remember, they arrested us and threw us in jail for a night before releasing us and dropping the charges – that was a clear warning.'

'True.'

'Okay then, off to work.' She saw a slight shadow on her brother's face. 'Hey, everything alright with you?'

He grimaced. 'It's just Alex. He's being a grumpy bastard. Since the logging stopped and we can't protest or do anything, he's been like a caged lion.'

'If you need a bed, there's a spare room at my place.'

'Thanks.'

She walked back to where she had parked the Chicken. That was the longest conversation she'd had with her brother since moving back to Pietermaritzburg. Maybe he was thawing towards her. But she worried about his relationship with Alex. Living and working with someone was intense; you were subject to their moods and foibles. It had seemed a good option a couple of months ago when he'd been released from hospital. Maybe now, especially since he had become part of Field's group of protestors, it was too much being a slave to Alex's moods.

A shadow in front of her brought her to the here and now. Strong hands gripped her arms. She wriggled but felt cold steel pressed into her belly. They had a gun.

'Wallet, phone, quick.' Two young men wearing beanies pulled down low over their faces jostled her up against the window of a jeweller's.

One looked over his shoulder. The alley was quiet, but not for long. 'Hurry up.' She heard his breath, ragged in her ear, panicky. She couldn't work out which one was holding the gun, but she hoped it wasn't the panicky one.

She dug in in her bag, but it was hard to get purchase with both of their bodies pressed against hers.

'Fuck this.' One tore her bag off her shoulder.

He stared into her eyes. 'I have a message for you: stop your investigation.'

Then they both ran, disappearing around a corner.

'Come back!' She ran after them, following two sets of legs and their heavy breathing. One held her bag. She ran faster, air tearing through her lungs, pain in her legs, chasing them into Church Street. Here they ducked and dived between crowds of people, all weaving their way to their places of work. Stallholders were setting up their wares for the day, shop owners were sweeping the street in front of their stores. The two heads vanished in the crowd.

'Shit.' Maggie stopped.

'You okay, ma?' A woman asked. She was dressed in the uniform of a nearby fashion palace and spritzing something from a bottle onto the shop window.

'I've just been robbed,' Maggie said.

'Lot of skabengas around here. Lots of robberies. You must be careful.'

She hadn't been careful. She had lost focus. Stop which investigation? Was this a message from the high circles in Joburg or was someone pissed off at her investigation right here in Pietermaritzburg?

Maggie walked back to Christo's shop, the City Hall chiming eight. The doors of World Shoes were now open. She went in.

'Back so soon?'

'I was robbed. They had a gun.' She slumped down on a chair.
'What did they take?' Christo kept his distance, but there was concern on his face.
'My bag. Computer, phone, wallet. Fucking everything.' She stood up and slapped her jeans pockets. She felt a slice of metal. 'I've still got the bike key, thank God.'
He went behind the counter and got back to polishing a pair of shoes. Not much compassion there, then.
'May I use the phone?'
He nodded.
Maggie dialled *The Gazette* on the shop phone. She asked Fortunate to tell Naidoo and anyone who was already in in the news room that she would be late. They could get the day started without her.
'So was it a work phone?' Christo asked.
'Nope, my private one. But all my contacts are on it.'
'Do you back it up?'
'Sure I do. To the computer they just stole.'
'You should be more careful.'
'Excuse me?'
'I said be more careful. You need to be alert around here, not wander around in a daydream.'
'Thanks for the words of advice.' Maggie headed for the door. 'I'll be off then.'
As she left the shop, she noticed a small smile playing on her brother's face. He was enjoying having the upper hand.
She headed for the police station. The closest one was the main Pietermaritzburg station, just around the corner. It hadn't changed in the years since she'd been away. Same depressing ten-storey building, same depressing grey concrete tower rearing up over the street. She'd been here for press conferences over the years, but she'd never visited as a common or garden-crime victim.
'I'm here to report a crime,' she told the receptionist.
The man pointed a thumb to the left. 'Next door please.'
Maggie walked through a glass door to the left of the receptionist's desk into the chaos of the police station. There was a man with a bleeding bandage around his head, a woman with three small children, all of whom were crying, two teenagers looking surly

and a businessman in a suit all trying to get the attention of one cop, who was typing notes into a computer with one finger and no sense of urgency.

Maggie muscled her way past the others to his desk. 'I need to report a crime.'

'Take a number,' the cop pointed to a small machine mounted at head height on the wall. 'These people are all in front of you.'

Maggie pulled a number and sat down on a bench next to the businessman. She had no phone to stare at it, so instead she stared at police posters. The cop called the next number and the woman got up with all three children attached to some part of her – one on her hip, one holding her bag strap and one trying to crawl under her skirt. She kept swatting him with her free hand as she talked to the policeman.

Maggie felt impatience rise. How long was this going to take? She had a newspaper to get out, and her bank cards and phone to cancel before the muggers cleaned out her bank account. Right now, they were probably already playing computer games on her laptop and one of them had just scored a nice leather backpack.

Unless her mugging was related to Jabu's and they were hacking her files.

She stared through the glass door to the police station, cops coming and going. Eventually the women and the three kids were done, and it was the turn of the bandaged man. Maggie read the poster about road safety for the twelfth time.

Then through the glass, she spotted a tall figure. Njima. She leapt up.

'Solomon,' she said, pushing the door open.

Njima was standing at reception, having a quiet word with the guy on duty there. He looked up. 'Maggie. What are you doing here?'

'I've just been mugged. Reporting it.'

'I'm sorry.' He stepped closer, put a hand on her arm. She could feel the imprint of his fingers through her leather jacket. They were warm and comforting. 'Are you okay?'

'I'm fine. Just frustrated because that—' she pointed her thumb in the direction of the station '— is taking so long. There's only one guy on duty.'

He removed his hand from her arm and she could still feel a patch of warmth where it had been.

He shook his head. 'There are supposed to be two. The other one is probably have a smoke break outside.'

Njima opened the door, put his head in and barked something at the duty policeman. He smiled at her. 'That should speed things up.' Then he looked closer. 'That's quite a bruise you've got there.'

'From that idiot at Barry's the other night.'

'I remember. What was going on?'

'He was abusing my friends.' She told him about Hope's abduction.

'Please tell her to report it as soon as possible,' he said. 'The longer she waits, the more details disappear, the harder it will be to apprehend the perpetrators.'

Maggie promised to do so.

'I'd better get back to work.' He stepped away.

'Before you go, how are the forensics on the forest bodies coming along?'

'They are definitely apartheid era. Now the guys are trying to work out how they died.'

'Bullet wounds?' Maggie asked.

'None, and no signs of knife wounds either.'

Maggie glanced through the glass door. There were now two policeman typing one-fingered onto computers.

'Looks like things are moving in there,' she smiled. 'Thanks to you.'

'Our duty is to serve,' he bowed slightly, and turned to go. 'See you, Maggie.'

'Before you go, can we report on the forensics?'

'Not yet, please. We'll issue a statement in the next twenty-four hours. Keep it to yourself for now.'

Maggie went in and reported the mugging to the cop. He typed her details in laboriously and assured her that there was little chance of ever seeing her bag, phone or laptop again. Best thing would be for to phone her insurance company. She didn't mention that she didn't have insurance.

Next she stopped at the bank and cancelled her bank cards. She withdrew cash to tide her over until her new bank card arrived.

As she stood in line at the phone provider to cancel her phone and phone contract and buy a new one, she rubbed her arms. They ached where the muggers had grabbed her.

'Here's your new phone, ma'am,' the sales guy said.

'Thanks,' she took the packet and signed the contract. Later she would check for bruising. Right now, she had to get to work.

Chapter 19
Wednesday, 1.35pm

Fortunate looked concerned. 'Maggie, how are you?'

'A bit bruised and battered. Minus a significant number of my belongings. Otherwise fine.'

'You've had some calls. Here's a list.' Fortunate handed her a piece of paper. 'If you're hungry, I still have some rolls left in the fridge.'

'Thanks, Fortunate. I'm okay right now.' Maggie glanced at the list. Chloe had phoned. There was a number she didn't know. She checked her email. Johnny Cupido had sent her the day's proposed story list. Ed was working on his roundabout photo essay. That was good.

She breathed deeply, picked up her desk phone and called Chloe. 'It's Maggie.'

'Hello.' Chloe sounded stiff.

'How's Hope?'

'Really not good. My brother is a doctor. He came to see her this morning. She was ...' she faltered. 'It turns out, she was not raped.' Maggie closed her eyes, and exhaled slowly. 'I am so glad.' That sounded terrible. 'I mean, I am not glad that she was beaten up. Just relieved that they didn't rape her.'

'Me too. Listen, she has bruising and a couple of broken ribs. Worst of all, significant emotional trauma.'

'Is she prepared to report it to the police?'

'Absolutely not. Refuses point-blank. No hospitals, no police.'

'Did she recognise anyone?'

'I haven't asked that. I am just trying to deal with her pain, moment by moment.'

Maggie regretted her question. It was a reporter's question, not a friend's one. 'Can I see her?'

'Well, that's why I've been calling. She keeps asking for you, over and over. I am not particularly keen to see you right now, but Hope insists.'

'I can, but it will be late.'

'No problem. Come when you can.' Chloe put the phone down. She started to read what copy she had, but images of Hope's face last night kept floating into her mind. Chloe's blame chafed against her.

Aslan had submitted a book review, which she checked. It was perfect, not an error in sight. The book sounded boring, though.

Her phone buzzed. It was Naidoo. 'I heard you had an incident. Are you okay?'

'I lost some belongings and a bit of dignity. Otherwise fine.'

'Do you need some time off?'

'No thanks.'

'Okay.' Maggie could hear the relief in Naidoo's voice. 'So while you were gone' – the editor made it sound as though she was out getting a pedicure – 'I had a chat with Johan.'

'Uh huh.'

'He told me that his mother is extremely ill, and he needs some time to look after her. He can't be over-stressed. No outside meetings or research trips to the homes of former gangsters. So I'm taking him off the environment beat. I said you would find something for him to do.'

'And who writes the environment stories?'

'You can, Maggie.'

So now she had to find something for Johan Liebenberg to do while also doing his job. The man was such an irritant. She made her way to the photo studio. Ed was sitting in front of a large screen, looking at images.

'Hi Maggie!' he looked up. 'Just checking out my roundabout pics.'

'Can I see?' She leant over his shoulder. Ed's photos were really good.

'You're an artist,' she said, standing up. 'Who knew Pietermaritzburg's roundabouts could look this good?'

'You flatter me,' he smiled. 'Now, are you here for make-up?'

'Nope, I've decided to own my status as a brawler.'

'I heard you had another altercation today.'

'I was a victim of crime, actually. A mugging.'

'Sorry, man.'

'Listen, do you have any spare work in the photo lab? I have a floating team member.' She told him about Johan.

'We're digitising the photo archives, all the way back to the 1900s. It's a huge job and we need all the help we can get.'

'Thanks, Ed. That's great.' She flopped down on a nearby chair.

'What's up?'

'A woman I know was abducted and beaten up last night,' she told him. 'I think it happened because we quoted her in a story. I feel terrible.'

'That's bad,' Ed acknowledged. He dug in a cabinet and pulled out a bottle. 'Need something medicinal?'

He handed her the bottle. It was a mini of brandy, nothing special. It fired her throat and then her belly.

'Which story?'

'The forest one.'

He pursed his lips and nodded. 'How's that going it?'

'It's not. I seem to hit deadends, every time I think I have a lead.'

'And then after the deadends?'

'What do you mean after?'

'You hit deadends, but weird things keep happening. Follow the weird things. You usually do.'

Ed was right.

For instance, was her mugging that morning a weird thing, or just a coincidence? If someone had mugged her to get their hands on her computer, they would be disappointed. There wasn't much on it but links to motorcycling forums. If they had mugged her as a threat, it hadn't worked either.

Finally, after all the copy was assembled in the vague approximation of a newspaper, she left the office, grabbing one of Fortunate's leftover rolls on the way.

When she got to Hope and Chloe's, there was a figure at the gate. She pulled up, stopped and lifted the visor of her helmet.

'Brad?'

Chloe's former boyfriend shuffled over to Maggie, dressed in a huge overcoat and his ever-present beanie. 'I'm guarding them.'

'Did they ask you to?'

'No, it's a service I am offering voluntarily.'

'Very kind.' Maggie wondered what kind of service Brad would really be able to offer if Hope's attackers returned. 'May I go in?'

'Yes, just wait.' He buzzed the intercom and let Chloe know Maggie was on her way in.

'Before you go, there's something I want you to know.'

'What's that?'

'I've deleted my Twitter account.'

'Well done, Brad.' She started the Chicken and drove down the driveway. There were some people in life who excelled in making themselves the centre of every drama, no matter what.

She parked the bike, took off her helmet and walked to the front door. It was dark now. Maggie knocked. Chloe answered immediately, her face drawn and her eyes full of accusation.

'It's so bad. She's in a terrible state. When she's not sleeping, she's crying. When she's not crying, she's sleeping. She won't talk, won't see anyone. The only person she's asked for is you.'

Maggie followed Chloe in and put her helmet down near the front door.

Hope was lying on the sofa, wrapped in the same blanket as last night. One lamp was on, the rest of the house in darkness. Maggie knelt down next to her and put a hand on her shoulder. Hope's eyes, still puffy and bruised, flickered open.

'Hi.' Maggie said, quietly.

'Hi.' Her voice was tiny, but it was there.

'How are you?'

'I hurt.'

'I know.'

Hope's eyes closed again. Maggie stayed kneeling next to her. Chloe sat in an armchair near to Hope's head. Her hand stroked Hope's head.

'They pulled me into the car and blindfolded me,' Hope said, eyes still closed. Chloe put a hand up over her mouth, tears welling. 'We drove for a while, maybe half an hour. At one point, they opened the car window and threw something out.'

'Her cell phone,' Chloe said. 'It's gone.'

'Then they made me walk through long grass. I could sense sunlight through the blindfold and on my skin. Then they made me walk down some stairs. The place they took me seemed very dark. It was underground or some kind of cave, because the floor was made of earth. I could hear water.'

She sighed. Maggie rubbed her shoulder gently. 'We are here, Hope.'

Hope continued, as if she had not heard Maggie. 'In the car there were two men. I could tell by the voices. Both Zulu. At the cave place, there were more men. I could hear their footsteps as they came down the stairs. They beat me until I was crunched up in a little ball on the floor.'

Her face crumpled. Tears ran down her cheeks. Under her hand, Maggie could feel the tension in Hope's body. As she retold the story, she was reliving the experience and by tensing up, she was protecting herself against the blows and the pain that would come.

Chloe sobbed. Maggie pulled a tissue out of the box on the coffee table and passed it to Chloe. Then she used another tissue to wipe Hope's tears.

'One even kicked me, like a dog.'

Her eyes opened and she looked at Maggie. 'I almost didn't mind the pain. The worst was the fear. I was frightened I would never see Chloe again. I was terrified that they would rape me.'

She sighed. 'Finally, they stopped. One man spoke to me. He said that I was a bad woman and they were punishing me. He said that if I told the police, they would come for my girlfriend.'

'Did they say anything else?'

'Yes, he said I must stop telling people what I know about the butterfly and about the forest. Nobody wanted to listen to me, and I should stop shouting loudly in places because nobody would listen to me when I was dead.'

'Did you recognise his voice?'

'No. He was one from the car, but I didn't recognise him.'

'Were any of them known to you?'

Chloe frowned furiously at Maggie and shook her head. Hope echoed with a slight shake. 'No, none of them.'

Maggie leaned in even closer. 'Hope, I know you were blindfolded, but is there anything you remember about any of these men? Something distinguishing.'

Chloe made frantic slashing motions across her throat. She

didn't want Maggie to pursue this. She just wanted her to listen. It was natural, the urge to protect.

'Nothing at all.'

'And then what happened?' She touched Hope's arm.

'They tied me up and left me. I don't for how long. I thought I was going to die there. I thought I would never—' she choked and the tears flowed down her cheeks— 'I thought I would never see Chloe again.'

Maggie wiped her tears, gently touching her cheeks. Chloe cupped her head. 'And then they came, tightened the blindfold and told me I was going home. I was so scared then, more scared than during the whole day, because I didn't know if I could believe them. It was like they gave me hope, but at any minute they could take that hope away. It was the worst moment of all.'

'My darling,' Chloe whispered.

'They took me up the stairs, and back through the long grass. The warmth of the sun was gone and I knew it was night.'

'Did you hear anything while you were out there?'

'I heard chickens. A few voices in the distance. And then they put me in the car, and drove me here.'

'Did anyone talk in the car?'

'No, there was no talking. No radio, no nothing, just the car sounds.'

Hope closed her eyes again. She didn't open them for a long time. Maggie and Chloe sat in silence and listened to her breath slowly deepen and become regular.

Once she was asleep, Chloe tucked the blanket over her. She looked at Maggie, eyes darkening.

'You see what you did.'

Maggie felt dizzy. 'I'm sorry you feel this way.'

'I do.' Chloe bent over Hope. 'Now, please just go.'

Chapter 20
Thursday, 6.30am

She had not slept well, Chloe's accusation going round and round in her head. There was still no food in her fridge. She found a half-empty packet of spearmint chewing-gum in her backpack. The flavour reminded her of *The Gazette*'s previous news editor, Zacharius Patel. He was a spearmint gum junkie who devoured a couple of packs a day. That had been his only vice.

What would he think of what she was doing now? He would tell her to concentrate on getting the job done and stop messing around with an investigation that was going nowhere. 'Spare us the saviour complex, Maggie,' he used to say, 'and get me a story.'

A black BMW followed her in to *The Gazette*'s parking lot. A window at the back slid down as she pulled off her helmet.

'Ms Cloete, Chief Mjoli can meet with you today,' said Lucky Bean Msomi. 'He has called his elders for a meeting.'

This was the moment where Zacharius Patel would be telling her to back the hell out. She had an office job now, not a reporting job. Then again, Naidoo had asked her to cover for Johan.

'What time?'

'I'll fetch you at 2pm.'

'Okay.'

The window slid up, and Msomi's driver executed a flawless turn in *The Gazette*'s parking lot. The BMW purred away.

She grabbed her second coffee of the day. Her phone rang. It was Christo.

'I might have to take you up on your offer.'

'What do you mean?'

'Alex is really losing it. Last night he went on a rampage, saying he was going to pull the plug on the Forest Keepers, that we were all a bunch of idlers, not properly committed to the cause. Some people walked out. Now we are down to half the numbers.'

'How is he today?'

'I haven't seen him. He's still sleeping. I'm leaving for the shop now.'

'Christo, there is space for you at my place. Just let me know, okay?'

'Okay. So far he doesn't seem too cross with me, but I am sure the time will come.'

The time would come, Maggie thought as she put down the phone. Field was a firebrand, not scared of burning bridges. At some point, something that Christo did would tip him over the edge and he would lose it with her brother. Would Christo be strong enough to handle that? She wasn't sure.

Maggie wrote a to-do list. Apparently leaders made lists. First on the list was a call to Dr Kruger. Second on the list she wrote 'Work'.

At eight she called the doctor. Ina Kruger had looked after Christo in Kitchener Clinic for many years. She knew him well and had been a key part of his release programme.

'Kruger.'

'Dr K, it's Maggie Cloete.'

'Hello, Maggie.' This was Dr K at her effusive best. 'What can I do for you?'

'I have some concerns about Christo. Is now a good time?'

'It is.'

Dr K knew about Alex Field and Christo's living and working arrangements. She had given them her blessing when he had been released from the clinic. Maggie explained that Alex was showing signs of being emotionally unreliable.

'I think it's a bit of a roller coaster living with him.'

'How is Christo coping?'

'He's calm. He sees what's going on with Alex, but he doesn't seem to let it impinge on him.'

'That's a sign of psychological good health. He is aware of another person's behaviour but does not blame himself or get too closely involved.'

'So you would advise me not to be worried?'

'Exactly. You have offered Christo a refuge, and he knows that. If he needs it, he will let you know.'

Next on the list was work. At nine, she went into conference, Johan trailing her.

'Hey, Johan. I've spoken to Naidoo. We've organised you some temporary work in the photo lab. Ed's going to show you around.'

Johan put a warm hand on Maggie's arm. Even through her shirt, she could feel his sweaty palm. 'Appreciate it, Maggie. You and Naidoo are really looking after me.'

'No problem.' Maggie turned to go.

'Can I still come to conference?' Johan asked, looking like a small lost boy. 'At least pretend I am still a journalist?'

He had never really got going as a journalist, but Maggie didn't say so. 'Sure you can.'

After conference, she called Chloe. The academic's voice was cool. 'I don't really want to speak to you.'

'How is Hope?'

'She's still either sleeping or crying, sometimes both at the same time.'

'What are the chances she'll report the attack to the police?'

'None. She refuses. Didn't you hear what she said? She's terrified they'll come for me. She also doesn't believe the police would be much good.'

Maggie could understand that.

'Look Chloe, I know a really good cop. A decent guy. He is working on the forest case already. He could come round and talk to you and Hope.'

'Just drop it. And leave us alone. You caused this and I don't want to talk to you any more.'

Chloe put the phone down. Maggie rested her head in her hands. Then she took refuge in her inbox and the acres of copy.

Mid-morning, Ed messaged her from the photo studio.

How long do I have to have this guy here?

Two to three weeks. Maggie decided blunt was best.

If I don't kill him before.

Why? What's he doing?

He's spent the last two hours telling me how he turned down a position on the board of Sentinel for lifestyle reasons. How they begged and pleaded with him to stay.

He is a nightmare, Maggie wrote. *Just tell him to shut up.*

Can I gag him?
Feel free.

Maggie went back to editing Johnny Cupido's op-ed. He'd done a long interview with the leader of the opposition in KwaZulu-Natal. She was twenty-seven, the daughter of a chief and educated at the London School of Economics. Maggie could tell from Johnny's breathy prose that he was more than a little bit in love with her. She deleted all references to her physical attributes and made a mental note to tell Johnny that length of leg was not a quality to be mentioned in any interview with any politician, male or female.

She grabbed a roll off Fortunate's trolley for lunch. Tuna and watercress. Things were looking up. Downed with a cup of scalding black coffee, it wasn't a bad lunch.

Maggie ate at her desk, getting through as much copy as she could, well aware that she would be heading out shortly on a jaunt with Lucky Bean Msomi. When it was time, she told Fortunate she was going to a meeting, and then stood outside the building. Within seconds, Msomi's BMW slid silently to the kerb. Vincent got out and opened the back door for her. She climbed in.

'Hello, Ms Cloete.' Lucky Bean Msomi gave her his full megawatt smile. He sat in the back, dressed in a navy suit and shiny brown leather brogues.

'Hi.' She sat and buckled herself in. The interior of the car was pale cream leather. It smelled new and expensive.

'How are you?' Msomi asked as the car slid away.

'Just fine. And you?'

'I am well. Disappointed that you are not with your colleague today.'

'Oh.' She remembered Johan's discomfort when they visited Msomi at home. He would have been more than grateful to be spared today's expedition. 'He has other tasks.'

'The Chief would have been happy to see him again. He was part of the Sentinel negotiating team.'

'Really, was he?' Johan had said he had met Msomi during a community meeting. he had not said he was one of the negotiators. The guy was a mess of contradictions. Better known as lies.

'Yes, it was mostly their legal people, but Liebenberg was often there as the communicator.'

Maggie glanced out of the window. They were now on the highway, heading towards Howick. 'What were you negotiating?' 'A settlement.' Msomi's smile grew wider. 'Sentinel paid off the tribe to drop their land claim on Karkloof Extension 7.'

'Is that legal?'

'Perfectly.'

Maggie wasn't sure if it was. It was certainly the way of big business: pay off the small fry who get in your way to ensure that they get right out of it. By buying off the tribe, Sentinel could move without conscience on the forest. Except that, inconveniently, it turned out that their bit of forest was an apartheid graveyard. No one could have predicted that except the people who put the bodies there. They would have done anything to stop the forest being razed.

The car crested the rise at Hilton and the Midlands spread out before them in a bucolic haze of distant mountains and nearer rolling hills, all dressed in shades of winter yellow. Clutches of pine trees made dark gashes on the hillsides, echoed by patches of black where farmers had burned firebreaks. Msomi gazed out of the window.

'Tell me about the chief,' Maggie said. 'What can I expect?'

Msomi turned back to her. 'Mjoli? He is very traditional, very Zulu. He is a member of Contralesa. However, his tribe and chieftaincy are small. He is bitter that the government has mostly ignored him.'

It was rumoured that, during the election process, the government had given handouts to traditional chiefs to ensure their loyalty. If Chief Mjoli had been ignored during elections, then perhaps it was understandable that he had taken his handout from industry instead.

Vincent clicked the indicator and turned off the highway, guiding the car back over the highway bridge towards Howick. Maggie and Msomi were silent as they approached the village. Was this the route Hope had been taken? She talked about water. Did her captors bring her near the Howick Falls?

Maggie looked down at her feet. There were black scuff-marks on the back of the seat, as if someone had been rubbing their shoes against the leather. A captive? Someone as small as Hope could easily have been bundled into the footwell.

She felt a chill go through her. Maybe leaping into Msomi's car and trusting him with her welfare had not been her brightest idea. No one knew where she was.

The car stopped at a traffic light in the middle of town. A beggar knocked on the window, and Msomi waved him away like a fly.

'So much unemployment here. These people have nothing better to do,' he said conversationally.

The car pulled out of town, passing farmlands to left and right. Eventually, the henchman signalled a right turn and they pulled off the main road onto a dirt track. The car bounced over numerous potholes.

Msomi pointed through a screen of eucalyptus trees. 'The village is down there.'

Maggie looked over his shoulder. She could see a collection of modest houses, a mix of rondavels and small modern houses. Each house had a large satellite dish affixed to its roof. As they drew closer, Maggie saw a number of brand-new cars, amongst them a couple of Mercedes.

Vincent parked the car next to one of the Mercs and Msomi climbed out.

'Lucky! Lucky!' There were cries from nearby houses, and three pre-school age children ran out to greet him. Msomi dug into his pockets and gave them each a handful of sweets. They grabbed them and ran off.

Maggie walked round to Msomi's side the of the car. A tall, elderly man approached them and he and Msomi greeted each other in the traditional way, with their left hands resting above their right elbows and a three-part handshake: shake, clutch thumbs, shake again.

'This is Cele,' Msomi told Maggie. 'He is one of Mjoli's headmen.'

Cele inclined his head courteously to Maggie, without offering her his hand. He said something to Msomi in Zulu.

'He will take us to the meeting room. We can wait there for Chief Mjoli to join us. He is busy at the moment, but he will come soon.'

Cele led Maggie and Msomi to the meeting room. It was inside one of the bigger rondavels, dark and windowless. The only light spilled in from the door. Maggie's eyes took a while to adjust. Cele indicated a couple of stools for them to sit on.

'I will be back,' he said.

They sat. Msomi pulled a sweet out of his pocket, unwrapped it and put it in his mouth. As an afterthought, he offered Maggie one. She shook her head.

Slowly, elderly men began to trickle into the room. Each one greeted Msomi with a traditional handshake and Maggie with a nod of the head. They gathered around a large chair set at the head of the room, talking to each other in rumbling tones. Being a headman was not a young man's business. They had all left the village to chase work, she thought. Many had probably died. HIV/AIDS had cruelly targeted the young.

The old men stood and rumbled while Maggie and Lucky Bean Msomi sat and waited. Chief Mjoli was in no hurry to greet his guests. He was either keeping them waiting deliberately or had much more important things to do elsewhere in the village.

As if reading her thoughts, Msomi turned to her and said, 'He will come.'

Maggie didn't doubt that. She just wondered when.

Eventually there was a cough at the door. Msomi stood up as did Maggie. The old men stopped their rumbles and stared respectfully in the direction of their chief. He stopped just inside the door, shadowed against the light.

Msomi moved to greet him, indicating that Maggie should follow. They held a terse conversation in Zulu. The chief nodded at Maggie and then proceeded to his chair. He sat heavily and, in the half-light, she could see that he was a large man dressed in modern clothes, but with a leopard skin slung over his shoulder.

'We welcome our guests,' he boomed. 'We welcome our brother Msomi and we welcome the journalist, Ms Cloete.'

He stared at Maggie and continued.

'Ms Cloete wishes to understand how we exchanged our rights to Karkloof Extension 7 for a financial settlement.'

The old men rumbled behind him.

'Ms Cloete needs to understand that our government has

continuously failed to provide services to the rural areas. Those of us who live here and try to maintain a life of tradition and respect for the African ways do not have the benefit of the infrastructure and services that exist in towns. The government has ignored the tribal ways.'

He coughed again. 'We, as *iikosi* and *iinkosana*, are office bearers and yet we receive no pay from the government. They remunerate politicians, but not us.'

Mjoli leaned forward and pointed a finger at Maggie. 'Take a look at our village! It is a very poor village. Our young have gone. Many have died. We are a village of old people and children. What good is a forest to us? Yes, we can forage there and find food. Yes, we have the pride of saying this forest belongs to us. Yes, we can arrange tours and get tourists to visit, but the forest does not bring our young people back. It does not bring economically active people back to their roots, where they belong.

'When the government ignores rural communities and their needs, the forest is nothing to us but trees. Trees are no good, except for burning.'

He leaned back in his chair, comfortable that he had made his point. He folded his fingers over his belly, hands resting on the leopard skin.

'So we took the offer from the forest company. They offered each of us – me and my iinkosana – some money. This money was owing to us. The government owed it. But because they refused to respect our tenure as traditional leaders, we took the money from another source.'

Maggie glanced at Msomi. 'May I speak?' she asked quietly.

Msomi spoke in Zulu. The chief nodded.

'In exchange for the money the tree company paid you, you have withdrawn your claim on the land?'

'We have,' Chief Mjoli said. 'We have taken the pragmatic approach.' His headmen nodded at this. 'We have chosen funding over years of fighting in the law courts. We still believe that Karkloof Extension 7, and indeed much more of Sentinel's land, rightfully belongs to us. But we have ceded our rights.'

'Is there a time limit on your rights claim?' Maggie asked.

The chief frowned. 'Explain.'

'Did you relinquish your claim forever, or can you reinstate it in, say, ten years' time?'

'We have relinquished our claim. However, there is no saying what our descendants will do when we are dead and gone.'

The chief rumbled with laughter and his headmen followed him. 'In the meantime, we have food to feed these descendants. You see Ms Cloete, it was the only way for us. We could starve and fight a court case, or give up the case and feed our families. We had no choice.'

Maggie wondered how far satellite dishes and spanking new sedans went towards feeding families. The children that had grabbed sweets off Msomi had not looked particularly well fed.

'And what about Sentinel? Do they have a responsibility to your village? Do they hire your people and give them jobs?'

'We have some men at Sentinel.' Chief Mjoli conferred with Cele. 'Yes, we have eleven Sentinel workers in our village. Eleven jobs that we did not have before.'

'But they are not working at the moment,' Maggie said. 'The work in the forest has stopped, because of the police activity. The bodies in the forest.'

The warm atmosphere in the room chilled. The old men went silent and all smiles and friendliness left Chief Mjoli's face. Msomi grabbed her arm in warning.

'Shut up,' he hissed.

'What about the bodies, Chief Mjoli?' Maggie asked. She looked at all the faces, locked down, angry. 'Does anyone in this village know anything about them?'

Chief Mjoli stood. 'Get this woman out of my sight!'

'I am sorry, Chief,' Msomi stammered.

'Get her out!' the chief bellowed.

Msomi grabbed Maggie's arm and ran.

Chapter 21
Thursday, 4pm

'What's wrong?' Maggie asked. 'What did I do?'

'Are you crazy? Trying to get yourself killed?' Msomi still had his fingers around her arm, tight like wire. He pulled her towards the car. Vincent was in the driver's seat revving the engine.

'It's common knowledge that there were bodies in the forest. What's wrong with asking?'

'Maybe some people want to bury the past. Have you not thought of that?' Msomi pulled open the back door of the car and shoved Maggie in. He slammed the door, just missing her foot.

He opened his door and got in. A chicken squawked and churned into the sky, trying to get out from under the car's wheels. Maggie turned to look at the village with its satellite dishes and large sedans. A couple of children made a desultory effort to run after the car, but gave up and waved. She waved back.

She turned to Msomi, who was wiping his face. 'So what's your role in this?'

'I was the negotiator. I helped negotiate the settlement between Chief Mjoli and Sentinel.'

A well-remunerated role, Maggie was sure.

'Where did the meetings take place?'

'Mostly at the Sentinel office. Sometimes in the village.'

'How much money was it?'

Msomi turned and stared at her. A cold, hard stare. 'I am not at liberty to say.'

He dropped her back at work without another word passing between them. Maggie got out and thanked him. He nodded wordlessly and the car slid away.

Maggie headed inside. Fortunate handed her a pile of messages. 'Your brother called. Someone called Jack Lyall calling for the second time in two days.'

Her heart contracted. Jack was Spike's real name, the name he used when he was trying to be professional. What would it be like to talk to him after all these years?

She pocketed the pile and climbed the stairs to the newsroom. First, she read through Aslan's stories. She pushed one on a gallery opening through to the subs for the next day and kept two for the Saturday edition.

She dialled Njima's cell phone. It went to voicemail. She called the police station and got put through to a secretary. 'Captain is not available at the moment.'

'Well listen, you tell Captain that *The Gazette* is running a story on the progress of the forensics on the bodies in the forest tomorrow. If the Captain has any reason to stop the story, he should call me in the next hour.'

She put the phone down, and opened Twitter to check if any other journalists had updates on the forest story. There was nothing. This meant Njima hadn't talked to anyone else.

Her desk phone buzzed. 'Cloete.'

'Maggie, it's Sol here.'

'That was quick. Now I know why they call you Takkies.'

'Very funny.'

'Listen, you said you needed twenty-four hours on the forensics. I am desperate for something new on the forest story. Can I go ahead and write it?'

Njima went silent. Then he said, 'We've finished running the toxicology tests. They died of poisoning.'

'What?'

'Yes. Poisoned. All seven of them. Poisoned, burned and then thrown into a mass grave.'

'Any identification on the bodies?'

'No, this is what's going to take a long time. We're trying to match them against the lists of those who went missing, but, as you know, there are so many.'

'Have you tried Vuyani Mshenge?'

'I got that message, but I didn't understand it. Too cryptic for this cop.'

'My source thinks his body was buried in the mass grave. She suspects he might be one of the Umlazi Seven.'

Njima harrumphed. 'You keep getting information before the police. Is this standard behaviour?'

'Just try the name. So, Captain, are you giving me this for tomorrow's edition?'

'Yes, it's okay. Just don't quote me.'

'From a source in the police department, I get it. Ernest Radebe is going to be furious. You do know that.'

'Ernest Radebe is a pencil-pusher and an idiot. He's already had his press conference and his moment of fame.'

Maggie laughed.

'I like it when you laugh,' he said quietly.

Was Captain Solomon Njima flirting with her?

'How's the bruise?' he asked.

Maggie touched her jaw. 'Less puffy and painful. Listen, Sol, thanks a lot. I'd better get moving on this.'

'You wouldn't want to thank me for the inside info by having dinner with me?' He definitely was flirting with her.

'I would, but not now,' she told him. 'When this story's over, let's have dinner.'

'Okay, but you could have a long wait for my charming company. This one could go on for a long time.'

'I think your charming company is worth waiting for,' Maggie said, before ringing off.

Then she pulled her grown-up boots on and dialled Spike.

'Lyall.'

Her heart softened as she heard his voice.

'Hi Spike, it's Maggie here.'

'Hi Maggie.' He altered his tone as soon as he heard her, made it brusque and businesslike.

'No friendly hello, howzit?'

'Not today.'

Two could play at this game. She could be brusque. 'So. You called?'

'I've been following your Sentinel story.'

'Yup.'

'Nice work. Look, there's a friend of mine in town for a couple of days. He used to work for Sentinel. Says he could shed some light on a couple of things.'

'Great. Where can I meet him?' She scrolled through her inbox. Menzi had produced some fine copy today on the various misdemeanours of the local populace, all hell-bent on murdering, robbing and defrauding each other.

'How about Barry's? Tonight, at 9pm?'

'Barry's Bar? Isn't that a bit noisy and crowded?'

'He says he prefers to hide in plain sight.'

The guy she was meeting at Barry's was called Etienne Schofield, Spike said. She looked him up on LinkedIn, where he was described as professor of plant sciences at Rutgers University. Not bad for a Maritzburg boy.

She bashed out a front page lead on new findings in the bodies in the forest investigation and mailed it to Patti and the subs. She copied Naidoo on the mail, but got an out of office response.

Fatima had a story on clinics in northern KwaZulu-Natal where stocks of antiretrovirals had run out three months before and still not been replaced. Johnny Cupido's piece was on a meeting of the provincial MECs that had broken out into fisticuffs over ticket privileges for a big soccer match.

Maggie signed them all off. Just as she was getting ready to leave and finally get some groceries in, her cell rang. It was Chloe.

'She wants to talk you. She insists.'

'How is she?'

'Following me from room to room. She stands outside the door when I'm on the toilet. She panics if she can't see or hear me.'

Maggie went home for a shower and changed into fresh jeans. She glanced into the fridge. She found a wrinkled apple in the fresh container, cut off the soggy bits and ate that. On the way through town, she stopped at Bugsy's, a well-known student joint, to wolf down a bunny chow and slug a cold-drink. She buzzed at Hope and Chloe's gate a little later. There was no sign of Brad. He had clearly given on up his self-appointed guard duty.

'Hello.' Chloe's voice sounded reedy and vulnerable through the intercom. The gate rattled open. Maggie went down the driveway and parked outside the cottage. Tonight, light poured out of all the windows.

Chloe opened the door. She was wearing the same clothes as yesterday and there were black bags under her eyes. She shook her head at Maggie's unspoken question.

Maggie walked in. Hope was sitting up on the couch, the blanket draped around her shoulders.

'Is he still out there?' she asked Maggie.

'You mean Brad?'

'Yes, him.'

'No, he's gone actually.'

'Good,' Hope said. 'I don't trust him. I'm glad he's gone.'

She was right. There was no reason to trust Brad. He was the keeper of his ego, and everything and everyone else was secondary to that.

Maggie sat down next to Hope. She put a hand on her arm. 'How are you doing?'

Hope turned to look at her. A fire burned in her eyes. 'Angry. So fucking angry. If someone gave me a knife and one of those guys, I would murder him with no compunction.' She turned to Chloe. 'And I think I would enjoy it.'

Chloe sat in the armchair, hands folded between her knees. She rocked slightly as if this was not new to her. Maybe the conversation had taken this turn already today. Perhaps more than once.

'I just want them gone,' Hope declared. 'Gone from this earth.'

Her eyes lit. 'I know! I should ask Dumi. He used to have some underworld connections. He could find a hitman for me.'

'You feel like you want to take revenge,' Maggie said.

'I do! I can't sit around here, waiting to get better, to feel normal again, without doing something.'

'I can't help feeling—' Chloe began, but Hope interrupted. 'Dumi knows all kinds of people. He is connected. He can help me.'

'We do need to identify them first,' Maggie said gently. Chloe frowned at her for entertaining Hope's fantasy, but she nodded back.

'That's true,' Hope said.

'And the best way to do that is via the police.'

Hope sank back into the sofa. 'I can't do that. They said they would come for Chloe if I reported it.'

Maggie looked at Chloe. 'Can you get time off work?'

'Yes, I have compassionate leave. My brother has written Hope off for a month. The winter holiday starts in three weeks. Altogether, we have about six weeks. Why?'

'How about you report to the police and then disappear? I'm sure Brad would make his Ballito beach cottage available to you.'

'What do you think, Hope?'

'Right now, I want to report the fuckers and murder them, preferably at the same time. Tomorrow, I'm going to be lying in bed crying, too scared to go to the toilet.'

'What if we act today then?' Maggie said. 'I can get the cops here in ten minutes. Chloe can talk to Brad about the cottage. What do you think?'

Chloe leaned in and whispered something in Hope's ear. Hope listened, nodding. 'Okay, but I need to know we have the cottage first, before you call the police.'

Chloe got up to find her cell phone and call Brad. Maggie could hear her talking in the bedroom.

Hope took Maggie's hand and lay back on the sofa. 'How did I become the victim, Maggie? That sickens me more than anything. All the things women hear: keep safe, dress sensibly, don't go out at night alone, let someone know where you are going. I didn't break any of the rules. It was morning, I was wearing jeans, Chloe knew where I was, I have a five-minute walk from here to varsity that I have done safely for the last five months. I just don't get it.'

'I think it means the rules are a crock of shit,' Maggie said. 'They picked you out for a reason, Hope. You spoke out and they decided to cut you down. Simple as that. Women with voices are dangerous.'

'But to whom? Who is threatened by me?'

'People with an interest in the status quo. Because the status quo pays big bucks.'

Chloe came out of the bedroom. 'We have the cottage. Brad is bringing the key now. He is going to drive there with us in convoy, spend the night and come back tomorrow.'

Hope stiffened. 'He'd better stay far away from me.'

'He will,' Chloe said. 'Now, I'll just pack us some things.'

Maggie called the police station. Luckily Njima was still on duty. 'Have you called to accept my offer?' She could hear the smile in his voice.

'No, not yet. But I do have a request.'

She stood up and walked away from Hope, down the corridor to the bedroom. 'Sol, remember the abduction victim I told you about? She is ready to make a statement right now, but she might lose courage if she has to wait.'

'Can she come in?'

'She's in a bad way emotionally. If you could come here, it would really help her.'

'Give me the address.'

Maggie gave him Hope and Chloe's address and went into the sitting room. Hope wasn't on the sofa. She found her curled up on the bed watching Chloe pack.

'He's on his way.'

'Okay,' Hope said in a small voice. A tear trickled from her eye and traversed her cheek to touch the pillow. 'I'm really scared.'

'Darling.' Chloe put down the jeans in her hand and climbed onto the bed with Hope. She lay behind her and held her tightly.

'I'll go and wait for them.' Maggie stepped out to give Chloe and Hope their privacy.

She sat in their sitting room, a haven of calm. Only Chloe's quiet voice and Hope's sobs gave any indication of the horror that had struck them, their peaceful life destroyed. Now they were about to report the crime, to tie their names to police dockets that would dog them forever.

Hope would always be the academic who was abducted and beaten. Chloe would always be the academic whose partner was abducted and beaten.

A bell rang and Maggie got up to answer it. She found the intercom with a video screen at the front door. There was a car outside, some kind of four-wheel drive. She could make out the burly shoulders of Solomon Njima at the wheel. She pushed the button and watched the gate slide open. She stepped outside and waved as the car came down the driveway. Njima parked next to the Chicken, his giant SUV dwarfing her bike.

He stepped out. 'This nifty ride belong to you?'

'It does.'

He whistled, a breathy intake. 'Nice.'

Maggie led the way into the cottage. Chloe and Hope sat on the sofa, holding hands. Hope's blanket was safely tucked around her.

'Hope, Chloe, this Captain Njima. Sol, Hope Phiri and Chloe Steyn.'

Njima shook hands with the two women and then sat in the armchair.

'Are you okay?' he asked. Hope nodded and then shook her head. She brushed away a tear.

'What are you feeling right now is like nothing you have ever felt before,' the detective said. 'It feels huge and overwhelming, but I promise you, you are bigger than this. And we—' he indicated Chloe and Maggie '— are going to help you.'

Hope nodded again, tears falling freely down her cheeks. Chloe moved the tissue box from the coffee table to her knee so that Hope could reach them.

'Now, in your own time, tell me what happened. I will take notes and afterwards I will ask you to read them and see if you would like to make any changes. Now, Ms Phiri, start on the day that it happened.'

Maggie leaned against the kitchen counter and listened as Hope told her story again. Even the second time around, it did not make for easy listening. Njima took notes as Hope spoke. Occasionally, he interrupted her to ask a question or clarify something.

Then he read Hope's report back to her. 'Is there anything you want to change?'

'No. It is correct.'

'And the subject of threat is that if you reported this to the police, they would attack your partner.'

'Yes,' Hope said.

'Which is why you have taken a few days to come forward?'

Hope nodded. Chloe explained that they were leaving town that night. She gave him her cell phone number and the address of the beach cottage.

'When you are back in town, please let us know,' Njima said. 'We might be able to organise some police presence outside the house.'

'Thank you,' Chloe said.

Njima stood up to go. 'We will be in touch via Ms Steyn's cell phone if we have any news or if we need you to come to the station.'

Maggie walked outside with him.

'An intelligent woman,' Njima said. 'Very clear thinking. If this ever comes to court, she will make an excellent witness for the prosecution.'

'If,' Maggie repeated.

'You know it isn't very likely,' he smiled down at her, almost in apology. 'since she was blindfolded the whole time.'

'Sure it isn't likely. But there is a clear link from this case to Sentinel. And a clear link from Sentinel to Dave Bloom's death.'

'Which was suicide.'

'Say some people,' Maggie retorted. She folded her arms.

Njima bleeped the car open but did not climb in. He hovered over Maggie, irritatingly tall and handsome.

'My offer for tomorrow night still stands.'

'I won't forget,' she told the policeman and then watched his retreating back as he got into the cab of his unnecessarily huge car. He leaned out of the window as he reversed.

'Some day I want a ride on that.' He pointed to the Chicken.

'I won't let you anywhere near it.'

Chapter 22
Thursday, 9.30pm

Maggie pulled off her helmet and walked into Barry's Bar. She was now over half an hour late, so she was not sure if Spike and the visiting professor would still be there. The Thursday night crowd was well on its way to extreme, raucous drunkenness. There were hoots of laughter as bodies pushed against each other in the fight to get to the bar.

'Maggie.' Spike materialised at her shoulder. He was at least half a head shorter than Sol Njima. 'You're here.'

'Sorry I'm late. I got caught up in something.'

'What can I get you?' Spike's usually genial face was serious, but his eyes were still the same sparkling green. Just that they were not sparkling at her.

'A beer would be good.'

'Etienne's through the back. I'll get drinks and find you.'

How long would Spike play cool with her? His natural tendency was to extreme gregariousness, but tonight he was impersonating an iceberg.

Maggie walked in the direction Spike had indicated. The crowded front room of Barry's gave way to a second, smaller room that was a couple of decibels quieter. She hadn't noticed this space on Monday when she'd been here with Aslan.

She recognised Schofield from his LinkedIn profile. His was in his fifties and balding.

'Maggie Cloete, from *The Gazette*, how do you do?'

'Etienne Schofield. Pleased to meet you.' He had a faint South African accent, now overlaid with an American twang.

'So you're at Rutgers?'

'Yes. I lecture in plant studies there.'

'Spike tells me you're a former Sentinel employee.'

The man's face darkened. 'Yes.'

'Did you know Dave Bloom?'

'Yes, he joined Sentinel shortly after me. We were both scientists, both environmentalists at heart, and so glad and grateful to get jobs in an industry that kept us tied to the great outdoors.'

Spike returned, putting drinks on the table. 'I see you've met each other.'

'Sure have.' Schofield lifted his glass of red wine in a toast. 'Great to have a glass of good Cape red. Wine is so expensive in the States, I hardly drink it.'

Maggie raised her beer and sipped it. After hearing Hope's story again tonight, she needed the kick of alcohol. The yeasty flavour was satisfying, like liquid bread.

'So you were saying about the early days at Sentinel?' she prompted Schofield. Anything to ward off his oh-poor-me-the-expat line. She had zero sympathy for his lack of fine reds. And she really didn't want to hear how expensive and difficult life was overseas. Being abducted and beaten by a gang of thugs was difficult. Cold winters were not.

'Yeah, I came from plant sciences, and he came from a more general environmental background, but when Dave joined, we quickly found common ground. We were really grateful and happy to work at such a great company. And I thought it was,' he turned to Spike, who nodded. 'I really did.'

Maggie shrugged. She had never worked in a corporation and never intended to. What corporate people had in common was a tendency to believe their company's own PR.

'What was it doing then that was so great?'

'Then it was taking empty or degraded wasteland and planting plantations. We thought it was wonderful: regeneration, job creation, giving back to the communities, all that.'

'But it was always a paper milling company, right?'

'Sure, it was. But we saw that as a necessary evil while we were saving the planet.'

'How were you saving the planet?

'We honestly believed that by growing plantations on wasteland, we were at least redeveloping land and repaying carbon debt.'

Maggie remembered the professor and his lively description of the difference between real live forests and plantations.

'And the scales fell from your eyes when?'

Spike lifted his eyebrows. The old Spike would have kicked her under the table. Now he just gave her a cool, appraising look.

'When we saw a drop-off in paper prices. In order to maintain revenue, the company started growing more plantations. In this case, they didn't just use wastelands; they started buying up the grasslands. These are South Africa's natural heritage, packed with flora and fauna, just humming with life. They would slash and burn them and then plant alien trees. We started to see the number of grassland species fall, and the whole biomass replaced by a monoculture – an alien, invasive monoculture that destroyed everything in its path.'

'And did you do something about it?'

'Yes, Dave and I both motivated strongly to management to stop. I joined an environmental group and wrote pamphlets. At that stage, they were also letting workers go. I spoke to the paper workers' union. I thought we could work together.' He stopped and sipped his wine.

'Dave and I went to a first meeting with the union. We discovered that they had a different, more urgent issue. Because of the pulp-mill pollutants, a lot of them were getting sick: cancer, heart disease, infertility, all kinds of things, that they – and later we – believed were a direct result of the chemicals used in the mills.'

Maggie thought back to the lunch at Sentinel on Tuesday and Max Govender telling her about the MD of the Pietermaritzburg mill who had died recently of some kind of cancer. Lifelong exposure, perhaps, to the chemicals?

'Did you take this to management?'

'Sure we did. As soon as possible. We were starting to see the environmental impact upstream and downstream. And the company, caught in the middle, obsessed, as companies are, with making profits. We took it to them.'

'What did they do?'

'They offered the union an across-the-board pay raise, and better medical care.'

'And you and Dave?'

'Dave got offered a shiny new job in marketing. They were

interested in a new kind of forestry certificate to show that the plantations were carbon neutral. He got to sell that campaign to the willing and credulous public.'

'What about you?'

'Well our MD offered me a job on a special project.'

Maggie glanced at Spike. His eyes were conscientiously trained on Schofield.

'How special?' she asked.

'We always knew Sentinel had a lab within a lab. He pulled me aside and offered me the chance to work there, doing research into the effects of certain toxins. It was highly secret and I would be highly paid.'

'What kind of chemicals?'

Schofield drained the dregs of his wine, then put the glass down firmly on the table. 'These toxins were not chemicals.'

'Biological?'

He nodded. 'Indeed.'

'But why would a forestry company get involved with research into biological poisons?'

'That's what I wanted to know.'

'And what did you find out?'

'The guy was a member of the Broederbond. He was offering certain high-up members of the government our research facilities in return for favours.'

'What kind of favours?'

'Access to land that Sentinel could turn into plantations, logging permits, fewer obstacles in buying up pristine grasslands. That kind of thing.'

Maggie shook her head. 'I don't believe it.'

Spike looked down at his hands. 'People think that the present government is corrupt. Let's just say they have nothing on the previous lot. Evil personified.'

'What did you do about the offer?' she asked Schofield.

'I turned it down.' He sighed. 'But I was told in no certain terms if I didn't shut up and take the role they offered me, they, quote unquote, could not guarantee the safety of my family in the unstable nature of South African society.'

'They threatened you?'

'Absolutely. A bald and barefaced threat.'

'What did you do?'

'We got the hell out. My wife, three kids and I were on the plane to London that week.'

Maggie looked at the pleasant-faced man in front of her. He didn't look like someone who had been the victim of industrial espionage. He just looked like a normal guy with a penchant for red wine.

'I got a job as a junior lecturer at Middlesex. My wife worked as a secretary. Kids went to state schools. It was tough.'

'I'm sure.'

He looked around the room. 'And I'm not particularly happy to be back. I always have an uncomfortable feeling when I'm here.'

'Why are you back?'

'My mother is dying.' Maggie regretted her earlier feelings of irritation with him.

'So have you seen Natalie Bloom?'

'I called once. She couldn't wait to get off the phone. It's like I'm tainted.' He pursed his lips, looked resigned. 'Sentinel are the ones who should be tainted, not me.'

'So what do you think happened to Dave?'

He put his fingers on either side of the wineglass. 'I've been out of touch with Dave for years. The old Dave would never have killed himself. He was a positive person, did everything for his family, including taking that crap job in marketing.'

'But he became an advocate for the Karkloof Blue. That was something.'

'Sure. But it's quite easy to hide behind a minor environmental cause. There's a kind of safety there.'

'Did he hide?' Maggie mused. Everything everyone had said about Dave Bloom suggested he was no wilting flower. She turned to Spike, who had remained silent throughout the conversation. 'How about you? What's your take on Dave?'

'Like many, I can't believe he killed himself. As Etienne says, he was the kind of guy to accept a dull job in order to be there for his family. I just don't see him leaping off a waterfall.'

'Then maybe he was involved in something else? Maybe he had come across something that was genuinely threatening to the company?'

'Like what?'

'Bodies, maybe? Seven people, who died of poisoning a long time ago and whose bodies had been hidden in a forest. Maybe that's what he knew about. Or a secret lab?'

Schofield got up. 'Need to get going, I'm afraid. Nice to meet you Maggie.'

She shook his hand and watched him go. Then she turned to Spike, 'Can I get you another beer?'

He looked at her, the green eyes serious. 'Sure.'

She brought back two bottles and sat down next to him. He had picked the labels off the two empties on the table. Spike turned to her. 'You look exactly the same.'

'I presume that's a compliment.'

'Sure it is. Haven't you seen what's happening to our generation? They're all getting fat and turning into versions of their parents.'

Maggie didn't want to talk about parents. Especially not his.

'How are your children? Your wife? I'm sorry; I don't know their names.'

'They're great.' Spike pulled out his cell phone, and showed her a picture. 'That's them at the game reserve. Sue and the three little ones – Mark, Gemma and little Oscar. We've just come back from Hluhluwe; great trip.'

'They look lovely.' To her surprise, she was able to say this with complete sincerity.

'They are.'

He sighed, then lifted his eyes to hers. Electricity sparked down her spine.

'So what brings you back to town? Last I heard you were never coming back to this hellhole.' A half-smile played at his lips. Those might have been words she'd thrown at him.

'I've got a desk job at *The Gazette* so I can keep an eye on my brother's rehabilitation. The doctors wanted me here since he has no other family around. Chris Cloete – I think you've met him.'

'Sure – he's in the Forest Keepers, with Alex Field. What's he rehabbing from?'

'A long stint in Kitchener Clinic. PTSD, alcohol abuse, paranoid delusions, extreme depression.'

'I remember now.' During their time together, she had told Spike about Christo. 'But when I met him, I didn't put two and two together. He seems so sorted.'

'He is,' Maggie said, with a wave of pride. 'So I am here for a bit, but it's not permanent. I've still got my place in Joburg.' Joburg really was her place. The city's frenetic heartbeat had become her own.

'Also,' she said, 'my son is there.'

'Hey, that's great!' Spike smiled, for the first time that evening. 'I had no idea you had a kid. How old is he?'

'Eleven.'

'Great age,' he said. 'Old enough to do fun things with, but not so old that you're the most embarrassing person on earth.'

Yes, and lucky Joachim was getting to spend time with Leo while she fought provincialism and petty-mindedness at *The Gazette*.

'So I hear it's more than a desk job, Maggie,' he said.

'Ja, I'm news editor, but it's killing me. I'm not meant for office work. I need to be out there, in the field, investigating.' She sighed. 'And being a manager sucks. Some of the journalists are decent. But some are a nightmare.'

She told him about Johan Liebenberg: the boasting about his corporate job, the inability to get even a basic news story out the door, the disappearing to look after his mother.

'Show me this bozo,' Spike said.

'Hang on,' she smiled as she flicked to LinkedIn to show him. Bozo was one of his favourite insults. To be a bozo in Spike's world was to be complete and outright idiot in anyone else's.

'Here you go,' she flashed her phone's screen towards him.

'Jesus,' he said, leaning in and squinting at the screen. 'Maggie, that guy's not Johan Liebenberg.'

'What do you mean?' she said, staring at Liebenberg's familiar pasty face.

'His name is Marius van Heerden. When I was at Stellenbosch, he was outed as a police spy who had infiltrated NUSAS. He vanished overseas, but I see he's come back and reinvented himself.'

Chills coursed up and down her spine. What in God's name was former apartheid police spy doing in *The Gazette*'s newsroom?

Chapter 23
Thursday, 10pm

Maggie said goodnight to Spike and headed home, her head spinning. On top of all the information Schofield had given her, she couldn't get her mind around Liebenberg. Once a spy, always a spy. Who was his spymaster now?

She parked the Chicken under a carport and took the stairs two at a time to the second floor. The corridor to her apartment was well-lit and she knew immediately who the figure slumped against her front door was.

'Christo.'

'Hi Maggie.' He stood up and ran a hand through his hair. 'You said I could come and crash here.'

'Course you can. Always.' She put the key in the lock and glanced at her brother as she pushed the door open. 'Alex have a bad day?'

'Crazy one. I told him I can't take it any more, so he fired me.'

'Oh shit, Christo, that's bad.' Disaster scenarios ran through her head: unemployment, alcohol, return to the clinic.

As they got inside, Christo said, 'Maggie, I need you to stop playing the big sister. You've done nothing but patronise me since I got out of hospital. I would like to stay here, but on condition that you treat me as a fully functioning adult.'

She sighed. 'Agreed. And apologies for my behaviour before. It was only out of concern and love.'

'I get that. But I've had enough of the china doll treatment.'

Maggie looked into the fridge. 'I can't offer you any food.'

'No problem. I ate at the Wimpy earlier.'

She looked in the cupboard. 'I have some instant coffee.' She opened the lid and looked inside. 'Looks okay.'

'Maggie, seriously, I'm fine.'

She slumped on the sofa next to him. 'So how bad was it?'

Alex had first lost it at home about someone drinking his organic rooibos tea. Then he shouted at everyone in the commune for some imagined grains of dirt in the bathroom. At work, he had made Christo unpick some perfectly straight seams in a new pair of boots. And lastly, he had yelled at him for not putting the shop phone to voicemail while he was out at lunch, even though Alex was in the shop.

'I told him he was out of line. Then he told me I was fired, and I should fuck off. So I did.'

'You left him alone in the shop?'

'Yup.'

Maggie laughed. One of Alex's stipulations was that Christo permanently man the shop so that Alex could attend to some of his lifestyle needs. These apparently included sitting in cafes with his laptop, visiting other shop owners to pass the time of day, and going for languid and boozy lunches at the Tatham Cafe.

'So it sounds like Alex did some actual work today,' she said.

'He did. Which means he's going to be even more pissed off with me.' Christo yawned.

Maggie got up and pulled two towels out of a drawer. 'The second bedroom's all yours. I'm going for a quick shower, and then I'm going to crash.'

When she woke the next morning, Christo was still fast asleep. She threw on some jeans and a pair of takkies, and took a brisk walk to the nearest cafe where she bought some bacon, eggs and milk. By the time he woke up, she was frying breakfast in the kitchen.

'Appreciate the hospitality, sis,' Christo said, crunching bacon.

'Can't have you starving as well as unemployed.'

'Hilarious. Is there anything I can do for you today?'

Maggie stared at him. 'You mean, domestically?'

'Sure.'

'Well if you feel like going to Spar and getting a few groceries, that would be great.' Maybe her housekeeping fairy had arrived after all. She just hadn't expected him to be six foot tall and muscly.

'Can I do one last big-sister deed?'

'Okay.'

She explained how her Golf was in police lock-up after her

arrest in the forest and she had started using the Chicken again. 'I want you to have it.'

'Thanks, Maggie. I appreciate that.'

As she put her helmet on to drive to work, she again felt the weight of last night's information. She missed Jabu, and their teamwork. Two heads were always better than one. She made a mental note to call him and find out how he was doing. The knowledge that she had gathered around Dave Bloom's death was starting to overwhelm her, not least Spike's conviction that Johan Liebenberg was a former police spy. There was no sign of him in the newsroom, and Fortunate told her he had a day's leave to take his mother to hospital.

An email from Naidoo awaited her.

I gave you strict instructions not to cover the forest story without my express permission and once again you have deliberately and maliciously ignored my requests. I am beginning to have second thoughts about this relationship, Maggie, as I cannot have insubordination on my staff. How can you be a leader of people if you yourself cannot be led? Please see me at 10am. Yours, Tina

That was ugly. She racked her brains. Naidoo had asked her lay off the forest story, but she had also asked her to cover for Johan. In Maggie's mind, covering for Johan meant covering the forest story, but it clearly did not in Naidoo's. She was in for a bollocking.

She went to the kitchen to get her coffee and met Patti.

'Naidoo's in a rage again.'

Patti sipped the toxic office coffee. 'Getting into trouble with Naidoo seems to be your speciality.'

'I have trouble with bosses full stop.'

Patti walked out of the kitchen smirking, clearly thinking of her windfall in the office betting pool.

While she waited for her meeting with the editor, she googled Marius van Heerden. A person of that name had been outed at Stellenbosch in the late eighties as a police spy. He had infiltrated a student organisation and reported back on their activities to the police. There were no photos. In the pre-digital age, anonymity had been a breeze.

At ten, Maggie knocked on Naidoo's door. There was silence,

so she waited. After a couple of minutes, she knocked again and cracked the door open. Naidoo was on the phone. She put up her hand imperiously. Maggie closed the door.

After ten minutes, Naidoo opened it. 'Come in.'

Maggie sat in the chair opposite the editor's desk.

'I feel we have already been here,' Naidoo said. 'Just last week. This is getting both boring and tedious, Maggie. At what point does it sink in? I am the editor, not you.'

'I copied you when I sent the story to Patti,' Maggie began. 'And I got an out of office.'

'At which point, you pick up the phone and call me.'

'Fortunate said you were at a reception.'

'Even if I am at a reception. You call me and say, "I'm thinking about changing the lead to this story about bodies in the forest. Is that okay, dear Tina?"'

'If it's any comfort, my phone has been ringing off the hook all morning from stringers and editors around the country wanting to find out where my tip-off came from.'

Naidoo gave her a cold stare. 'It is of no comfort, Maggie. Zero. Right now, your scoop is meaningless to me. Especially since I have had both Xolani Mpondo and Timothy Richardson shouting at me on the phone again this morning. We are at an intensely sensitive point in our paper price negotiation with Mpondo's company. We cannot afford to piss him off again. If that happens, there will be no newspaper for you to write your scoops for. Understand?'

Maggie nodded.

'So,' Naidoo stood up. 'This is an official warning. Stay off the forest story. Do not – and I mean do not – report on Sentinel, the forest or any bodies without my express permission beforehand. If you disregard this, you will be fired on the spot. Timothy Richardson is behind me on this. I have his full back-up.'

'OK,' Maggie stood too.

Naidoo paused, clearly expecting some kind of apology. Maggie wasn't sorry. She had done her job, and done it well. Should she tell Naidoo Spike's contention that Liebenberg was a spy? She decided to hold onto that information. Its time would come.

Naidoo shook her head, her shiny hair a waterfall all the way down her back. 'What are you waiting for? Get out there and run a paper, please.'

She put on her designer reading glasses and sat down. Maggie left the room. Now that Christo was unemployed, she couldn't jeopardise her job. But she was an investigative reporter. She couldn't stop investigating. It would be like asking her to stop breathing.

She would investigate, but she would not write anything. She opened her email and looked at the floods of mails. People were begging to know who had tipped her off. Maybe, if the worst came to the worst, she could go back to being a stringer. Here at *The Gazette* the kind of work she was good at, the investigative journalism that meant quiet digging, talking to people, following leads, was not respected. This was not a gig that was going to last. She would need to move on, soon.

Maggie felt rattled and distracted all day. She wondered how Hope and Chloe were doing at the beach. She thought of Etienne Schofield, looking over his shoulder while sitting at his mother's deathbed. She thought of Dave Bloom, cold and naked, standing on the edge of the Howick Falls, desperate and vulnerable. She thought of the plump chief and his elderly minders and the village children running next to Msomi's car, their hands outstretched for food.

It was a horrible, sordid mess, and sitting right in the middle of it, smug as a cat, was Xolani Mpondo. He was the reason why she couldn't write interesting leads about bodies in the forest, and she suspected that he or someone in his company was responsible for Dave's death and Hope's abduction.

She read people's stories, edited them, asked questions, asked for new intros or second paragraphs, discussed with Patti what should go where and where the gaps were, read the wires to find copy to fill those gaps and plugged them. The main story, which should have been a follow-up from yesterday's lead on the poisoned bodies, was a story that Menzi found at court about train theft. Someone had attempted to steal goods from a train carriage between Pretoria and Durban. And this was the news of the day. It was nauseating.

Then she picked up the phone.

'Does the offer of dinner still stand?'

'Sure it does,' said Sol Njima, his voice warm at the sound of hers. 'I'll make a reservation and email you the details.'

Maggie signed off her work and went home. She was not one to primp before a meal with a man, but she could change out of her sweaty work clothes into something fresher. Christo was home, eating cereal in front of the TV. It felt like being thrown back twenty years, a starving teenage brother wolfing down cornflakes after rugby training.

'All okay?'

'Mmmhmm,' he said through a mouthful of muesli. 'Alex phoned. He wants me back at work.'

'Couldn't take the actual work all by himself?'

'Think so.'

'And? Will you accept his offer?'

'Ja, I'll go back on Monday. I need the job. Plus he's not such a bad oke. But Maggie?'

'Ja?'

'I think I'd rather live here for a bit, if that's okay. It was getting too intense being around Alex all the time.'

'What a great idea.' She leaned over and gave her brother a hug. 'You are so welcome here.'

She showered and changed her jeans. 'I'm heading out. Are you going to be okay?'

'Just fine. After being at Alex's and always having people around, it's quite a relief to be on my own for a bit.'

He pulled his laptop onto his lap. 'Just have a bit of research to do.'

Chapter 24
Friday, 8pm

Maggie shrugged on her leather jacket and grabbed her helmet. Njima had emailed her to say he had booked a table at the Tatham Cafe. It was the hangout of hipsters in the mould of Alex Field and Brad MacKenzie, the kind of place that did fiddly bits of food dotted with tiny flowers and things drizzled on it. Not her kind of place at all.

Njima had probably booked it thinking it was the sort of restaurant women liked, not knowing her preference for heart-clogging, stomach-distending junk food.

She parked in the lot and walked up the gracious steps of the art gallery. The City Hall rose in front of her in its red-brick glory. Town was sleeping now. Darkness had fallen on all the soft hills. While it appeared peaceful and innocent, behind closed doors, in alleyways, in boardrooms, in the City Hall itself, in shacks, on farms, people were doing things to other people. Bad things.

As a journalist, she could separate herself from the relentless drum-beat of crimes committed and regard them as stories that had to be written, deadlines that had to be met. But after twenty years of covering people's inhumanity to other people, it had begun to exhaust her.

Her attempt at management was not working out well. Where would she go next? Would she fling herself back into the fray? She had seen many journalists move into corporate PR and lose their spirit. She could never write lies for a corporation. Teach maybe? Write a book? They all seemed like soft options. Perhaps she was addicted to the relentless rhythm, so much so that everything else seemed second best beside it.

'Waiting for me?' Solomon Njima appeared out of the darkness, broad shoulders wrapped in a trench coat. The police station was just around the corner; he had probably walked.

'Just pondering my future,' she glanced at him, not for too long, as he looked too good. 'My job is looking dicey.'

'But you're a prize-winning journalist,' he said. '*The Gazette* should be happy to have you.'

They walked in and up the stairs to the restaurant.

'*The Gazette* doesn't want me as a newshound, *The Gazette* wants me as a back-office manager.'

'And how is that working out?'

'Not well.' A waiter showed them to their table. Maggie ordered a beer and Njima ordered water.

'Not a drinker?'

'No,' he smiled. 'My father drank. He was a mean bastard. I swore as a kid that I never would, and I never have.'

'I admire your determination.'

He shrugged. 'I didn't want to become what he became.'

Maggie's beer arrived and she took the first sip. It tasted gorgeous.

'I have to admit,' she said, 'no sip tastes better than the first one.'

'So you could stop right there.' He leaned in and curled a hand around her glass. 'I could take away this glass and you would be fine, because you've had that wonderful first sip.'

'You could do that, but then I'd have to punch you.'

He clapped his hands together and laughed. 'Always the pugilist. I'll never forget the look on that guy's face the other night when you knocked him down. He couldn't believe what had happened to him.'

'He was abusing my friends. And look what happened to Hope – kidnapped, beaten. You know what the worst thing is? She has been through this terrible trauma, but people keep expecting her to be grateful that she wasn't raped. Is that where we are in this country now?'

The waiter appeared. 'Are you ready to order?'

'Let me see.' Maggie picked up the menu and looked for the heartiest thing she could find. 'I'll have the beef curry, please, extra hot.'

Njima ordered a steak. He closed his menu and handed it to the waiter.

'Why do men rape? I just don't get it.'

'Why do men rape? That's a big question for a first date.'

'This is a date?' Maggie smiled. 'I had no idea.'

'Sure it is,' he said, sipping his water. 'In this country, men rape because they want to get their power back. They have spent their lives being disempowered – by apartheid, but probably also by their fathers and grandfathers, in some cases their mothers. They are told they are useless, worthless, no good. They have no money, no love, no power. They find power in the eyes of other men when they drink, when they fight and when they rape.'

'So it's about power in the eyes of other men.'

'Yes, that is why we have gang-rape.'

'Do they feel powerful afterwards?'

'No, they find that it is fleeting, which is why they will probably rape again.'

'It makes me sick,' she stared down in the golden liquid of her beer. 'I can't imagine what so many women in this country go through. It's a rape epidemic, just so that some pathetic men can feel power for a few short seconds.'

He went silent. Their food arrived and Maggie was happy to see that hers was a large portion that did not involve tiny flowers, minute morsels or drizzling. There were hunks of beef in a mighty curry sauce with a generous portion of rice. She attacked it with gusto.

'So I want your opinion on something,' she said as she chewed.

'Go ahead.'

'It's a bit of a long story.'

'I don't mind.'

'A long time ago, a guy called Dave Bloom and a colleague of his became aware that not only were Sentinel's plantations damaging the environment, but so were their paper mills. And the damage was not only to the environment but to the workers who laboured in the mills. Many of them were getting ill, with cancer and lung diseases. Dave and his colleague started to partner with the paper mill workers' union in order to force Sentinel to start facing up to the environmental hazards its industry created. They approached management. The workers got a raise and better medical care, so they dropped the case.'

Njima listened, focused.

'Dave got shipped to a nothing job in marketing, but the

colleague received an interesting offer. He was given the chance to work in a secret lab at Sentinel testing biological agents.'

'Did he do it?'

'No, he refused. Then he got death threats against his family so he left the country.'

The cop shook his head. 'I find this hard to believe.'

'Skip forward many years, and Dave Bloom slips, jumps or is forced over Howick Falls while naked in the middle of a winter's night. He had moved on at work to do research into better solvents, and was motivating to save the Karkloof Blue, a butterfly whose habitat and existence is threatened by Sentinel's intention to raze the natural forest where it lives. A group of environmentalists protest the proposed logging of the forest, but apart from them – and Dave Bloom – no one seems to care. The local community, which has had a land claim on the forest, has been bought off following negotiations with Sentinel.

'A PhD student whose speciality is the Karkloof Blue speaks to the local press and is quoted in the story saying the logging of the forest is bad for the butterfly and for the environment. She is abducted and beaten to a pulp and warned to keep her mouth shut.'

Njima sliced off a piece of steak, and put it in his mouth. His eyes were fixed on her face in a way that might make someone else feel awkward but was comforting to Maggie. She continued.

'Logging is stopped because workers find seven bodies in the forest. These have been there for nearly two decades, and appear to have been poisoned. The bodies could be those of anti-apartheid activists. When a local journalist writes this up as a lead story, the MD of the company phones her editor and the paper's CEO to complain, saying that the story puts their paper price negotiations in jeopardy. The reporter is told not to report on the story any longer without her editor's express permission.'

He nodded.

'So, what do the disparate elements of the story have in common?' she asked.

Njima pointed a fork in her direction. 'You.'

'Very funny. Now try harder.'

'Forests, land, the age-old South African debate about who has rights to what.'

'Yes and no. The main common denominator is Sentinel, a company that intimidates and buys people off in order to get what it wants.'

'Maggie, that makes you sound naive. That's what all companies do.'

She shook her head. 'I don't think all companies get involved with testing biological agents or intimidate their employees into running away overseas. I don't think all companies get bunches of thugs to abduct their detractors and beat them or throw them off cliffs. I think this whole thing revolves around Sentinel and its poisonous intent not to let anything get in its way. And I think Xolani Mpondo is in it all the way up to his well-scrubbed, fragrant, fucking designer-clad elbows.'

'You paint a good story.'

'That's my job.' She sat back and folded her arms. 'But seriously, what do you think?'

'It's hard to prove. Either we have to find fiscal misdemeanours, or we have to show Mpondo directly involved in crime himself.'

'You mean hiring thugs or actually being present to observe or participate in a crime.'

'Pretty much.'

'So if Hope could identify him, that would be something?'

'Yes, sure, but a voice identification would be difficult to hold up in court.'

She rested her arms on the table and put her head in her hands. 'It's such a fucking mess.'

'It is a mess, but we have competent police officers on it and we are doing our best.'

'How competent?' Maggie peered at him through a mesh of fingers.

'Well, me. I'm very competent.'

'I don't doubt that, Captain, but the rest of the police force does not have the world's best reputation. For example, the quote unquote community organiser who brokered the deal between the iinkosi and Sentinel is a well-known gangster and fraudster who has slipped through police nets many times.'

He sighed. 'Msomi, you mean?'

182

'The very one. Doesn't any deal brokered by Lucky Bean Msomi stink to high heaven to you?'

'Very stinky.'

'Can we take it from that angle?'

'Get the Fraud guys on it, you mean?'

She nodded enthusiastically.

'Yes, I'll ask them to take a long look at the negotiations. See what they come up with.'

The waiter removed their plates. 'Anything else?'

'I'll have a black coffee,' Maggie said.

'Me too,' Njima agreed. 'And can we have it on the balcony please?'

He stood up. 'Coming?'

'Isn't it a bit cold for outside?'

'Yes, but I'm hoping that you'll join me and I'll be forced to keep you warm.' The smile that played on his lips was reflected in his eyes.

'Well if you put it that way.' She stood up and followed him to the balcony, a narrow strip with red-brick tiles, two white wicker chairs and a white balustrade. It had a beautiful view of the City Hall and its waving palm trees.

Maggie shivered. She had left her jacket inside.

'Good,' Njima said, opening his arms. 'Now I can keep you warm.'

She slid into his solid embrace. It was like hugging a tree trunk. Her head pressed against his chest and she could feel his pulse. He smelled clean and delicious, as if he had lifted a freshly laundered shirt off a pile just before coming to meet her.

'This feels good,' he said. Maggie nodded against his chest. She didn't need words.

She also didn't need words when she lifted her head and his lips found hers, soft and warm and deep.

He pulled his head away and stared at her. 'I find you so attractive.'

'I'm sure you say that to all the women you kiss.'

'What? All the women? Which women?'

'I seem to remember that you had a hot date with you on Tuesday night.'

He pushed a piece of hair out of her eyes, his body still pressed against hers, his arms still wrapped around her. 'That, my dear Ms Cloete, was my little sister Nomsa. She is a successful Joburg lawyer who was in Maritzburg for one day to represent a client. She demanded that her big brother take her out for dinner, and then spent the whole night communicating with her client via SMS. Not the hottest date of my life, I can tell you.'

He laughed. It was something that came easily to him, along with his smile. Maggie wanted more of his easy access to joy. She pulled his head down to hers and kissed him again. Their tongues met and she swam with desire, but also with a sense of rightness, as if she had been waiting for this moment since the day she met him.

'Coffee?' the waiter said, putting two cups down on a small table between the wicker chairs.

They pulled apart slightly, but his hands still held her close. 'I didn't want coffee,' he said. 'It was just an excuse to get you outside.'

'I do.' Maggie pulled away. She sat down and the wicker chair squeaked. The coffee was dark, bitter and delicious. She downed hers and drank his too.

When she had finished, he grabbed her hand and pulled her to her feet again. 'Listen I need a lift.'

'To your place?'

'I'm still hoping you'll take me to yours.'

Maggie stared into his eyes. 'Okay, but I am not sure if the Chicken will manage a fine specimen of a man like you. We'll have to take it slowly.'

'Oh, I like it slow.'

'Stop it.' She slapped him on the arm and he laughed again.

'Let's pay.' She walked inside, holding his hand. It engulfed hers.

They split the bill and walked downstairs to her bike. 'I don't have a spare helmet, and since you represent the law on this motorcycle, you are going to have to go without.'

'I will take the risk.'

The Chicken sagged dangerously with Sol on the back, its hubcaps scraping the tarmac. She drove slowly, acutely aware of his arms around her waist and his breath in her ear. The winter night was cloudless and a scattering of stars sparkled at Maggie from above. She felt as she could drive forever, Sol's warmth behind her and the roar of the Chicken carrying them wherever they needed to go.

She pulled up to her gate, but there was no need to press the gate-opener on her key ring. It stood open. The flashing light of an ambulance strobed the dark walls of the apartment block.

'Someone's sick,' she said to Sol as she drove in a low gear down the driveway to her parking spot. He got off the bike first and she followed. As she turned towards the ambulance, time elongated and extended as she looked at the body on the stretcher. The person was wrapped in silver insulation blankets, ambulance staff working furiously to resuscitate him. Blood ran from his face into his hair and all along one arm which had flopped out of its restraining blanket.

'Christo!' she screamed, racing forward.

A medic restrained her, holding onto to her arms, which reached out to Christo. 'Please miss, we are trying to save him.'

'That's my brother! What are you doing? What happened to him?'

'It was a knife attack. We are trying to save his life.' The medic turned to Sol. 'Can you help her please?'

Sol's arms wrapped around her again, but she felt nothing of his body as she watched the medics work on her brother through a wash – and then another wash – of tears. She shoved her knuckles into her mouth, biting down hard enough to draw blood, her body rocking.

'Oh God,' she prayed, to a deity she didn't believe in. 'Oh God, oh God, save him please.'

Her breath failed her and she began to crumple. Sol lifted her to her feet, silent, arms holding her up. The medics were a frantic hive buzzing around her brother. Then their activity slowed and, finally, stopped.

'We are sorry. We did our best.' One turned to her. 'So sorry you had to see this ma'am. We really did our best.'

'Christo!' she pulled out of Njima's embrace and ran to her brother. She stroked his hair, streaked through with blood. There was a hastily applied bandage on his neck. He was still warm. She kissed his cheeks, her tears falling on his face, mingling with his blood and running in a pink stream down his neck. She rocked and cried, barely able to breathe.

'Oh God, I want to die!' she screamed to the pitch-black sky yawning mercilessly above her head.

Chapter 25
Friday, 11pm

Maggie's apartment was now a crime scene and Solomon Njima was in charge. She sat wrapped in blankets in her neighbour's flat, rocking backwards and forwards in an attempt to nullify the pain washing over her in excruciating tides.

The neighbours, a couple in their sixties, were already in their pyjamas, but the wife sat patting Maggie's back and repeating her story.

'We heard crashing from next door. From your place, dear. Bill said we should call the police, but I said no, because I was taught never to get involved with domestics. Not that we have any reason to complain about you as a neighbour, my dear, you've been lovely—' she patted Maggie's knee. 'Anyway, the crashing got louder and there was shouting. We did call. They took a while to come. The ambulance took that poor boy outside. He was bleeding terribly from a stab wound in his neck.'

Maggie rocked and rocked. She could still feel Christo's rapidly chilling skin under her fingertips, feel the blood in his hair as she kissed and held him. Her heart was living in some place outside her body, a place that was cold and cruel and where pain was endless and remorseless. Her skin felt raw, her throat dry from screaming.

'I think you should go to bed,' she told Mrs Moffet. 'Seriously, do. I will just wait here until the police tell me what to do next.'

'Well, if you say so, my dear. Please help yourself to anything you want. There's tea, coffee, anything you want. Come on, Bill.'

They shuffled off.

Maggie got up. She could not bear to be still. Being still was an insult to her brother. Doing nothing was a slap in his beautiful dead face. She could not sit and rest. She needed to move. Someone had carried her jacket and her helmet upstairs and left them on the floor of Mr and Mrs Moffett's flat. She put on the jacket, and, carrying the helmet, opened their door and let herself out. To her right was the crime scene; people in protective gear, moving quickly in and quickly out, lights flashing, shouting and orders from Njima.

To her left was freedom. She eased her helmet over her head.

Outside, the ambulance was gone, Christo with it. There were streaks of blood on the tarmac, black marks where her brother's life had ended. She toed them with her Docs.

Then she rocked the Chicken off its stand, put the key in the ignition, turned it and roared off up the driveway.

She headed right for Alex's place. The Forest Keepers would have to know. She opened the throttle and roared up the hill. Inside the helmet, she opened her mouth and screamed. The Chicken's power drowned out the noise, but she could hear it in her head. She screamed until her eyes ran with tears and the road in front of her was a mist.

Then she stopped. Leo needed to her to stay alive. Dicing with death on a dark road was not an indulgence she could afford.

She buzzed at Alex's gate. Minutes passed. A light went on in the house. Then, through the intercom, a voice. 'Who's there?'

'It's Maggie. Christo's sister.'

The gate squeaked open. She drove in and parked and it closed behind her.

She pulled off the helmet and went up the two steps to the front door. As she got there, the door opened. Bettina was standing there.

'Hi Maggie.'

Maggie walked past her into the house. 'Who's here?'

'Just me and Patrick.'

'Where's Alex?'

'Not here. He came home after work, changed his clothes and left again.'

'Did he say where he was going?'

'No.'

'Christo says Alex's been acting weirdly lately.'

'Ja, for sure. He has been shouting at us for small things that we did not do or for touching his things. He has been stressed.'

'Did he say anything to you about Christo?'

'When Christo left yesterday, he said he was disloyal. That a movement needed loyalty in its foot soldiers, and that Christo was too power-hungry.'

Maggie stood in the hallway, helmet in her hand. She felt on the cusp of something. 'Bettina, do you remember anything, anything about the last couple of days that Alex might have said or done?'

'Why do you ask me this?'

Maggie took her wrist lightly between her forefinger and thumb. 'Christo is dead. He was killed tonight at my apartment. The place is a bloodbath. If Alex is missing too, then I am not sure if you and Patrick are safe. It seems as if someone is picking off the Forest Keepers. These people are brutal. Do you have anywhere to go?'

Bettina's hands rose up over her face. Her eyes widened and began to fill. 'I am so sorry. Christo! I can't believe it.'

Maggie patted her shoulder. 'I know. But I do not think this house is safe. Seriously, can you go somewhere?'

Patrick wondered in topless, hair sleep-tousled. 'What's going on?' He was wide awake by the time Bettina told him the news.

'God. Let's pack. We can go to my folks in Balgowan.'

He and Bettina scurried off to gather some belongings. Maggie wondered into Alex's room. It was spotless, organised and tidy. He had a single bed. She wondered what middle-aged man voluntarily purchased himself a single bed. One that was monk-like? One that didn't expect or want sex? One so committed to his cause that he never expected to find love?

She sat at his desk and opened some drawers. She pulled a couple of things out – bank statements and electricity accounts. Nothing personal.

'Maggie we are ready.' Bettina was at the door.

'Okay.'

'Are you leaving too?'

'Hmm, not yet. I want to take a look in Christo's room, if that's okay.'

'But if they are after the Forest Keepers, they might come here.' Bettina looked at her strangely. Maggie knew her calmness was puzzling. She was operating on two levels, the one where her skin felt flayed and her mouth was still screaming and another where her brain was preternaturally sharp. She needed to use up the sharpness before it faded and everything was screaming again.

'I won't stay long,' she promised the woman. 'I just want to go through a couple of my brother's things.' She remembered something. 'I need to choose some clothes. You know, for his body.'

Bettina nodded, backing out of the room.

'If you could just leave me a key so that I can let myself out.'

'Take mine,' Bettina said, throwing it to Maggie.

'Thanks, I'll get them back to you next week.' Maggie turned and went into Christo's room. She heard them slam the front door behind them. She heard the gate clang open and closed. She opened the door to Christo's room.

This was the space that belonged to a normal human being: an unmade bed, clothes on the floor, a couple of newspapers on the bedside table, more clothes hanging over an old armchair in the corner.

She sat down on the bed. Her brother had slept here two nights ago. Two nights ago, his veins had been pumping with blood, his cells regenerating as he slept, his chest rising and falling with breath. Now all that was gone. He was a slab of meat in a morgue. And a memory.

She pulled his duvet over her and rested her head on his pillow. It still smelt of him. She felt her body warm up the cold sheets. She listened to her own breath rise and fall. She slept.

Maggie woke in the cold dawn, a heavy weight on her heart. Her heart felt it before her brain acknowledged it. Christo's pillow was wet with her tears. He was gone. Her little brother, the one who she had admired from afar when he was a schoolboy, and then tried to rescue when he'd come back from jail, incarcerated as a conscientious objector. She tried to help him fight his demons but they'd been too big for both of them. He'd taken refuge in a clinic for many long years and was only beginning to get his life back. She had only just got him back.

Was it her fault? Could they have made better decisions about where he lived and worked? At the time, they'd seemed so right. They'd had advice from experts. Dr K had been so encouraging.

She sat up. Dr K had asked Christo to keep a diary. It was a way to maintain his mental balance and sort out his emotions. Where was it? She leapt up and began pulling open the desk drawers. It wasn't hard to find. Christo was not one to hide things. A black-covered notebook, in hardback with a red cotton spine. Blue lines on white pages. Blue ballpoint. She read her brother's words, accounts of meals and days at work. She featured too. As did the words judgmental and overbearing. Tears filled her eyes again. She had driven her brother away.

The house creaked. Houses made noises, but when they were full of people and life, no one noticed. This house was dead now.

On the way out, she glanced in the fridge. There was a plastic Spar packet with a sign on it. *Alex's food. Please don't touch.* She rifled in the bag and grabbed a banana. She ate it and threw the skin in the bin.

Maggie pressed the buzzer on the keys Bettina had given her and the gate opened. She swung a leg over the Chicken and drove away, the gate closing behind her. She drove with no idea of where she was going. She pointed the Chicken down roads and up hills. It was unconscious journeying and when she stopped, she found she was looking up at a big tree, its arms spread high and wide as if to embrace the sky.

Maggie buzzed at the gate to be let in.

'Hallo?' came a voice. It was natural to be cautious at six in the morning.

'Natalie, it's Maggie Cloete. I am sorry to do this to you, but we need to talk.'

Natalie opened the door a crack, regarding Maggie through the safety of the security gate.

'It really is you.'

She unlocked the gate. 'Are you okay? You don't look good.'

Maggie was silent. She looked at Natalie.

Natalie reached out, grabbed her hand and pulled her into the house.

'What is it, Maggie? What is it?'

'I am sorry, I didn't mean to come here.'

'Just tell me ...'

'Your kids ...'

'... are still sleeping.'

Natalie put either hand on Maggie's shoulders. 'Talk to me.'

'It's my brother. He was one of the forest protestors. He was killed last night.'

'Oh God.' Natalie pulled Maggie to her. Maggie let herself be hugged. Natalie was smaller than her but she felt like a rock. Maggie cried, her tears a wet mess on Natalie's shoulder.

'I am sure it was them,' she sobbed. 'I think they came for him. They wanted him out of the picture, and they succeeded. I watched him die, Natalie. He died right in front of my eyes.'

Natalie pulled her to the sitting room, where she put Maggie on the sofa and gave her a blanket. She handed her a glass with an inch of something golden in it.

'At six in the morning?'

'Just drink it,' Dave Bloom's widow said. 'You will feel a tiny, minuscule bit better. It will only last a moment, but that moment will be worth it.'

Maggie swallowed it. The whisky soothed her throat, but the bitterness remained.

'Now tell me what happened.'

Maggie told her of the night before. Natalie held her hand as she spoke.

'Alex Field has disappeared. I've told the other Forest Keepers to keep a low profile. I am worried that Sentinel is picking them off, just like they did with Dave.'

Natalie looked down at their intertwined hands. 'Maggie, have you thought about the fact that they might have been coming for you?'

'You mean because of my articles?'

'Yes. And they found Christo instead.'

A bolus of air was trapped in her throat. She fought it down. The thought of her brother standing in the way of killers hunting her was too much to bear.

'Possible, but I suspect not. As a journalist I'm an obvious target, but too obvious.'

'The Forest Keepers are obvious targets too.'

As Hope had been. She told Natalie of Hope's ordeal. The woman's face went white. 'These people are evil.'

'Yes, evil, but also nameless and faceless. How can we even begin to bring them to justice, if we can't name them? It's too murky. I can't see my way through it.'

'Maybe the police investigation will be successful.'

Maggie thought of Njima. Their flirtation, carried out while Christo was being murdered, seemed vapid and insulting now. She should have been home with her brother, defending him against the threat that had knocked on the door.

Natalie picked up the whisky glass and stood up. 'Tea or coffee?'

'Coffee, please,' Maggie said. 'I'll have it black.'

When Natalie came back, a mug in each hand, Maggie said, 'It's just dawned on me. My intercom. People have to buzz to be let in. Christo would never have let a random stranger into the apartment complex.'

'Someone he knew, then.'

'Knew and trusted.'

Maggie's skin prickled. She could feel hairs rise on her arms. 'Apart from me, there was only one person. Alex Field.'

'Head of the Forest Keepers.'

'And no one knows where he is.'

'What do you know about him?'

'Nothing, apart from the fact that he owns a shop and has inspired a loyal band of activists.'

Maggie drained the coffee and put the cup down on a nearby table. 'I need to go and report in with the police now.'

'Please be careful.' Natalie stood up. 'Listen, I imagine your place is very unwelcoming. Feel free to sleep here tonight if you need to.'

Maggie thanked her. Much as she liked Natalie Bloom and appreciated the offer, she felt marked. She couldn't afford to infect others any more than she already had.

Chapter 26
Saturday, 7am

Maggie drove to the police station through the early morning light. The streets were still Saturday-morning quiet. People would be getting on with their weekends: cooking breakfast for their families, reading the paper, making plans, shopping lists. The patchwork of life carried on, even when hers had been ripped apart.

Daily lives filled with minor decisions, ones which had recently filled up her life too but now seemed meaningless. Her life had been scraped empty, a curettage of such extreme cruelty that the only parts of it left were the bit that breathed and the bit that grieved. All the shades in between, all the charming greys of life, were black and white.

The fact: Christo was dead. Another fact: she had not protected him from death. The third fact: she was flirting while he was fighting for his life.

All of this, all of it, made her feel as if her skin had been flayed. She was travelling through life without a protective layer. The only solution was to grow one. It did not matter what it was made of. It did not have to be skin. It could be blood or bone. It could be plastic or alarming chemicals. All that mattered was that it was there, stopping her heart from bleeding out onto the pavement.

She parked in the street and walked into the building. She stopped at reception. This time it was a uniformed policewoman sitting there, who had lovely long braids. Maggie admired them but as if at a great distance. They were cinematic or scientific, those braids, so far were they from her life.

'Captain Njima?' she asked the woman. 'Is he in?'

The woman made a call. 'Yes, he is. You may go to the fourth floor. He will meet you there.'

Maggie went through security, submitted to having her bag

checked and then pushed the button for the fourth floor and got into the lift.

Njima was waiting for her, his face thunderous. 'Where have you been?'

'I left. I couldn't stand the Moffetts a second longer. I went to Alex's. He's gone. The other Forest Keepers left too.'

Words spilled out of her as Njima led her down a grey corridor to a room called 'Family Room'. For the families of dead people. She was glad it was empty. She had too much grief spilling out of her to witness anyone else's.

'Maggie, we are doing our best, but it is hard to do when our key witness walks out. Please don't do that again.'

'What witness? I wasn't there. I was out with you. I saw nothing, except my brother's death throes.'

'Of that I am perfectly aware. Now I am going to have to ask you to put that into a statement.'

'To you?'

'To me.'

Maggie laughed. It sounded like a bark in the empty room. 'You know exactly where I was.'

'I know that, but the we have to follow the process.'

'Then fire away. God forbid I should impede the process.'

He picked up a clipboard on the table.

'Tell me about Friday night, starting from when you got home from work.'

Maggie talked him through the evening, remembering how Christo had said he wanted to stay with her as things with Alex were getting too intense.

'Intense?' Njima asked. 'That was the word?'

'Yes, apparently Alex was being moody and irritable. Christo had decided that working and living with him was too much. He was going to dial it down a bit.'

'Did he mention any incidents? Anything specific?'

'Field fired him on Thursday for some minor infraction. Then he called and apologised and said Christo could have the job back.'

'Did he take it?'

'He said he would start again on Monday. He said Alex wasn't such a bad guy.'

'And how did he seem?'

'Christo? Relaxed. He was eating muesli, feet up, watching TV. He was looking forward to a night of peace and quiet. He had his laptop out. Was that still in the flat?'

'It's gone.'

'And then you left.'

'I left and went to the restaurant. You know the rest.'

Njima put a hand on her arm. 'Maggie, I am so sorry.'

'I know you are.' She stared at the hand and he removed it. She looked into his lovely brown eyes. 'Wherever we were heading last night is a place we will now never go. I hope you understand that.'

'I do,' he said quietly.

'So when can I go home?'

'Not yet. We are still completing work there. Maybe Monday.'

She might have to take up Natalie Bloom's offer.

'And what about his body?'

At some point, she would have to arrange some kind of farewell. Right now, that seemed as likely as her climbing Everest, but she was dimly aware that form would have to be followed. She and Leo would stand at the grave, two lonely figures in black. How would Leo handle the news? He had met his uncle a couple of times. Christo had always been kind to him.

'I will let you know when we can release it. There will be an autopsy first.'

Maggie stifled a gag and put her head in her hands. She took a few deep breaths. She needed to get out of here, find some fresh air, try to think about what she should do next.

'Can I go?'

'Yes.' He got up. 'Maggie, please be careful.'

She left, walked downstairs, and out of the building. Habit took her down Church Street and then she turned right down the lane towards World Shoes. The shop was closed, grille gate pulled firmly across the glass door. All locked up.

She went into the shop next door. It was a florist, flush with shoppers. The smell of their different perfumes combined with the sharp tang of newly chopped stems nauseated her.

'Just a quick question,' she said to the woman at the till. Her name was Pumla, a name tag stated. Pumla nodded, her hands busy ringing up a customer's bill.

'I'm trying to find Alex, from the shop next door. When did you last see him?'

'He closed up last night. I don't think he's been back.' Pumla handed the customer her bill and a large bunch of something pink and red.

'No sign of him today?'

'None at all.'

Maggie left. She stood outside in the lane while shoppers flowed around her. Someone's bags bumped against her legs and still she stood. Everyone had a destination. She had none. She was unmoored. Christo was gone. Panic rose. She looked up at the sky. It was a clear winter blue, strong and deep, a colour that would once have brought her peace. Now its blue scraped against her skin like an insult. She staggered further down the lane, not knowing where her legs were taking her.

She could use a drink, or something narcotic. She needed an injection of something, straight into her veins, to remind her what it was supposed to feel like to be alive. She felt ghostly, a shadow of Maggie, floating down the street.

Every cell in her body felt pain.

She doubled over, clutching her stomach. 'Oh God.' She could sense people swelling away from her as if she were drunk or mad. She didn't care. Public humiliation was nothing to the pain of loss, of grieving. She groaned out loud, and a woman jumped away from her.

'Maggie?'

She saw a pair of brogues, eyelets in neat rows, brown and tidy. A slim pair of dark jeans. Kind eyes.

'Aslan.'

He lifted her into a standing position, hands around her upper arms. 'Maggie, you look terrible. What's wrong?'

'It's Christo.' A sob shook her. She could not hold it in. 'He's dead.'

Aslan held her in a firm hug. He stroked her back as she wept wave upon wave of sobs. She had no sense of the street or of the people around them, just his arms around her and the grief that poured from her body.

'Let's get you a cup of tea.' He started guiding her towards a coffee shop. 'With lots of sugar.'

Through her tears and mucus, Maggie could see people inside the coffee shop. They were sipping lattes and cappuccinos while discussing their Saturday-morning purchases, oblivious to the fact that her life had fallen apart.

'Don't make me go in there,' she held onto him. 'Please get me out of here.'

'Okay.' Instead he led her to his car, parked around the corner. He bleeped the lock and opened the passenger door. She climbed in and Aslan plugged in the safety belt. Maggie leaned her forehead against the window.

'Where to?' Aslan put the key in the ignition.

'I don't care.'

She closed her eyes and felt the car rumble into gear. The window rattled slightly against her forehead. Waves of pain floated up and down her body. The need to escape, to be out of the body that was causing her so much pain, was overwhelming.

She didn't open her eyes when the car came to a halt. She heard the engine switch off and then him climb out and slam his door. Footsteps approached her side. He tapped gently on the window and she moved her head. The door clicked open.

'Come,' he said, taking her arm and helping her out.

They were at a house she remembered. A small suburban house with a neatly tended front garden surrounded by a wall topped with razor wire.

Aslan opened the door, and the smell of spices reached her. The taste of the banana she had stolen from Alex Field made her gorge rise.

'You're here,' a small woman in a sari bustled up the corridor towards them. 'And you've got Maggie with you.'

'She needs a bed, Mom,' Aslan said.

Mrs Chetty put her arm around Maggie and led her into a bedroom. Maggie sat on the bed, immobile, and Mrs Chetty pulled her shoes off, helped her into a lying down position and covered her with blankets.

'I can't sleep,' Maggie said, closing her eyes again. She heard

Mrs Chetty leave the room, was dimly aware of a whispered conversation. She heard a hadedah call in the garden, a drawn-out series of unrelated notes that was as mournful as it was ugly, and then she remembered nothing more.

She awoke to drawn curtains and darkness. Somewhere in the house she heard a TV. Judging by the pitch of the commentator's voice it was a rugby match. The smell of spices still lingered but now it made her hungry. She was covered in a pile of blankets so heavy it was hard to move.

Mrs Chetty must have heard her stirring. She put her head around the door. 'Stay right there. I will bring you some soup.'

The broth was thin and hot and salty. It seared Maggie's tongue slightly, but she was too hungry to stop eating. She put the bowl down on the bedside table and covered herself with blankets again.

The next time she awoke there were cracks of light coming through the curtains and the hadedah in the garden had been joined by a friend. Their conversation was raucous, like two old drunks scrapping over the last beer.

What time had Aslan brought her? Early afternoon maybe? And she had slept from then until morning, the heavy, dark sleep of the bereaved.

She padded down the corridor in her socks to find the bathroom. Cold winter air seeped in through the window. She peed and then stared at her face in the mirror. She saw lines, her hair sticking up in a million directions and heavy dark bags under her eyes. The bruising on her jaw had been reduced to a pale, sickly green.

Maggie went back to bed. It was too warm to leave and the world outside was too scary to face. At this moment, she did not want to think about anything, not Christo, not Hope, not Dave Bloom. The world was too cruel.

Mrs Chetty brought respite in the form of three more meals, each eaten in bed. She brought Maggie a pair of pyjamas, coaxed her out of her jeans and brought soft socks for her feet. Then she left her alone.

In between meals, Maggie slept, waking every couple of hours to visit the bathroom or stare at the ceiling until she fell asleep again, giant thundering rollers that overcame her and tumbled her under with their force. She slipped under them and slept again.

In the early evening she woke, and walked down the corridor to watch a news show with Mr and Mrs Chetty. She lasted fifteen minutes but found the outside world exhausting and returned to bed. She slept again, this time with furious dreams of Christo, chasing him down corridors as he laughed each time he managed to escape her.

She woke again to an ice-cold morning and lay under the blankets, shivering. It was too cold to get up, to even try to make it to the bathroom. Eventually, Mrs Chetty arrived, attired in a pale blue dressing-gown.

'Tea?' she said.

'Yes please.' Maggie got up, pulling a blanket over her shoulders, and followed Aslan's mother to the kitchen. Mrs Chetty got mugs out of a cupboard while Maggie settled herself at the breakfast nook. She fiddled with the sugar jar, taking the lid off and putting it back on again.

'Thank you for looking after me,' she said.

'My dear,' Mrs Chetty said, sitting down opposite her and passing her a hot mug. 'You have been through so much. I am just so sorry about your brother.'

Maggie held the mug with both hands, the heat scalding her skin. 'I...' She coughed. 'I cannot believe that he is gone.'

'Do you know that we lost a child?'

Maggie shook her head.

'Before Aslan was born, we had a daughter. She only lived for two days. When we lost her, we never thought we'd be able to breathe again, let alone eat three meals a day, bath and talk to people.'

Mrs Chetty gave a sweet, sad smile. 'But you do. You get up and you get through the day, even if it feels like walking through syrup.'

'It feels like that now.'

'And it will continue to do so.' Mrs Chetty sipped her tea. 'For a long time. But think of this, did Christo want to die?'

Maggie thought of him the last time she saw him, a bowl of cereal balancing on his stomach, boots off, feet up, one hand on the TV remote. She shook her head.

'He would want to live, correct? So by hiding from the world, you are doing him a disservice. If Christo were here, right now, what would he say to you?'

'He would say get out there and find out who the hell killed him.'

'Well, then.' Mrs Chetty smiled again.

Chapter 27
Monday, 8.20am

Aslan drove her back to the Chicken, still parked near the police station. She put on her helmet and swung a leg over the bike. All the rest and sleep and good food of the weekend had helped her, and she felt scoured clean. The wind was freezing and her eyes teared up under her helmet. Icy air lashed her face. She had to get some gloves. The cold focused her mind on what she had to do.

First stop was the office. Maggie knocked at Naidoo's door and opened it when she heard the editor's voice. She walked out five minutes later with permission for a pool laptop and two weeks' compassionate leave. Johnny Cupido would deputise as news editor in Maggie's absence. Patti would be thrilled.

Then she walked up to the archives, one floor higher than the newsroom and next to the photo studio. Instead of rows of paper files, the archives had been replaced with a bank of computers. Alicia Labuschagne, the former archivist of those paper files, would be turning in her grave. Alicia had relished her position as keeper of the paper's memory and she would have hated this new world, now run by Ed's team of digital lackeys.

Maggie searched her memory for the password and user name that she'd been given on her first day. After a few false tries, she remembered the right ones. She typed in 'Alex Field' and waited while the computer's search engine did its thing. This was no Google. The algorithms were clearly somewhat outdated.

The computer threw up a short list. Maggie clicked on each link: all recent stories, all mostly written by her. The earliest report was from a year ago, covering a Forest Keepers meeting.

The guy owned a shop in town and seemed to know everyone. How could he have appeared from nowhere?

She typed in 'World Shoes' and the computer came up with nothing. Perhaps Field's shop had also not existed a year ago. She tried 'leather shoes' plus the shop's address, and discovered that it had been called Fancye Footworke and owned by a woman named Iris Botha. The article related incidents of shoplifting in the street and Ms Botha, as the owner, was fulsomely quoted.

She tried searching for Forest Keepers. There were no links earlier than July the previous year.

So Alex Field and his organisation had arrived in town fully formed only a year ago? Where had be been before and where had he come from? She made a note to Google him once she was back at her own computer. Right now, she had to come at this from a different angle.

She looked up Xolani Mpondo. He was all over the newspaper, going back eight years when he'd become MD. Sentinel announces that the streams downriver from its KZN mills are all effluent-free, Sentinel announces that it will plough millions into environmental projects, Sentinel announces that it will sponsor the protection of rhinos, Sentinel announces a network of mountain bike trails through the Underberg.

Sentinel trying to prove itself to be a good corporate citizen. What had Alex Field called it? Greenwashing. Xolani Mpondo had done such a great job of it that no one thought anything of it when his employees started dying off.

She heard a creak on the stairs and then Johan Liebenberg came in.

'Morning Maggie,' he said. 'I just heard in conference that you have compassionate leave.'

She stood up. 'Morning Marius.'

His eyelids fluttered, but he kept his face blank. A master of control.

'What do you mean?'

'Let's not pretend any more,' she said. 'You are not who you say you are. This has worked for you for a long time, but it's not going to work any more. Either you tell me everything or I'll go right down to Tina Naidoo and blow your cover.' She spread her hands. 'Your call.'

He flopped into a chair. 'OK, so I used to be Marius van Heerden. I've been Liebenberg for a long time. Since I came back from London.'

'Where you ran.'

'Yes, I ran when my cover fell away.'

'You don't seem ashamed.' Maggie stared at him.

'I'm not. Every side had their spies. The guerrillas had their own people infiltrating the cops.'

'I don't believe that.' Stories of covert activities on the side of the apartheid government had been rife during her early days as a crime reporter; her own detention without trial in 1989 had been her personal proof. Later, the Truth and Reconciliation Commission had revealed the full extent of the former government's spying and killing network.

He shrugged. 'Believe it or don't. I don't care what you think.

'So who are you to Xolani Mpondo?'

'He doesn't care who I am.'

'But you are very useful to him.'

The man nodded. 'Sure I am. I got my gig at Sentinel a long time ago, long before Mpondo made his way up through the ranks.'

'And now, just as Sentinel goes in to log a piece of precious natural history, a place of secrets and bones, Mpondo gets you a job on the local newspaper so that you can spy on us.'

'Correct.' He coughed. 'Not only spy. I ran interference.'

'Which means?'

'The idea was to keep him informed, as well as keep the story off the front page as much as possible.'

Maggie laughed. 'That didn't work too well.'

'Neither Mpondo nor I reckoned on you. You did your job far too well.' He showed his teeth in a display of self-satisfaction. 'Though you did fuck up once.'

'When?'

'You told me the Forest Keepers were going into the forest to guard the trees. I told Mpondo and he sent the cops in to get you.'

'You slimy, underhanded bastard.'

Liebenberg grinned. 'Insults mean nothing to me. Believe me, I have heard it all.'

'So is your job here done?'

He examined his pudgy white fingers and then glanced at her, almost coyly. 'Not entirely. The forest investigation is by no means over. But when it is I'm moving to a cushy new job in Mpumalanga.'

'Seeing you know so much about everything, maybe you can help me,' Maggie said, turning back to the computer screen. 'I'm doing some research before I go,' she pointed to the photo of Mpondo. 'Your good friend.'

Liebenberg leaned over her chair and stared at the screen.

'I'm also trying to find out more about Alex Field, the head of the Forest Keepers,' she said, typing his name into the search engine. 'Thing is, there is nothing about him in the paper before July 2014. Guy didn't seem to exist.'

'So he came from nowhere?'

'Looks like it.'

'Either that or he wanted to cover his tracks.'

'What do you mean?'

'Maybe he's undercover.'

The skin on the back of her neck crawled. She looked up. He leaned against one of the tables, hands in pockets. She clicked on one of the links and enlarged the photo of Field.

Liebenberg peered over her shoulder. 'That guy's not Alex Field.'

Maggie frowned.

'His name is John Evans. He was a paymaster in the South African Police right up till 1993, when he and all of his records conveniently disappeared.'

Maggie stood up. 'And you know this because?'

'Because he ran me. Along with numerous others.'

'And you knew this, while I was running stories on him as head of the Forest Keepers?'

'Sure I knew it.' An insouciant smile played on his fleshy lips. Another moment of one-upmanship over the news editor. 'But John got me my gig at Sentinel, back in the days when white men still had influence. I'm in his debt. I wasn't about to break his cover.'

Maggie paced, trying to put things together. She turned to him. 'I have every reason to believe that the person who killed my brother on Friday night was John Evans. Having kept this information from me, information that might have saved his life, you are now under obligation to help me find him.'

'Killed your brother?'

'Yes, he died from a knife wound to the inner carotid artery. Outside my flat. While I watched.'

'Not the first person John's killed.' His face was blank. No remorse.

Rage boiled inside her and then erupted. She rushed him, her shoulder to his fleshy side, and he stumbled backwards. He righted himself and she pushed him again. This time he stumbled over a chair, arms spinning as he tried to balance. He fell heavily and she heard a crack as his head hit the lino flooring.

Maggie knelt on his chest and held his hands down. He struggled and flailed to escape, but the layers of flesh on his body meant he was neither supple nor strong.

'Where the fuck is John Evans now?' she spat at the prostrate man. 'How can I find him?'

'I don't know,' he twisted under her grip. 'I haven't seen the guy in twenty years.'

'Except every day in the paper.'

'Let me get up!'

She got off him and Liebenberg struggled to his feet. 'Maggie, I am sorry that your brother is dead.' He paused.

'Show me how sorry you are. Sit down, there,' she pointed at the desk, 'take that pen and paper and write down every place you met Evans and every place and person you ever heard him mention. If you don't, I'm going straight to Naidoo and your precious cover will be broken.'

He sat and wrote the list, which she pocketed.

She roared the Chicken over to Sentinel's offices. The butterfly dome rose up behind the glass head office, an impressive testimony to greed. She phoned Mbali, who came to meet her outside, dressed in a chic red winter coat. She rubbed her upper arms.

'What's this all about?'

'This is about spying,' Maggie told her. 'Spying and secrets, and a company that has entwined itself with South Africa's dirty history.'

She outlined her theory to the young woman. Mbali's face was incredulous.

'I don't believe any of this!'

'I understand that you don't, Mbali.'

'So why are you telling me then?'

Maggie stopped. 'Remember fourteen years ago?'

Mbali nodded, eyes on the pavement. It was not easy to remember. She had been abducted by a madman who had killed her adoptive father and had been intent on killing her.

'Mbali, what saved you then was not me storming to the farm. It was information. My brother is dead, and the only way I can find out who killed him – and other people who have died – is with information.'

'And you are asking me to risk my job? I am just starting my career. I can't afford to become a whistleblower.'

Maggie held Mbali's upper arm. 'That is your personal choice, Mbali, if you like working for a company that spies and extorts and tests biological poisons on young apartheid activists. If you like it, then find me someone who doesn't. Or find me some information that points to Sentinel's dirty past. And do it fast.'

She turned and walked away, leaving a small red figure behind her.

She straddled the Chicken and dialed Njima. 'Maggie? You vanished. Are you okay?'

'Better, thanks.' She didn't want to have personal discussions any more. Not with him. 'I need an update.'

'Well, the autopsy is today. We are finished at your flat. You can go back if you want to.'

She didn't. 'What about the bodies?'

'Forensics are still identifying the nature of the poison. When we have something definite, I'll let you know.'

'And the attack on Hope?'

'I wish we had progress on that, Maggie, but there's none. We can't find unknown perpetrators.'

'There's something else you need to know. Alex Field's real name is John Evans. He is a former apartheid-era secret policeman who used to be a spymaster for other police spies. I think he might have been leader of the squad that killed the people in the forest, which was why he was so desperate to stop the logging.'

'I know that Alex Field was Evans,' Njima said quietly. 'We do keep an eye on our former staffers – especially when they return to their old haunts.'

'If you had told me he was dangerous, that might have saved my brother.'

'Maggie, there is no reason, I repeat no reason, to believe that Evans killed Christo.'

'He wouldn't have let a stranger into the apartment complex. It had to be someone he knew.'

'Evans was not the only person Christo knew. There were others.'

'I've got some details for you on Evans from someone who knew him well. I'll drop it off.'

She hung up. Police work was far too slow and pedantic for her. She drove back to the office, put Johan's list in an envelope and asked Fortunate to have it couriered to Njima at the station. Then she walked out of *The Gazette*'s offices, saying goodbye to no one, and with the feeling that she would never be back.

She had her own trail to follow. And it started with the bodies. She drove to the sprawling mall to the east of the city and found a coffee shop with the twin offerings of wifi and power supply. The coffee was also decent. She found the website of the Truth and Reconciliation Commission and read the testimony of the families of the Umlazi Seven. She found the words of Prudence Mshenge, Vuyani's mother. She described how he returned from the police, his body covered with bruises.

'In his mind, he was still strong. He believed in the ANC cause of fighting for a non-racial South Africa. He believed that the time for non-violence was over, but he promised me he would never target innocent people. I believe that is why he worked on the power station attack.'

Mrs Mshenge described how her son had come home from Durban one night and said that they had done 'something big'. In the papers the next day she read the story that a power station in Umlazi had been blown up. Two days later, he disappeared. She never saw him again. She described the pain of not knowing what happened to her son. Six other families described similar stories.

The TRC had given apartheid-era police the chance to confess to their crimes in exchange for amnesty. Maggie searched the amnesty section of the website. No Evans. The guy had vanished until two decades later when he turned up in Pietermaritzburg reinvented as an evangelistic environmentalist determined above all else to prevent the logging of Karkloof Extension 7.

And why would he have killed Christo? Her brother must have suspected something about the true nature of Alex Field. And if she hadn't behaved in a such a high-handed way towards Christo, he might have confided in her.

Maggie felt a wash of despair. She groaned and put her head in her hands.

'Everything alright ma'am?' the waiter asked.

She shook her head. It was not alright. It was definitely not alright. Evans and Xolani Mpondo were involved in some horrible death waltz in which they needed each other. Christo had understood it, and now he was dead.

It was too much for her. She called over the waiter, paid up and left. She needed to empty her mind. The only way to do that was on the Chicken. She took the highway towards Hilton. There was nothing left for her in this town. An anonymous flat where her brother had been brutally murdered. A job that had not been a good fit. A relationship that had not got beyond the first date. Without Christo, Pietermaritzburg had no centre for her. It was empty and cold. She would go home to Leo.

Then she saw the Howick turn-off, leading her to where it began.

Chapter 28
Monday, 2pm

Maggie parked the Chicken and walked past the curio sellers, one of whom shouted 'Hey, ma'am' and held up a carved elephant in her direction. She put her hand up, shouted back, 'No, thanks.'

The guy got up and followed her, an elephant in one hand and a giraffe in the other. 'Buy one, ma'am. Please buy one.' He bobbed at her side as she made her way towards the restaurant.

'Not buying today, thanks.'

'Come on, just one.' He thrust the giraffe in front of her face.

Maggie put a hand to his arm. It was threaded with muscle. 'I am not a tourist. Stop trying to sell me stuff.'

He wrenched his hand away. 'And I am not a beggar.'

He stood tall and watched her as she entered Ishmael's Cafe. The proprietor hurried eagerly towards her. There were only two other tables occupied.

'Where would you like to sit?'

Maggie headed for a window seat and Mr Ishmael pressed a menu into her hands. She leaned her head against the glass. She really could leave, right now. There was nothing to stop her. Nothing at all. Leave this godforsaken place and never come back. Back to Leo, where her real life was.

'What will it be?' Mr Ishmael stood before her in his pristine white shirt, a crisp ironed seam down each sleeve.

'Coffee and a bacon and banana toasted please.'

'Good,' he turned to head back to the kitchen.

'Just one question first,' she said. 'Who are those guys outside?'

'The curio sellers?'

She nodded.

'They are from Malawi. Nice, well-spoken. They have a hard time. Not many tourists at this time of year so they make few sales. But they keep trying, they don't give up.'

There was a fine line between being determined to sell and badgering people.

'They are much better than the other lot,' Mr Ishmael said. 'At least they work, they try. I can respect that.'

'Which other lot?'

'The squatters.' He indicated towards the waterfall with his notepad. 'I've had so many break-ins this year. They wait around for me to leave and as soon as it's dark, they're trying to get in here. Sometimes they succeed, sometimes not. The police are sick of me calling.'

He went off to give the kitchen her order and returned with a steaming cup of coffee. Maggie sipped it gratefully.

'So the squatters at the waterfall, where do they come from?'

'Oh, all over,' Mr Ishmael said. 'Don't get me wrong; I feel sorry for them. It must be horrible to live like that. To have a respectable job one day, then have nothing the next. That must be terrible.'

'What do you mean?'

He hovered, and Maggie indicated the chair opposite her. He glanced at the other two tables, both focused on their eating, and sat down gratefully.

'There was no squatter camp when I first opened the cafe in 1982. That was just empty land. In 2008, there were a lot of lay-offs in the area, and suddenly many people were unemployed.'

Maggie went cold, remembering Joshua Ntombe's words. 'Lay-offs from which companies?'

'From many different ones, but in this area, it was mostly Sentinel that retrenched people.'

'Are you telling me people in the squatter camp are former Sentinel employees?'

'Many of them, yes.'

He got up to fetch her sandwich and Maggie ate it, salty bacon and sweet banana mingling in her mouth. Then she paid Mr Ishmael and headed out.

She stopped at the curio seller's blanket where he had laid out his wares, and pointed to a small sandstone elephant.

'I'll take that one.'

She paid him thirty rand and put the elephant in her jacket

pocket. 'So Mr Ishmael says you guys are from Malawi.'

'Yes,' he nodded, glancing at his colleagues, who nodded too from their sitting positions. 'There's more work here.'

'Do you like it here?'

'It's not too bad. Sometimes the people don't like us.'

'Which people?'

He thumbed towards the squatter camp. 'Those ones. They don't like it because we work and they don't.'

'Is that where you live?'

'No way! That place is crazy. Full of devils and witches. We stay at Midmar.'

So the Malawian curio-sellers would rather commute into Howick every day all the way from Midmar than sleep in the camp next door to their place of work. That was interesting.

'Thanks.' She turned and headed for the Chicken.

'Nice wheels!' The guy shouted after her. She gave him the thumbs up before putting on her helmet.

She drove the short distance to the squatter camp, bumping over the dirt road, and parked where the road ended. Holding her helmet, she walked towards the first row of dwellings. Sandile's house was a burnt-out shell. Just ten days ago, his mother had stood there, with a baby on her back, stirring her cooking pot.

Some kids were playing nearby, plastic bags rolled up into a football.

'Where's Sandile?' she asked them.

'He's gone. His mother died.' Maggie remembered how ill Sandile's mother had seemed. Did she die of something AIDS-related?

'And the baby?'

'The baby died too.' The kids clustered around her, interested in her questions. One taller boy hung back.

She looked to the left, where Sandile's mother had crouched over her cooking fire. Their house was reduced to rubble and ash.

'What happened to their house?'

'People burned it.'

'Where did Sandile go?'

'He ran away,' another kid chimed in, 'when they burnt his house.'

Maggie felt ill. Sandile had become an orphan and was now homeless, joining the ranks of lost children on the streets. It was too sad.

'Got money for us, miss?' the big boy at the back called.

'Maybe I do.'

The smaller children went back to kicking the football. He stood near her, watching them, torn between joining the game and earning some money.

She remembered Hope's description of the place where she was held. 'Is there a cave anywhere here? Somewhere underground?'

He nodded slowly, but Maggie saw caution in his eyes.

'Would you show me?'

His eyes widened and he shook his head. 'We don't go there. Children not allowed.'

'OK, then will you take me to Xoliswa?' She didn't believe that the children wouldn't play in a cave. They must have been warned off, if it was a dangerous place where adults played their dangerous games.

'Money first,' he put out his hand.

She gave him five rand. 'Half now, half after you bring me to Xoliswa.'

The last time she'd seen the community leader he'd been playing dice under a tree. She didn't know which of the houses was his.

The boy led her down the same path Sandile had taken, a path flattened by feet. Instead of heading to the water and the big tree, he bore right and walked up a slight incline passing houses left and right. Maggie felt the atmosphere around her thicken. Even if she saw no one, her presence had been clocked. She felt the back of her neck prickle, as if many eyes were on her.

Xoliswa's house was at the top of the incline, cobbled together with sheets of corrugated iron. The boy called out and a corresponding shout came from inside.

'He says he's sleeping.' The boy turned to Maggie.

'Tell him I am here. The journalist from *The Gazette*.'

The boy shouted something in Zulu, and there was a returning yell. Again Maggie kicked herself for forgetting her Zulu.

'He says he is busy.'

'Tell him I want to talk about Xolani Mpondo, his old boss.'

There was another exchange, then a flurry of yells. A teenage girl stumbled out of the shack, adjusting her T-shirt as she did so. She carried her shoes in her hands. She looked relieved to be getting out of there.

Xoliswa appeared moments later, also pulling on a jersey. 'You interrupted me.' He looked smug and Maggie had the sudden urge to brain him with her motorbike helmet. Men in positions of power the world over were all the same.

The kid held out his hand and Maggie put another five rand in it. Xoliswa barked an instruction to him in Zulu as he left. The kid waved a hand and ran off without a word.

'I hear that many of the people here used to work for Sentinel,' she said.

Xoliswa finished dressing. The jersey hung over his stump, untied. 'Yes.'

'Were you also a Sentinel worker?'

'I was. Why do you care?'

'I care because I am trying to understand Xolani Mpondo better.'

'Mpondo is a boss, and bosses get what they want.'

'Including getting people to shut up? People such as environmental protestors, journalists, academics?'

'Bosses can get anyone to shut up, if they pay enough.' Xoliswa glanced around him. Maggie had the feeling that he was waiting for something or someone to join them.

'Did he pay you? To push Dave Bloom over the waterfall? To beat up Hope Phiri?'

'You don't know what you are saying. You are one very stupid woman.'

Maggie saw a shadow to her right and then felt a clanging blow to her head.

Chapter 29
Late Monday night

Awareness came to her bones first. They ached from lying on a cold earthen floor. Her head ached too, a deep throb that started inside her brain and radiated outwards.

She shivered. She was in utter darkness. She could smell a tang of soil and something worse, something human and foul. This was a place where people had lost all hope and where others had lost their humanity. It stank of evil, another layer of cold below the cold itself. And she could hear water, just as Hope had said, the sound of water.

This was the cave, the cave below the waterfall, where a group of men had taken Hope and pounded her to a pulp. Fear shot through Maggie's veins. She didn't want to be their next victim.

She struggled to a sitting position, realising as she did so that her hands and feet were tied. She tried to stand up, but only got as far as crouching because another rope joined her hands and feet together. She was hog-tied like a pig.

She fell back heavily onto her backside, and then inched up against the wall of the cave so that she could rest her head. The walls were damp with moisture and craggy with layers of rock that jutted unevenly into her back and her skull.

She waited.

There was nothing worse than waiting. Waiting for a bunch of thugs to come and beat her up again, or worse, was torture. She was a person of action, not a passive victim.

'Help!' she screamed, her patience giving out quickly. 'Help me! Someone help me.'

Silence radiated back at her, cruel waves of nothing.

Maggie tested the rock face behind her with her fingers. It was a landscape of craters and crevices. She crouched on her feet and made her way further down the cave wall, fingers on the alert for one sharp, pointed piece of rock.

Eventually she found it, a piece sticking sharply out of the landscape like a horizontal stalactite. She crouched near it and began rubbing the rope around her wrists against it. If she could work the rope loose, she could untie her feet and get out of there.

She rubbed the rope vigorously, occasionally stopping to test if it had loosened. She caught her wrist on the rock and felt warm blood drip down her hand. If the rock was sharp enough to pierce skin, it was sharp enough to wear down plastic rope.

Maggie worked so long that her legs began to shake from exhaustion. She couldn't hold this crouching position much longer. She felt the toasted sandwich rise in her gut and she heaved.

She slid down to a sitting position and rested. Once her legs stopped shaking, she resumed the crouching position, found the rock with her fingers and resumed the rubbing. She ignored the tremors in her legs and carried on the process for as long as she could. She rested again and then started trying to free herself once more.

There was nothing else to do in the godforsaken cave. And there was no way she was going to lie there like a pig awaiting its fate.

She rested and crouched and rubbed, rested and crouched and rubbed. Her wrists ached, her back ached, her thighs ached.

After what seemed like hours of work, she heard the twang of one string go. She tested the rope around her wrists. It seemed looser. With renewed vigor, she continued rubbing and had the satisfaction of hearing more strings go. She was nearly there.

And then she heard footsteps and saw the flickering lights of torches.

'Help!' she screamed. 'Help, I am here!'

'Yes, we know you there, Ms Cloete.' It was a familiar voice, smooth and warm and bitter as coffee.

In the torchlight she saw Lucky Bean Msomi duck to enter the cave, followed by Xoliswa and a man unknown to Maggie. Not one of Msomi's entourage. Perhaps he was the one who had bashed her on the head. Both he and Xoliswa carried the torches, and their erratic light-play on the walls, floor and ceiling of the cave made her dizzy.

Msomi directed Xoliswa to check Maggie's bonds.

'I see our little reporter has kept herself busy,' Msomi said, his ever-present smile more menacing now. He barked an order in Zulu and the man wrestled Maggie back into a lying position and, keeping one knee on her, pulled more rope out of his pocket and retied her wrists. He also shortened the rope tying her wrists to her feet.

'Get off me!'

When he was done, she struggled to a sitting position.

'What the hell are you trying to do, hitting me over the head and keeping me tied up in this bloody cave?'

'That is a very good question, Ms Cloete. But I don't owe you any answers.'

'I want to understand who made Dave Bloom jump off the waterfall against his will and who beat up Hope Phiri so that she would shut her mouth. I want to know who did that and why. And most of all, I want to know who gave the orders.'

Xoliswa said something short and sharp in Zulu and the other man made a noise of assent.

'No we will not do that,' Msomi said. 'At least, not yet.'

He crouched down so that his face was close to Maggie's. His breath was hot and sour. 'You are one lucky bitch. These two want to rape you and throw you over the waterfall. I said no. We are waiting to hear from the boss. He is still deciding. You are safe here and we can take our time to decide what to do with you. Maybe we will let you quietly starve. A long, slow, hopeless death, rather than a sharp and nasty one.'

'For what? What have I done?'

'You have gone too far. People are sick and tired of your interminable questions and your prying. People are sick of you.'

'Which people?'

He put his hands in his pockets. He wore thick-roped corduroys, expensive as velvet, and shiny polished brown brogues. 'Wouldn't you like to know.'

'I do know,' she spat. 'I know that Xolani Mpondo is your paymaster.'

He smiled, a long grin that cut his face wide open. 'Mr Mpondo is a gentleman. He would never get involved in such matters.'

'So you do the dirty work. Tell me,' she looked Msomi in the eye. 'Did you also break Hope Phiri's ribs? Is beating up women one of the perks of your job?'

He barked an order, and the third man klapped the side of her head. Pain shot through her body.

The men turned to go, their torches flickering in the direction of the stairs.

'Wait!' she said. 'Can I have some water?'

Msomi said something in Zulu, and Xoliswa answered.

The gangster turned back to her. 'Xoliswa will bring you water. But do not think this is the thin edge of the wedge of kindness. We are making decisions and we will know by daylight what we plan to do with you.'

'Just kill me now, you coward. What are you waiting for? More orders from the puppet-master? You can tell him that Captain Njima is already looking for me. I have left a trail and he will find me.'

It was a lie. No one knew where she was. But maybe it would make them think twice about murdering her.

'Try as you might, Ms Cloete, you instil no fear in me whatsoever. The police are an incompetent bunch of fools, as you well know.'

Police incompetence, or police susceptibility to bribes, had led to Msomi being freed years ago, as Maggie knew only too well.

Msomi left and she heard his footsteps going up the stairs. She was alone with the noise of the water again.

She slept, exhausted, and woke again to footsteps. She didn't know if it was ten minutes later or ten hours. Xoliswa was there, with water in a plastic bottle. He held it to her lips with his good arm, in the bizarrely tender parody of a mother feeding a child. She gulped it down greedily.

'Thanks,' she breathed and then he held the bottle to her lips a second time.

When she was finished, she turned her head away. He threw the empty bottle aside.

She looked up him. 'So you used to work for Sentinel. Why did they retrench you?'

'They didn't say. But with only one arm, I was useless to them.'

'What happened?'

'Logging. I got in the way of a saw.' He screwed up his mouth. The memory was not a happy one.

'Did you get compensation?'

'Some. But not enough to keep my wife. She left with another man.'

'But you still work for Mpondo. How much does he pay you to kill people?'

In one supple movement, Xoliswa grabbed her by the throat and pushed her head against the cave wall. His fingers tightened around her air passage; she gasped. His eyes lit with a strange flame, one of pleasure at inflicting pain.

'You – ask – too – many – questions.' With each word, he bumped the back of her head against the uneven cave wall.

Then he let her go. 'When I get the order to kill you, I will be back.'

He left the cave. She closed her eyes, panting until her breath returned to normal. Then she got up on her haunches and began sawing at the ropes around her hands. When the pain in her thigh muscles grew too much, she rested. Then she crouched and sawed.

Time was meaningless, punctuated only by moments of pain and effort. She saw Christo, sitting on the sofa in her flat, feet up, and crunching muesli; she saw Sol Njima's kind eyes and felt his warm arms; she saw Hope and Chloe in a fierce embrace against the rest of the world. All people who had fought battles and who wouldn't want her to give up on hers.

As she crouched again, her feet tingled and grew numb. She swayed. She had no idea how long she had been trapped here or how long it had been since the toasted sandwich she'd had in Ishmael's cafe. Her head throbbed and began to fizz.

She rested and tried again.

As she grew more exhausted, the periods of rest grew longer and the periods when she crouched and sawed grew shorter. Soon she would only manage to be on her feet for a couple of seconds. Her body was giving in on her. Soon she would have no energy left.

She heard footsteps on the stairs, a light footfall. She lay down quickly with her hands behind her back so that her captors would not see what she had been doing. She could feel her pulse throbbing in her chest. A small figure stood at the entrance to the cave, holding a candle.

'Ma'am, are you okay?'

'Who are you?' she croaked.

'I am Sandile.'

Chapter 30
Tuesday morning

Sandile. Whose mother and baby sister had died, whose house had been burned down by the community.

'What are you doing here?'

'The bad men killed my family. I don't want them to kill you.'

She sat up. 'I thought your mother and the baby died of illness.'

'They were sick, but they died in the fire. Xoliswa burned our house down.'

'Why?'

He looked Maggie in the eyes. 'My mother was a strong person. She told him she was tired of living in a place of evil and that she would go to the police unless he stopped killing people and using the teenage girls for sex.'

He moved behind her and she could feel his nimble fingers working the knots behind her back. 'So he killed her and my baby sister.'

'Where did you go?'

'I hid here. Until they brought the woman here. Then I hid in the forest.'

'You saw them bring a woman here?'

'Yes, it was terrible. She screamed, and there were so many of them. I was too scared of them to try and help her.'

'Did anyone see you come here?'

'I waited until they were gone. They went away in a big car.'

'Is my bike still there?'

'I saw no bike.'

She swore. 'What time is it?'

'It is the morning.' He finished untying her hands and then knelt at her feet.

'Can you get me to Ishmael's? Not through the village.'

'Yes, I know a way.'

Once her feet were untied, Maggie staggered to a standing position. Her legs buckled. After hours of crouching, they now shot through with pain.

'Come.'

Sandile led her up the set of stones heading upwards. At one point, he stopped.

'That way is to my old village.' He pointed to the rest of the stairs. 'But this way is to Howick.'

Maggie looked into the mouth of the tunnel. It was nothing more than a crawl space. Sandile blew out out the candle and put it in his pocket. He got on his hands and knees, and she followed him. In the deep of winter, he wore only a pair of shorts and a tiny jersey two sizes too small for him. The soles of his takkies were full of holes. She crept behind him, the palms of her hands and her knees in agony from the stony floor. Pain led to freedom so she tried to rise above it.

The tunnel was dark and damp. It felt interminable. Eventually she began to crawl uphill, towards light. Then sunlight streamed in, hurting her eyes. Sandile pulled himself out of the tunnel, turned around and gave her a hand. Maggie collapsed onto the wet earth.

'Get up, miss,' he said. 'You are nearly there.'

They walked through a short stretch of forest, branches whipping against their faces and reaching out to grab their ankles. Maggie could hear the waterfall to their right, plunging away to the dark pools below. Her body ached, but she pushed herself forward.

'There is the restaurant,' he said, pointing. Through the undergrowth she could see the outline of Ishmael's cafe.

She ran across the dry grass, Sandile at her side. The open space made her feel intensely vulnerable and she needed to get inside as quickly as possible.

She flung open the door to the cafe, and stumbled in.

From that moment, events were spots on a timeline with no obvious connection between them.

Mr Ishmael gasping and rushing towards them with a coffee pot in one hand; him wrapping her and Sandile in blankets, putting hot drinks in front of them; her sipping too fast and burning her tongue; him on the phone to Njima; Njima arriving and folding her in his arms; a child-protection officer arriving to take care of Sandile; Maggie putting her arms out to the boy; Njima sitting alone with him in a booth and asking questions in a quiet voice, the child-protection officer at his side; and finally, Maggie wrapped in the blanket, putting her head down on the table and sleeping.

A warm hand on her shoulder. 'Maggie.'

She sat up, and rubbed her eyes. 'Yes.'

'Sandile will be an excellent witness. We will issue arrest warrants for Xoliswa and Msomi immediately.'

'And Mpondo?'

'We have nothing against him yet. We will have to see what emerges when we question those two.'

'What will happen to Sandile?'

'We have a couple of excellent foster families who look after children in situations like his.'

'Are you sure he will be alright?'

'Maggie, the child has been living wild for the past ten days. He will have a roof over his head, food and clean clothes. It will seem like heaven to him.'

'Can I see him?'

'He's over there.' Njima indicated another table, where Sandile was eating a large plate of bacon and eggs, with toast on the side.

Maggie went to sit with him. 'Is that good?'

He nodded, mouth full and chewing.

'Thank you for what you did.'

'It's okay.'

'You saved my life, and thanks to you, the bad guys will go to jail.'

'That would make my mother happy.'

'When it is all over, I'd like to see you. Would you be okay with that?'

'Sharp, ma'am.'

She put her hands in her jacket pocket and felt something smooth. It was the sandstone elephant. She handed it to the boy. 'Would you like this?'

He gave her the thumbs up. Sandile was going to be alright.

She turned to Njima. 'Listen, can your guys go and search

Xoliswa's house? I think he's got my bag with all my stuff in it.'

'They already are.'

'And please get them to find my bike.' She got up and approached Mr Ishmael, who was pouring another coffee for Njima.

'Can I use the phone?'

He indicated to the phone mounted on the wall near the till. 'Go ahead.'

She dialled Chloe's cell. 'We have a witness. Looks like Hope's attackers will be charged.'

'Oh God,' said Chloe. 'That is both good and bad.'

It was indeed. Good because the criminals would be brought to justice; bad because Hope would have to give evidence and relive her day of torture in court with people looking on and judging her.

Chloe gave the phone to Hope. 'Thank you, Maggie,' the academic said. She sounded exhausted, as if she had just finished climbing a rock-face. They both knew she had another mountain ahead of her.

Maggie sat opposite Njima. She took a sip of his coffee.

'I know where my brother's killer is,' she said.

Chapter 31
Tuesday afternoon

Police stationed themselves at the caravan, while Njima, Rankin, Maggie and three constables walked the path to Karkloof Extension 7. They trod in silence and in single file, only the sound of birdsong and a light breeze accompanying them. At the barbed wire fence, Rankin dropped back to wait, while Maggie, Njima and the constables climbed through and followed the path into the heart of the forest. A low winter sun sent dappled shade through the canopy, and Maggie was glad of her extra-thick fleece.

They had a plan, although Maggie had had difficulty getting Sol to commit to it.

'Count yourself lucky I told you where he is,' she retorted. 'I could have gone in to find him alone. That wouldn't be the first time.'

The big policeman had agreed reluctantly.

When they reached the chosen spot, Sol and his team stayed back and Maggie walked on by herself.

She focused on her feet, making sure they stayed on the tiny strip of path. This was a walkway for the delicate hooves of buck or the pattering paws of porcupine, not her clod-hopping boots. However, she made no attempt to conceal or lighten her footfall. She wanted him to know she was there.

Through the trees, she could see the clearing ahead. Abandoned machines sat stationary in the same positions they'd been parked when the foresters found the grave. Police tape surrounded the gravesite. Most of the bones would have been removed by now, taken to the police station for the forensic anthropologists to do their jobs, but the grave remained taped off.

'Alex, are you there?' she called. 'It's Maggie.'

Silence, except for the birds.

'Alex, I have some really bad news. I wanted to tell you myself.

Can you come down and talk to me?'

She paused and listened. The forest listened back.

The nearest tree had a rock conveniently placed beneath it. She sat. She was prepared to wait.

'I don't know how to tell you this, Alex, but Christo is dead. He was killed on Friday night. I wanted to warn you. I think Sentinel is picking off the Forest Keepers one by one and you could be next.'

She paused, and the silence around her grew thicker. It was no longer just the trees listening to her. Field was up there somewhere, listening to every word she said. If she chose the wrong ones, he would stay hidden. If she found the right words, he might come down.

She sighed. 'At some point I'm going to have to arrange his funeral. I hope you can be there. I'd like to ask you to give the eulogy. Christo admired you so much.'

Maggie's thoughts turned to Vuyani Mshenge, who had died in this same clearing while still a teenager. His family had not received his remains nor been able to give him the dignity of a funeral. It was a human right to bury your dead. She was not a believer, not by a long shot, but she would still want a memorial for Christo, something to honour the man he had been. She had to take up the right that the Mshenges had been denied.

'Alex, seriously. I know you are there. Come down and talk to me.'

It was easier if she thought of him as Alex, the gung-ho leader of a troupe of wild environmentalists doing what they could to save a forest. It was only in a much darker place that she thought of him as Evans. For now it was best if she didn't.

'So maybe you'd like to know that Dave Bloom's killers have been apprehended. Natalie is going to be so relieved when she hears that. It was a gang of enforcers probably hired by Mpondo. The trail might lead back to him. For once, Sentinel might get some really bad publicity.'

She paused. 'Though of course, the mass grave was pretty bad PR for them.'

An icy little wind lifted the leaves. She shivered. This wasn't working.

'The police are doing a great job on the DNA found at Christo's murder site. I am more than sure it will point to Sentinel. If not Mpondo, then at least his enforcers.'

Still the silence, the ongoing, ever-thickening silence that enveloped the secrets of the forest. 'It's getting cold, Alex. I'm heading back now.'

She stood up and started to walk back down the path towards the Anderson farm. She schooled herself not to turn around but to just keep going, one foot after the other.

There was a slithering noise behind her as Field came sliding down a tree trunk. She turned around to see him. He was dressed head to toe in combat gear with camouflage stripes painted on his cheeks. He held a gun in his hand.

'You are not going anywhere,' he said.

'Alex, what are you doing?' she asked. Somewhere behind her, Solomon Njima would be on red alert.

'Stop playing your little games with me,' her interlocutor hissed. 'You know who I am, just as I know you've got this patch of forest crawling with cops.'

'Okay, John.'

'Don't call me that!' He began to approach her, crouched low, head darting right and left as if he were expecting police to spring from every bush.

'Then what shall I call you?'

'Alex. I am now Alex.'

'Fine,' she said. 'Alex it is.'

He flicked the gun in his direction. 'Now come.'

She walked towards him. As she drew closer, he grabbed her and, holding her by one arm, made her march in front of him, the gun cold between her shoulder blades. They walked towards the clearing. She stumbled over some tree roots and he pulled her roughly to her feet.

Beyond the trees, the sun was starting to lower in the sky. He made her stand above the grave.

'This is where we burned them,' he said. 'Seven ANC guerrillas. We tracked them down, infiltrated their group, gained their trust and brought them here.'

'Why?'

'They attacked the state. We had to eliminate them.'

'They were boys, Alex, unarmed, harmless boys.'

'No they were not! They were terrorists, highly trained, armed and dangerous.'

Maggie stared into the grave where the Umlazi Seven had been buried. She could feel the snout of the gun in her kidneys. 'How did they die?'

'We gave them anthrax in their food. They grew very ill and died over a couple of days. We transported their bodies here. Then we burned the bodies and put the remains in the grave.'

She tried not to let the horror show on her face. 'Why did you burn them?'

'Anthrax is highly communicable. The spores can live in soil for years. We had to burn them to prevent an outbreak.'

'Why did you use it at all?'

'We were experimenting with different methods. Ones that we could use on a bigger population.'

'You mean biological warfare?'

'Yes, we were a special unit asked to test biological methods.'

'And that's why you were so desperate to stop the logging. Because the bodies in the forest led a trail directly to you. When you heard from Johan Liebenberg that Sentinel were due to start razing Extension 7, you moved to Pietermaritzburg, set up shop and launched the Forest Keepers.'

'Yes,' he said. 'And it would have worked, if it hadn't been for your brother.'

'What did he do?'

'Questioned my leadership, refused to listen, showed insubordination.'

'You killed him for questioning you?'

'I killed him because he was too clever. He found out that Mpondo was bribing me. How else can an ex-cop with no pension and no savings afford a house and a business and a lifestyle? Mpondo paid me because I am one of the few people alive who knows that Sentinel's evil little lab still exists.'

'You and Dave Bloom.'

'Exactly. Except he was too stupid to use the knowledge to his advantage.'

Maggie felt heat in her blood. 'If Christo found out, then you were too stupid to cover your tracks.'

'He was a meddler, like you are, and he deserved to die,' Evans spat. He raised the gun to her head. She could feel the metal against her skull, against the angry bruise that was growing there. 'And now you are going to die.'

Maggie saw a mist of red rage. She kicked backwards and heard her Doc make contact with his shin. It made a satisfying crunch. As he doubled over, she kicked him again and elbowed him in the throat. He dropped the gun, but instead of scrabbling in the dirt for it, he lunged forward and grabbed her by the throat. He pushed her up against a tree, fingers tightening. She choked. She was losing air. Her fingers struggled against his.

'You are a fighter,' he sneered. 'Just like your brother. He fought hard, but in the end, the knife slipped in, so gently.'

Rage made her wild. She kneed him in the groin and as he staggered, she followed with a sharp kick to his ribs. He fell to the ground and she picked up his gun. He tried to get to his feet, but she trained the gun to his face.

'Don't even think of it!' she said. Then she kicked his kidneys. 'That is for Christo.' She kicked him again. 'That is for Vuyani and the Umlazi Seven.'

He groaned and rolled onto his back.

She lifted her boot back to kick him again.

'Enough Maggie!' Sol ran into the clearing, followed by the two constables who locked John Evans into handcuffs, pulled him to his feet and began marching him towards the road where they had parked a van.

She bent over, engulfed by waves of exhaustion rolling over her body.

With some effort, she lifted her head. 'It's over, isn't it?'

Sol Njima smiled. 'Yes, Maggie, it's over.'

Chapter 32

The Gazette, front page.

Mass Graves – Apartheid-Era Deaths Explained
Menzi Gumede, Crime Reporter

Police have arrested five men in conjunction with the the apartheid-era killing of the Umlazi Seven, a group of young MK operatives believed to have been responsible for blowing up a power station in Umlazi in 1985. One of the men and an accomplice (now deceased) allegedly killed the teenagers with anthrax-laced food, while all of them burned their bodies and buried them in a shallow grave in the Karkloof Forest.

Police liaison officer, Captain Ernest Radebe told a press conference that John Evans (56) and Sthembiso Ngema were both security policemen trailing the Umlazi Seven at the time of the alleged bombing. The seven were Vuyani Mshenge (19), Lwanda Sibanda (18), Jonathan Hlongwa (18), Percy Mthembu (20), Map Maphumulo (17), Vuyo Vundla (21) and Jackie Mbatha (17).

Ngema kidnapped the seven youths in the Durban area in October 1985 under false pretences, alleging that he was an UmKhonto we Sizwe operative who had identified them for military training outside South Africa.

Ngema, who has since died of unknown causes, then took them to a remote farmhouse in the Midlands where he and Evans fed them anthrax-laced food, and left the boys to die. They returned days later, collected the seven bodies and transported them to the Karkloof Forest, where Winston Majoli (63), Mandla Cele (65), Tumelo Mokoene (59) and Dludlu Njonga (69) helped them burn and bury the bodies.

Thandi Mshenge, sister of Vuyani, told The Gazette *that her family was grateful that Vuyani's remains had been found. 'Not knowing where he was or what had happened to him was hard. Now that we know, we can give him a proper burial. The hole in our hearts will never be filled, but now we can mourn him.'*

According to South African laws, had Evans asked for amnesty during the Truth and Reconciliation Commission (TRC) hearings, he might have been a free man today. However, by concealing his role in the murder, burning and concealment of the bodies, Evans is now liable to receive a life sentence.

Evans is also in custody for the murder earlier this month of environmental activist and Forest Keepers' member, Christo Cloete (43). Cloete was found stabbed to death in a Pietermaritzburg apartment complex two weeks ago. The two men had worked together in Evans' shop World Shoes in Theatre Lane. At the time of the murder, Evans was out on bail pending a trespassing offence brought against him by forestry and logging company Sentinel.

Investigating officer Captain Solomon Njima said at the press conference that police were investigating the possibility that Evans had set up the Forest Keepers organisation in an attempt to prevent Sentinel's logging of the Karkloof Forest exactly where he had buried the bodies of the Umlazi Seven 30 years before.

Mjoli, Cele, Mokoena and Njonga are charged with aiding and abetting murder. Mjoli is the chief of a tribe that resides near the Karkloof Forest. He is a member of Contralesa, the Congress of Traditional Leaders of South Africa.

The men are remanded in custody.

Epilogue

Beautiful singing filled the tent. Women's and men's voices entwined in spirals rising up into the sky in sorrow and in thanks as guards of soldiers, dressed in Defence Force fatigues, carried in seven coffins and placed them, tenderly, respectfully, on seven tables. The guards moved to the sides of the tent, standing formally to attention.

The Mshenge family sat in the front row, dressed in sombre tones. Maggie could see Thandi, unmistakably tall and upright, her head wrapped in a black turban. She dwarfed the tiny figure of her mother. Prudence Mshenge had draped her body in an ANC flag in deference to the solemnity of the occasion and to the organisation both her husband and her son had fought and died for.

When the singing stopped, a man got up to speak. The provincial premier was a tall man usually given to large smiles, but today his face was serious.

'Families, friends, comrades, we are gathered here today to mourn and to celebrate. We mourn the passing of these seven brave soldiers whose lives were taken too soon by the forces of the apartheid state. We are here to honour them and their part in the struggle. They were never able to enjoy the freedom of democracy, never able to vote or to be full citizens of this beautiful land.'

Maggie heard a wail from the front, a cry of pain so acute that the skin on her arms grew goose pimples. She glanced at the young woman next to her and grabbed her hand. She and Mbali had attended more than one funeral together before.

'But we also celebrate, because, through the work of the police, we are able to hand the bodies of these seven brave freedom fighters back to the families. They will take them to their homes and bury their sons in the land where they belong.'

In front, Prudence and Thandi nodded. They had a hearse waiting to drive Vuyani back to Sweetwaters, to bury him next to the father he had loved.

Maggie had no land to bury Christo. Instead, she had taken his ashes to Karkloof Extension 7 where, with the permission of Sentinel's new chief executive, Temba Tlakane, she had scattered them deep amongst the trees. He was now part of the forest he had loved so much.

Tlakane was a new-style CEO. After Mpondo's arrest, he had declared K7 a piece of natural heritage. In time, Sentinel might donate it to the nation, but for now it was to remain a private reserve, where the butterfly colony would continue to live safely.

Xoliswa and Msomi had not protected their paymaster. Their confessions put Xolani Mpondo right at the centre of Dave Bloom's murder and Hope's abduction and subsequent beating.

On the other side of her, Natalie Bloom touched Maggie's arm. 'Are you OK?' she mouthed. Maggie nodded.

The information on the lab had not come from Mpondo or his henchmen. It had come from Mbali, who had discovered that Susannah Hynde's research was not into better cellulose solvents. She was queen of the secret lab, investigating biological agents and other tools of war. Mbali learned that Dave Bloom had become aware of his colleague's research. He had threatened Mpondo and demanded that he stop logging the forest. Instead, the executive had arranged his death.

The initial police investigation indicated that the research that interested the apartheid government had also interested the present government. After the lab had come to public attention, it had been rapidly shut down. Temba Tlakane had seen to that. Solomon Njima was expecting John Evans, with his historical knowledge of the lab, to testify against Mpondo in exchange for leniency in his sentencing.

Maggie wanted Evans to rot in jail for the rest of his life for killing her brother and Thandi's, but she knew that the evil cycle of secrecy and corruption had to end.

It was with no little pleasure that she resigned from *The Gazette*. Tina Naidoo had made an unenthusiastic attempt to persuade her to stay on. Maggie was having none of it even though Naidoo was a lot less bolshie since her best friend Xolani Mpondo had been arrested for murder and abduction.

Maggie squeezed the hand of her new business partner and Mbali squeezed back. Sibanyoni and Cloete would soon be setting up shop in Durban as private investigators. They already had their first case: a prostitution and drug ring that sent sexually exploited teenagers out of the country as drug mules. The *Joburg Sun* was paying. Jabu would be their main contact.

She was looking into schools for Leo, who had decided that he would learn to surf.

'And now, I will ask the families to collect their children and take them home.'

One by one, the families of the Umlazi Seven got up and accompanied the remains of their sons out of the tent.

Prudence Mshenge stood up and walked to her son's coffin. She placed a small hand on the top, where her boy's head would be. Her face was calm and dignified. The soldiers stood to attention and then lifted the coffin from its resting place. They left the tent, Vuyani's siblings following. Thandi gave Maggie a small smile and a nod as she passed.

Author's note

This novel was inspired by many conversations with my brother, Andrew James, who, in his work growing indigenous trees and plants, is trying to return the beautiful biodiversity of KwaZulu-Natal to its former glory. Andrew kindly allowed me to use his words, which I reseeded in the character of Mike Rankin.

Other South African experts were so helpful and gave of their time to help me get things right: I have to thank Madeleine Fullard of the Missing Persons Task Team, National Prosecuting Authority, for explaining how the apartheid police disposed of activists they killed and how her team is finding the remains of those missing people and returning them to their families today; Carol Campbell of *The Mercury* who explained how a modern newsroom functions and the responsibilities of a news editor; and Allan Alford for talking me through some police procedures.

In the interests of getting things right, I should admit that I played fast and loose with the location of the Karkloof Blue colony. There are a few remaining colonies of this threatened butterfly in the grasslands of the Midlands mist belt. However, for the purposes of the story, I moved one colony to a section of wild Karkloof forest in the middle of a plantation which exists, I have to admit, only in my imagination. There also may or may not be a cave underneath the Howick Falls.

I have been lucky once again to have a raft of wonderful early readers. For their time and wise words, I'd like to thank Lia Hadley, Victoria Best, Sarah Potter, Ute Carbone, Geoff Gudgion, Caroline Spencer, Emma Christie, Andrew James and Thomas Otter.

I am eternally grateful to my publisher Colleen Higgs and her superb team at Modjaji Books for taking Maggie on once again, and giving voice to women writers in a world where, inexplicably, female subjectivity is still silenced.

Many thanks to my family and friends, near and far, who

never cease to prop me up; to my team at home in Heidelberg who provide love and laughter; and to my husband, who makes the ultimate sacrifice to bring me coffee during the dawn writing hours.

For more about Modjaji Books, and any of our titles, go to

www.modjajibooks.co.za

Printed in the United States
By Bookmasters